When there's nowhere left to go
Do you keep running...

THE ONE

A DETECTIVE LUCY GAUTHIER THRILLER

THAT GOT

AWAY

NIAGARA NOIR SERIES BOOK 3
LIZA DROZDOV

BOOKS BY LIZA DROZDOV

BLOOD RELATIVE

DARK WATER

THE ONE THAT GOT AWAY

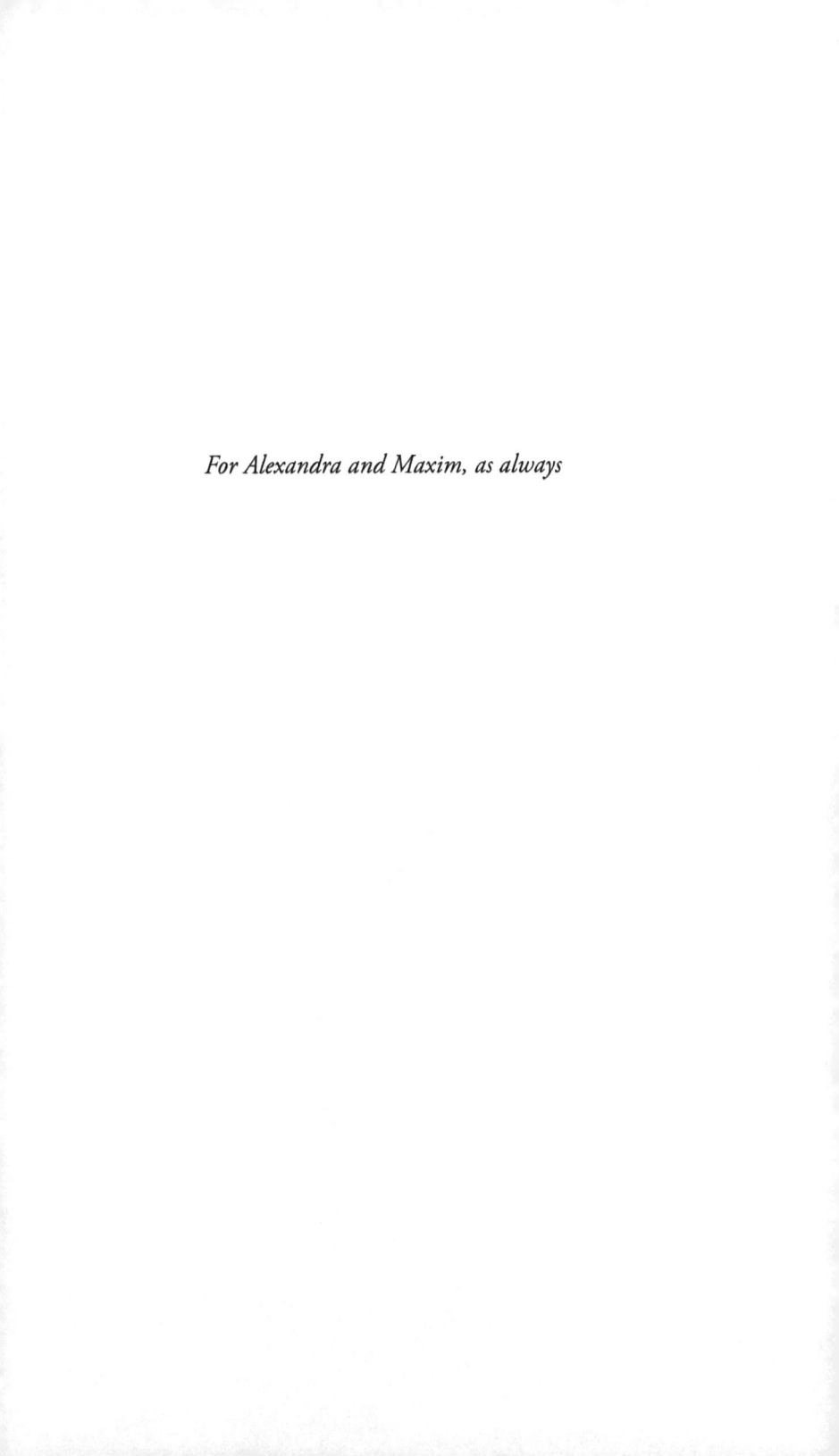

For Alexandra and Maxim, as always

ONE

YOU THINK YOU know me, you think you've beaten me, but you're wrong. You don't know me or what I'm capable of. I'm waiting and when you come tonight, I'll be ready for you.

How much time has passed since I first woke up down here? How long ago was it? A month? Two? At first I was counting the days, marking the number of times I tracked the sunrise as its reflection crept down the block wall across from the barred window—block by block as the sun rose in the sky. Then I gave up. I didn't help. Time had lost meaning, until now.

You gave me just enough chain to reach the toilet. I found I could pull the chair up to the high window and peer out through the bars. Twenty degrees of sight—that's all you allowed me, that's all I've had all this time. I could see between the end of the downspout at the corner of the house on the left and the propane tank sitting up against the window on the right. Twenty degrees of nothing. Just an empty field that stretches miles into the far distance. Never a car or a person, not even a dog. Just more nothing. Once a herd of deer stood in the distance, frozen in the long grass until as one they bounded out of my line of sight. It was like a dream and I wasn't even sure it was real. That had been just after the first snow. When was that? How many weeks ago?

You only come at night. Do you have a job that keeps you away during the day? A wife? A family that needs you at home? Where do they think you are when you come to me? What do you tell them? Do they know what you've done? Do they have any idea what kind of monster you are? They can't know you like I do.

Every night I hear the slam of your car door outside then your feet—first on the gravel driveway then creaking down the stairs before the click of the key in the lock. And every time was the same, until one night you finally trusted me enough to untie my hands. Maybe it wasn't trust, maybe you thought you've broken my spirit, that I'd lost hope, like the others, the ones who were here before me.

I know about them. I found their hair under the pillow and on the unwashed sheets, their clothes hanging in the closet. A bottle of cologne stuffed under the mattress, a bracelet in a drawer. Gifts you gave them, like you did me. How many were there? I don't dare think where they've gone.

I know you, but you don't know me. I'm not like them. I've been watching and planning, waiting for today and I'm ready for you. I broke that chair and hid all the pieces, except one leg. Now I'm behind the door waiting for the sound of the key. I'm ready and you won't notice a thing when you come for me. You'll see an outline of my body under the blanket and you'll come right in, not looking around, not looking behind you. You're no longer as careful as you used to be, when you first took me. I don't even know your name, but I know you and I'm ready.

I hear you on the stairs and it's just like I've been dreaming it for so many days. The door opens and you let it slam shut behind you as you walk toward the bed. I bring down the wooden leg onto your head. You stagger and I hit you again, and again, until you fall to the floor. I don't stop hitting you until I make sure I can walk out of here. I make sure that won't have to run away, afraid that you're right behind me and that you'll catch me, that you'll grab me from behind and pull me back down the stairs, back into this cage. I hit you to make sure you can't follow me, ever. You stop moving and I wait for a minute, to make sure. I take your keys from your pocket and carefully lock the door behind me as I leave. I hope nobody ever finds you.

I get in your car and drive it away, as fast as I dare.

TWO

Friday, January 10

THE WIND CUTS across Gravelly Bay, whipping my hair into my face. It's freezing cold—at least ten below Celsius for the second day in a row. The sun is out and the sky's a clear blue, promising more high pressure and intense cold. For a lot of people around here, that's exciting news. A couple more days of below eight or ten degrees and the Icewine harvest will begin. Vintners have been anxiously waiting, checking day and night temperatures for weeks, anticipating the time they can call in their crews and start to gather the frozen clusters of grapes that they'll magically turn into the nectar that we call Icewine. The rest of us just endure the cold like we do every year.

I park my patrol car in the lot next to Vogel's SUV and trudge through the snow toward the edge of the lake, my boots squeaking against the snow. My nostrils freeze shut every time I inhale, so I have to breathe through my mouth, creating a fog of vapour that freezes onto my eyelashes. A few hundred yards away out on the bay there's a cluster of people gathered around some portable ice fishing huts. I recognize one of them as DC Vogel, stamping his feet and clapping his hands trying to keep warm. He's standing next to the body and speaking to a guy who I'm guessing is Randy Delaware, the owner of Randy's Ice Fishing Rentals. In summer he runs fishing charters out of the Marina, but in the off-season Delaware has a contract with the Town to run the ice fishing operation out of a trailer parked here on shore of Gravelly Bay.

I take a deep breath and try to convince myself it'll be okay to step out onto the frozen surface. I know it's safe; I can see people out there, confidently walking around. There's even some heavy equipment over by the marina that weighs many times more than I do, but I just don't trust the ice. I know it can be unpredictable. Even though it may look thick, as soon as your weight is on it you'll break through into the frigid water below. I can't bring myself to go out there.

I'm starting to sweat with adrenaline but and I swallow hard, pull my earflaps down, tuck in my chin then place my boot onto the smooth icy lake. My mouth is dry. I can't do it.

Take a deep breath. Count to ten. Exhale. Count to ten. Inhale. I reach into my pocket and pull out my rescue medication. There's no way I can do this without help. I slip the Lorazepam under my tongue and continue my deep breathing to stave off a panic attack. *Deep breath. Count to ten.* I'm relieved to see Vogel and Delaware are making their way back to me. I can put off the inevitable, at least for a while.

"Good morning," I say, trying to sound confident once they make it back to shore. Vogel doesn't reply and I can tell from his miserable expression he hates the cold as much as I do. "I'm Detective Constable Gauthier," I say to Randy Delaware. He's warmly dressed in a down parka, snowmobile pants and good polar boots, unlike Vogel who's wearing leather dress shoes.

"Why don't you go into the car and warm up?" I suggest to Vogel. "I've left a thermos of coffee in there. Help yourself." He doesn't need to be told twice and before I've turned back to Delaware he's heading back to the car, slipping and sliding as he goes. The Forensic Team is already pulling into the parking lot and Vogel quickly gives them instructions as he climbs into the warm car and slams the door shut. I hope they're better dressed for this weather than he is.

A young woman steps out of the Randy's trailer and lights a cigarette. She's standing with her back to the wind and she averts her eyes from the body lying on the ice. I can tell she's watching us, hugging her coat tight to try and stay warm.

"Can you please show me where the body is now?" I ask Delaware, almost not recognizing my own voice, it's so high and squeaky from nerves.

Delaware gestures for me to follow as he sets off toward the fishing hut farthest away. It's several hundred yards out from shore—or from where shore would be if the lake weren't frozen over. I'm going slow and making a point of not looking down at the ice. *Deep breath. Count to ten.* It takes me ages to walk the short distance, thanks to the slippery surface and to my anxiety. I hear the ice cracking ominously; it's groaning and the vibrations under my feet resonate through my body. I freeze in terror.

Delaware realizes I'm not beside him and stops until I catch up. He looks amused.

"Nervous?"

"What's that sound? I whisper, my voice catching in my throat.

"That's the lake singing," he says as another loud boom sounds across the ice. "That means the ice is expanding," he chuckles. "Music to my ears."

He catches my terrified expression and slaps me on the back. "Nothing to worry about. The old timers always say that's the sound it makes when new ice is forming—it's just pressure from the expansion."

"You don't seem nervous."

"Wouldn't be much good out here if I was. This ice is almost eighteen inches thick," he assures me. "You'll see when you get out to the hole." Eighteen inches seems like it should support me, so I do my best to suppress my anxiety and follow him. I know the Lorazepam will kick in soon, but I keep up my deep breathing just in case.

We pass several portable ice fishing shanties that have been set up for people who've booked them for the day. It looks like Delaware is expecting a good crowd. Gravelly Bay is the most popular ice fishing spot nearby, and I bet Delaware is usually busy every weekend between freeze up and thaw. He won't be happy when I tell him he'll have to close down for the day.

Delaware stops short and points ahead, toward what looks like a pile of clothing lying on the ice, next to a large gas powered auger. He shakes his head, telling me that's as far as he'll go. I nod and pat his arm. There's no need for him to come any closer.

I approach the body, being careful to step into the fresh footprints Delaware and Vogel have already left and to ensure I minimize any contamination of the crime scene. That'll make the Forensic Services Unit's job a little easier I hope. Though looking around I can see that whatever footprints were left by either the victim or his killer have already been obliterated by the wind. There are small indentations everywhere, filled in with snow, with no discernable tread.

When I approach the victim, he's lying on his stomach on the ice, with his feet toward me. He's a large, very overweight man and the hood of his bright red parka is covering his head, or at least where his head would be if it hadn't been forced down into a hole in the ice. The ice has almost frozen again around his neck and face and all I can see is one of his ears and his bushy white beard, partially submerged in the slushy frozen water. Just a few more hours of this sharp cold will freeze the hole solid, encasing his head completely.

There's a bloodstain in the snow on the left side of his face, but I can't see the source. It looks like he has a cut on his ear, but I'll need the Coroner and FSU team to give me the details once they've done their investigation. It almost looks like someone has cut off the top inch of his ear, maybe as the first step in the journey that ended with his head stuffed into that hole.

As the forensic team comes up behind me, I'm staring through the hole in the ice, mesmerized by the darkness below. I feel dizzy, as if I'm about to faint, and I can't stop staring into the icy black water. I'm swaying on my feet when one of the technicians slaps me on the back, breaking me out of my trance.

They freeze when they see the victim in the red parka lying on the ice. "That's something new," says one.

"Do you think it's Santa?"

THREE

"WHO IS HE?" I ask Delaware, once I've left the FSU team to start their work. They'll take photos and mark any trace evidence while they wait for the Coroner. I got off the ice and back onto frozen land as fast as I could once they'd arrived and set up. I'd have run, but I was afraid I'd fall and I didn't need to do a faceplant in front of everyone.

"It's Martin Sanger," he says. "He works here, part-time."

"What's he do?"

"Helps me auger the fishing holes. Comes out every morning first thing and drills the ice. Then he helps me set up the portable shacks, if we need any for day rentals."

Delaware usually sets up several wooden ice shanties in late December, as soon as the ice is thick enough to support them. There are six out there now and they'll stay in place all winter, until the ice starts to break up in early spring. If it's a busy day, Randy can put up a few additional temporary shelters—just pop up nylon tents that get positioned over a hole in the ice. They're stored in the trailer he's got parked at the edge of the bay.

I've joined Delaware in the heated trailer, grateful to get out of the wind. I can watch the forensic team at work out on the ice through a small wire-meshed window in the door. Not that I can make out much at this distance, but I need to keep an eye out for when the Coroner arrives. I know Maja's on duty today and seeing her always makes my day.

There's a young dark-haired woman huddled in the corner of the trailer with her back to us, working on a laptop. It's the same one who'd stepped out for a cigarette earlier to watch us. Now she's uninterested. As far as I can tell she's doing her best to be invisible and is probably hoping I won't ask her any questions. It's not her lucky day.

"And who are you?" I say. "Do you work here too?"

"That's Patty," Delaware answers for her. "She's new."

"Does *new Patty* have a last name?" I feel a flash of irritation that she hasn't even turned to look at me.

"Smith," she mumbles in reply. I can barely hear her but decide I can't be bothered to pursue it right now, so I turn back to Delaware. I'm sure that's not her real name; she might as well have called herself Jane Doe.

"How long has Martin Sanger worked for you?"

"Ever since he retired. This is his third or fourth season," Delaware says. "He's crazy about ice fishing. I think he only works here so he can fish all day for free."

"Where did he work before he retired?"

"For the Township. Drove snowplow in winter and the Zamboni at the hockey arena." Now I remember Martin Sanger. I flash on a memory of him, dressed up like Santa Claus every Christmas season as he rode the Zamboni, clearing the ice between periods of every minor league hockey game. Why the hell would anyone want to murder a retired ice fisherman? It looks to me like he'd been tortured as well. What could anyone possibly want from Martin Sanger?

"Is that the augur he'd normally use to cut holes?"

Delaware shakes his head. "No. That's a ten-inch. We usually cut six or eight inch holes." Martin Sanger's head being forced through a smaller hole would definitely have been a challenge. I realize that whoever did this to Sanger had made him drill the hole too. Talk about digging your own grave. A chill goes through me in the over-heated trailer.

"Why not use a bigger hole for fishing? Isn't that more…accessible?" I know nothing whatsoever about ice fishing and it shows.

"A smaller hole is better—it lets less light through, so it doesn't scare the fish. And there are safety issues with a large hole, especially when there are little kids around." My mouth goes dry at the thought of a child falling through the hole. I know they'd never be found under the ice.

"I insist every child under five years of age wear a harness." He points to a few hanging on hooks next to the door. "They don't like it, but that's my rule. Generally the family groups are fine with a six-inch hole. They never stay long anyway, the kids get bored and restless." Who can blame them? I doubt I could stand sitting all day in a wooden ice shanty on a freezing winter day, waiting for some fish to bite, and I'm an adult. Supposedly.

"So why do you even have the larger auger?"

Delaware sighs. "Sometimes a group of people insists on it. They all want to fish the same hole. No idea why, but we aim to please. Maybe they think they're going to catch a fifty pound Lake Sturgeon and want to make sure they can pull it up." He shakes his head. "Usually one of them ends up stepping into it by the end of the day."

I can imagine a group of guys drinking beer and fishing all day. They probably get careless and end up soaking wet. Makes for a miserable ride home. They'd be much less likely to get a soaker with a smaller hole; they worst they could do is to lose their car keys or cell phones down into it.

"Can you please give me his address?"

While Randy starts going through what looks like a random mess of papers piled on the top of a filing cabinet, I look around the trailer. Next to the child harnesses are hanging dozens of pairs of ice claws, all with high-visibility orange and yellow cords so they won't easily be lost in the snow.

"You give them all ice claws too?" They're essential equipment for anyone working or playing on natural ice. If you fall through, you can use one in each hand to jab into the ice and pull yourself up out of the water to safety.

"Definitely. And I instruct them on how to use them. Nobody goes out on this ice without wearing them." I hope Delaware wouldn't ever let customers out onto the ice if there was any risk of them breaking through, but I'm sure they provide him some protection from liability, just in case a worst-case scenario happens.

"What do you fish for?" I ask while Delaware moves his searching for Martin Sanger's address to the mess of paperwork on the desk. I'd have been quicker just to look him up online myself.

"Perch, mostly. Also some Northern Pike and Walleye."

I approach *new Patty* to interview her. Presumably she knew Sanger if they worked together. She should have some insight into what might have happened to him. I'm sure she's been eavesdropping the whole time, so it's odd that she's acting disinterested and pretending not to notice me. It's not every day a man gets murdered where you work, so a little curiosity is only natural. Her feigned indifference is definitely unusual.

She does her best to ignore me, but eventually has to acknowledge I'm standing right behind her, looking over her shoulder at the laptop.

"How long have you worked here, Patty?"

"A few weeks," she mumbles.

"What do you do?"

"I manage the online reservations."

"She does all the computer stuff for me," Delaware chimes in, answering for her again. "I hate computers. And she helped Martin with the fishing parties—getting the holes drilled when the people arrive. Made sure they have minnows for bait, that the shanties have firewood for their woodstoves, that kind of thing."

"How well did you know Martin?" I direct my question to Patty, hoping Delaware keeps quiet.

She shrugs. "I work with him. We aren't friends."

Delaware passes me a note with Martin Sanger's home address. "Martin's wife's name is Natalie. She's a good lady. Bit crazy, like Martin."

"How *crazy?*" *Enough to do this to her husband* I can't help but wonder. What happened to Martin Sanger would definitely have taken some crazy.

"Just a crazy cat lady," he clarifies. "She and Martin run the cat sanctuary in town. They help feed feral cats, take them to the vet, that kind of thing." Delaware shakes his head. "The Sangers were the kindest, most generous people. Real salt of the earth types. Martin would give you the shirt off his back."

The Coroner's blue Subaru hatchback pulls up and parks next to Vogel, so I leave the trailer and intercept Maja. By the time I make it over to her, Vogel has climbed out of the car and is chatting away, as he always does. He's not what you would ever call a man of few words; Vogel has all of them, and he never stops demonstrating it, which has taken me a long time to get used to. I'm not fond of small talk and never have much to contribute to most social conversations. I don't really see the point of most of them, but Vogel makes up for that.

Dr. Maja Kaur is one of the Coroners and a local doctor at the walk-in clinic, and she also happens to be my girlfriend. We've been a couple—off and on—for over two years now, but I'm very private about our relationship. DC Vogel knows and he's been out to dinner a few times at our place with one of his many trial girlfriends, but that's about it, as far as the police force goes. I don't have any personal friends at work anyway, and the last thing I need is to deal with is more bullshit than I already face on a regular basis, just by being a young female.

"Hi Lucy," Maja says, laughing at Vogel's dress shoes. "Can you believe what this guy's wearing on his feet? On a day like this?"

"What can I tell you?" I shrug. "He clearly isn't capable of looking after himself."

"Excuse me," Vogel says. "In my defense, I wasn't home when I got the call this morning. I didn't bother to stop by my place to get my winter boots." There's no need to ask for details; Vogel is incapable of discretion so I know he'll spill everything in a few minutes, even if no one's interested. "If you must know, I had a date." Maja and I both look at him, awaiting the inevitable. "It went…well."

"When's the wedding?" I say with a wink at Maja. Vogel always goes too fast in all of his relationships: Sex on the first or second date, talking about living together or how many children they want by the third or fourth, and then she's gone shortly after, running for her life. I don't remember him ever getting to ten dates.

"The body's just over there." I grab Maja's arm and walk her away before he can reply.

My hand must have gripped her too tightly because she turns and stares at me. "Are you okay?" She studies me closely for a moment. "No, you're not. What happened?"

I take a deep breath. "The victim is out there." I point out to the frozen lake.

She understands immediately. "You don't have to come with me." She pats my arm reassuringly. "It'll be fine. Did you take something?" I nod. I'm not happy about it. I've been trying to reduce my anxiety medication and have been doing well for a long time. But if it comes down to having a full-blown panic attack at work, I don't feel I have a choice. I won't risk being without my medication.

"It's not a big deal," Maja continues. "Something like that would trigger most people, even without…you know," she trails off. Then she heads out onto the frozen lake.

I do know. But I wish I didn't.

FOUR

ONCE MAJA HAS pronounced Martin Sanger dead and the mortuary van removes his body, Vogel and I drive out the Sanger house together, first dropping off his car at the station. He runs in and puts on a pair of winter boots before joining me.

"Those aren't going to keep you warm sitting in your locker," I scold him.

"I hate wearing them," he says. "Reminds me of when I was a kid and my mother insisted I wear a snowsuit and mittens before I was allowed out to play. The other kids made fun of me."

"Losing toes to frostbite isn't funny either." Looking stylish is very important to him and snow boots don't fit the bill. I bet that even if he'd been home this morning when the call came in he wouldn't have worn them, in case they messed with his image.

Vogel has unsuccessfully worked his way through most of the single women in the entire Niagara region, looking for a partner who'll last for more than a couple of dates. He's good looking and fit, has a job, and his personal hygiene seems okay as far as I've noticed. So at least the basics are covered. I'm not really sure what his problem is or why they never stick around. My money's on him talking too much and being needy, but he hasn't asked for my opinion.

We drive out to Mill Creek Lane and find the Sanger house near the end of the road. It's a ranch style bungalow on a large lot, with an attached double garage and a car in the driveway, which I assume means that somebody's home.

Vogel and I take deep breaths before we knock on the front door. Delivering a death notice is never easy or pleasant and figuring out a way to tell Natalie Sanger her husband is dead, without revealing the details of his gruesome murder will take some discretion. I hope Vogel will manage it for us today; I'm not known for my emotional sensitivity and today I'm just not in the mood to try.

My anxiety about being on the lake is still weighing on me and I'm having a hard time shaking the feeling of cold dread and heavy despair. My disorder rules my life and it takes everything I've got just to function some days. I've learned how to mask it and only those closest to me would even notice when I'm not right. But even they don't know the whole story, of how deeply rooted my anxiety is in my past, and how impossible it's been for me to tear it out and destroy it.

I knock a few times but there's no answer, so Vogel heads around to try the back door while I peer into the windows. I'm sure someone is home; I can see lights on in the front room.

In a moment Vogel opens the front door from inside. "The back door was open. She's in the kitchen."

From the expression on his face I can tell it's not good news. I listen as Vogel calls it in then I head toward the kitchen, being careful where I put my feet. Natalie Sanger is lying next to the stove. There's a lot of blood on the floor from what appears to be at least one stab wound in her abdomen, as well as some more blood matting the grey hair above her left ear. I lean in closer and see that the top of her ear has been cut off, just the top inch or so. It also looks as though she may have hit her head on the stove as she fell, probably after she was stabbed.

I don't touch the body because I don't want to contaminate any trace evidence that might have been left by whoever did this. It's best to leave that to FSU. One thing about stabbing, the killer needs to get close to the victim in order to do it, much closer than using a gun. So, there's always a good chance they've left something behind: some DNA, or fibres, or possibly even fingerprints.

I study her body for a moment; Natalie Sanger is wearing a dressing gown over her pyjamas, so I guess someone surprised her early this morning. She's not wearing makeup and her hair looks like she hadn't managed to brush it yet, but I smell coffee and see there's a pot in the coffee maker. It smells bitter, so it's at least a couple of hours old. I'm about to go out to the car and retrieve a pair of booties and gloves, when her eyelids flicker.

"Vogel! Get an ambulance! She's alive."

Vogel and I stand back while the paramedics stabilize Natalie Sanger and take her out to the ambulance. She's in very bad shape and from the expressions on their faces it doesn't look as though they're confident she'll survive. She's lost a lot of blood from the stab wound, but the head wound looks to be the more serious concern.

Now we'll have to wait around for the FSU team to arrive. They've removed Martin Sanger's body to the morgue and are almost finished their investigation at the lake, but it'll be a while before they get here. They haven't had such a busy morning in…ever. Usually we go weeks without a crime scene to investigate and today we've got two at the same time. I'd say that's unprecedented in our township.

While we wait for them we begin our search of the house, being careful not to disturb the scene of Natalie's attack, where most trace evidence would be. I have no idea what we're looking for, since we don't have any insight yet into the motive for the crimes, but anything unusual needs to be noted, at least as a preliminary step in the investigation.

We search the living room, bedrooms and bathroom, and find nothing out of the ordinary.

"Did anyone else live here with them?" Vogel asks when we pass in the hallway.

"No idea. Why?"

"It looks like the spare bedroom has been in use." I follow him and see obvious signs that somebody has slept in the bed: the sheets are creased and the blankets thrown to one side. The closet door is open and it's empty, apart from some hangers on the floor. "I'd say someone left in a hurry," Vogel says then he asks the FSU team to check the room over for prints and trace evidence.

"I don't think they have any kids," I say, based on my look around. "There aren't any photos around. None on the walls or mantle." The only photos on display are of the Sangers' wedding day and one of him taken in the summer, grinning and holding a very large fish.

When we've finished checking the main floor, we head down to the basement together. At the foot of the stairs the door is closed and I cautiously open it, first flicking on the light switch I find on the wall outside. It smells musty, like the carpet is damp with mildew. My anxiety starts to run and I brace myself for whatever is down here. Mess and mould are triggers for me and I find it really difficult to be in dirty or cluttered spaces. Hoarders make my skin crawl and I've even had to leave crime scenes saying I needed fresh air, when I was really taking a rescue Lorazepam to stave off a panic attack.

As the large banks of fluorescent lights in the ceiling flicker on, I see the basement is a large finished space, probably decorated in the sixties or seventies when the house was first built. It's fully carpeted in rust-coloured shag broadloom, and the walls are covered with fake dark wood panelling. There's even a wet bar at the far end, with a few stools lined up in front.

There are also heavy-duty wooden shelves running the entire length of one wall, filled with metal crates. And those metal crates are filled with cats.

"What the hell?!" Vogel says. "How many cats has she got?"

"Delaware told me she was a crazy cat lady," I shrug. "Guess he wasn't kidding."

"There are nine cats here," Vogel informs me after he's done a head count. Most of them look terrified and have crouched into the back of their crates, trying to make themselves invisible by hiding under blankets and pet beds. One is oblivious to our presence; he's fast asleep in his litter tray. There's a lot of mess, thanks to water bowls being turned over and cat food spilled. But it doesn't stink, thankfully. Natalie Sanger must have changed the litter recently, possibly even this morning.

When we've finished checking out the basement and garage, Vogel and I meet back up in the kitchen. The FSU team is finished taking their photos, swabs and samples and are packing up to leave, and Vogel and I can now look more carefully through the only room we haven't had a chance to properly investigate.

A telephone is mounted on the wall next to the fridge. The Sangers are of a generation that still has a landline and the light is blinking, indicating there's a message waiting. Vogel presses the button and we listen as a woman's voice comes through the speaker.

"Hi Nat, it's Cathy. Just want to let you know we've had a report of a new mother with a litter. They're under a construction trailer at the colony by the marine scrapyard. We're going to rescue them this week if you want to join us. Call me."

On the wall next to the phone is a corkboard covered with lists of names and volunteer rotas, flyers for discounts on bulk pet food, and the phone numbers of three veterinarians.

There's nothing else of interest in the room. They were just a typical retired couple; one of them loves cats and the other one loves fish. Why would anyone want to kill Martin and Natalie Sanger?

I sign out for my lunch break and head to the gym for a quick work-out. If I don't do something physical after this morning I'll crawl out of my own skin. For years I've been dealing with my anxiety issues by daily workouts and weight training, just to keep the symptoms at bay and to allow me to function like a normal person. Since Maja's back in my life I've felt stronger and I've even been able to reduce my medication, but the daily workouts have been a lifesaver.

Unfortunately last summer I'd torn my rotator cuff while arresting a murder suspect, which meant I couldn't go to the gym for weeks. Before I could return to work I had to endure six months of rehab and physiotherapy and even now I'm only allowed to do a modified workout. It's made me irritable and anxious and I'm definitely getting fat, which even though I've been afraid to get on the scale, is undeniable now that I'm standing in front of the full-length mirror.

Inactivity and spending months being restricted to desk duty also nearly drove me insane, but the upside is that now I've learned ways to quickly retrieve and access files, documents and information, even restricted information, that will make my life as an investigator that much more efficient in future. Every cloud has a silver lining.

I'm finally at the point in my rehab that I can raise my left arm above my shoulder but I still have pain when I try, and I've lost a lot of my strength. It wasn't that long ago that I knew I could take down any suspect, even though I'm only five foot five inches tall. I'm angry that I don't feel that confidence anymore; I don't like feeling vulnerable. For too many years of my life I felt that way—weak and exposed, defenseless. I fought hard to escape that feeling and I never want to go back. I'll do whatever it takes to make sure it never happens.

FIVE

I'VE NEVER SEEN the briefing room so full. I can't even find a seat so I'm standing at the back of the room as DS Quinn Agu reads over his notes. What is everyone doing here? It looks as though every duty officer is present, in addition to the Homicide Unit and all support services in the building. There must be a major announcement coming and I feel a tingle of anticipation. I admit it's a bit creepy and disturbing that I'm getting excited about what is sure to be someone else's misfortune, but that's the nature of the job. It's also my nature, for whatever that says about me.

"Good afternoon everyone. Thanks for coming in," DS Quinn Agu begins, his deep voice resonating through the room. I've always thought he sounds like Darth Vader; everyone falls silent the second he speaks.

"Yesterday afternoon the body of a man was discovered in a farmhouse off Concession 8, near Pelham. He'd been battered and appears to have died from head wounds inflicted by this leg of a broken chair."

Behind him on the screen flash a series of images: the dead body of the man, splayed out on his stomach, his head a mass of trauma; the photo of the chair leg, lying a few feet from the body.

"It appears the man has been dead for approximately a month, but we are waiting for formal results from the forensic pathologists."

My first thought is why Maja didn't tell me about this? Surely she'd have heard from whichever Coroner on duty had been called in. My nose is a little out of joint and I miss some of what Agu is saying.

"The body was found locked in the basement of this house." An image of the house flashes up. "In a room that we now can only assume has been where he, or someone else, has been holding someone captive. A female, and likely more than one." There are a series of photos of the barred window and the bed with chains and a shackle. A horrified murmur rumbles through the room. Agu waits for the noise to die down.

"We've been keeping a tight lid on this since yesterday, but the Superintendent will be making an official statement shortly. And when he does, the media will be all over it. I've no doubt this will generate national, even international interest."

None of us in the room needs to be told why. The case would be sensational regardless, but everyone here remembers the horrific cases of Leslie Mahaffy and Kristen French—the two schoolgirls who were abducted and brutally murdered in the Niagara region over thirty years ago. Those crimes, and how they were so poorly handled by both our small police force and the larger, external groups we liaised with on the investigation, led to the creation of the first Serious Crimes Unit on the Niagara Police Force. It's now the Homicide Unit, and I'm the newest member to be recruited.

"The body was discovered by one of the new rural internet providers making a sales call to the house. He found the door open and the house empty. There was evidence that raccoons and possibly foxes have been inside looking for food or shelter, but the strong smell of decomposition made him call us in. Thankfully for him he did not go down to the cellar."

"Our initial speculation is that the man was killed by his captive and she was able to escape. Likely she took his car, as one has not been found and the farmhouse is too isolated to be reached without a vehicle. Based on decomposition and the estimated time of death, that person could have driven as far away as Vancouver—twice over, by now."

"Initial findings indicate trace evidence left by at least four different females in the cellar room. That number may change as we hear back from FSU. I fear it could go much higher. They are running fingerprints, looking for a possible matches with any reported missing persons."

A hand is raised. "Do we know who this man was?"

Agu shakes his head. "Not yet. We've now traced the property ownership, and we have a name on the bills from the heating company. We have a missing person's report on file that matches the individual in question. His wife reported him missing in early December. Additionally, this same individual owned a business in town, which was destroyed by arson on December 12.

A murmur goes through the room and Agu has to raise his voice to be heard. *Did they guy torch his business? Tried to run and got caught? Sound like an insurance scam.*

"We'll be contacting the next of kin today, but formal identification will be difficult, based on state of the body and decomposition. We'll need to resort to dental records. Once we have that we'll make an official announcement."

Agu holds up his hand, calling for silence. "We don't yet know if the man who owns the house, or the person whose body was found, is the same person who held the women captive. We have nothing to go on, except conjecture at this point."

"I know we have a couple of other serious crimes under investigation currently. However, we have no choice but to make this evolving situation a priority."

I understand that means that Martin Sanger's murder will be put on the back burner, at least for the short term while our department resources are put toward this new crime. The forensic evidence—fingerprints and any DNA taken at the scene of both crimes, will be put to the end of the queue while we turn our focus to the Cellar Man investigation. If it's as bad as DS Agu is implying, I have a feeling it will be a department focus for some time. I'm disappointed about that but there's not much I can do, unless Natalie Sanger survives and can provide something more for us to go on.

SIX

IT'S AFTER TEN o'clock and I've been starving and exhausted for the past few hours, but I've been reluctant to go home. My dinner consisted of two bags of peanuts from the vending machine, with a chocolate bar for dessert. Everyone else on the team left hours ago, apart from the clerk at the front desk. All officers on patrol duty are out in their cars and she's alone with her book and her knitting. She has to answer the phone, but it seldom rings late at night in our small town. And when it does she just puts the call through to dispatch, who'll send someone over. I know she's knitted enough scarves and mitts over the years to keep the area's homeless shelters well supplied and I bet she's read her way through the entire public library by now.

My phone rings again. It's Maja and I let it go to voicemail but she doesn't leave a message. Then I feel bad so I send her a quick text to say I'm at work and will be home soon, with a heart emoji to set her mind at ease. I know she's worried about me and probably thinks I'm at crime scene or possibly even in danger. Or maybe still dealing with the panic attack from this morning. But the truth is, I'm avoiding her. And I realize I'm doing it because I'm in a sulk, and I have no right to be, and it's childish, but I just can't seem to help myself so it seems the best thing for me to do is to avoid the whole issue. My basic relationship strategy in three words: Under Rug Swept.

My nose has been out of joint ever since DS Agu's briefing earlier today. Some of the police department had been made aware of the gruesome discovery of the body in the cellar yesterday. I know someone at the Coroners' Department would have certainly been on the scene. Maja, my girlfriend and the woman I love more than anyone is a Coroner, so ergo she knew about it. And she didn't tell me.

Rather than going home and picking an argument with her, which I have been known to do when I'm angry, I've just stayed on at the station. The added benefit of that is it makes me feel virtuous, like I've got the moral high ground. I've caught up on all my paperwork, as well as most of Vogel's. He can thank me later. I've also spent a long time thinking about the Sanger case and I can't come up with any reason why anyone would kill Martin, or attempt to kill Natalie.

Her stab wound wasn't lethal, thanks to her large amount of abdominal fat. I guess this is one instance when being overweight was good for her health. The knife did enter her abdominal cavity, but didn't strike any arteries or vital organs, apart from a small cut to her large bowel, which they've stitched and cleaned up and given her antibiotics for to prevent septicemia. However, she's in a medically induced coma while doctors try to reduce the swelling in her brain. They have her stabilized, but have no idea when—or if, she'll be conscious and able to answer questions about what happened in her kitchen this morning.

The now high profile Cellar Man case has been as ugly as expected; more details about the cellar murder have trickled in from FSU and the white board is filling up with images and notations. We don't have a positive ID on the body found in the cellar, but the house belongs to a man named James Landry. He's an insurance broker who hasn't turned up for work in almost a month, probably because he's busy being dead.

FSU has already found trace evidence of at least seven different women in the cellar, between fingerprints, hair found in the drains and DNA in the bed. Two sets of fingerprints were found—one on the toilet and one on the window, of women with previous criminal records. One of them was reported missing seven years ago.

There are fingerprints on the leg of the chair that had been used to kill Landry but they aren't a match to anything on file. Much of the chair leg was smeared with blood and brain matter and it's been wiped, so the prints aren't useable. So we're no closer to finding the one that got away.

Once the Superintendent held his press briefing at the end of the day the station became a madhouse: endless calls from media looking for statements, satellite news trucks lining the street outside the station and reporters huddling in the cold outside, ready to pounce on any member of the force and demand a sound bite from whoever came their way.

When my eyes start to droop I have to admit it's time to go home to bed. If I don't leave now I'll fall asleep at the wheel, which is a bad idea for anyone, let alone a police detective. I bundle up against the cold, say goodnight to the clerk then head out to my car. I remember—too late—that it's the first weekend of the Icewine Festival and most of the streets downtown are closed to traffic. That means I need to back up and turn around and figure out another way to navigate across town. The Niagara region is internationally famous for its Icewines; they are jewels that win awards internationally thanks to our unmatched climate and terroir, and every year we celebrate that fact. It's also great way to bring tourists into the region in the off-season.

I can't drive faster than a slow crawl thanks to the hundreds of pedestrians and tourists thronging the streets, which have been turned into an Icewine Village. There are twinkle lights on all the street trees and open fire pits and warming stations on every block, offering hot chocolate and mulled apple cider. All the shops are open until midnight, and several pop up stores have opened just for the Festival, selling award winning Icewine and souvenirs.

The restaurants I pass are all full and several have lines outside of people waiting in the cold for tables, even at this late hour. I feel a pang of regret; Maja and I were planning on attending the Festival this weekend. My mouth starts to water at the memory of the bottle we'd just finished: It was sweet but not cloying and had a perfectly balanced acidity; its flavour was full of apricot, with tropical notes of pineapple, lychee and citrus. At least the celebration is on for the rest of the month; maybe we can make it next weekend.

Once I've cleared the traffic downtown I then have to take the road past the Marina, thanks to an accident on Sugarloaf Road. As I drive along the waterfront I can see clearly out across the frozen expanse of Gravelly Bay. The deep indigo sky is full of stars and reflects the lights from town and the frozen bay is a blanket of white, extending all the way to the dark open water on the horizon. The lake doesn't look so frightening now and on an impulse I pull into the parking lot and look out across the ice.

It looks so tranquil now, like a scene from a greeting card. My earlier terror is gone, but it has left behind a heaviness and uncovered a sorrow I've been carrying for a long time, one that I work to forget about until events like this morning's force me to remember.

My friend Heather and I were playing one winter along the frozen river that stretched for miles like a white ribbon, lined and patterned with the tracks of snowmobiles and cross country skis. We were walking along the ice when suddenly Heather was gone. I could see a hole and when I looked into it saw the water flowing underneath the ice, but there was no sign of her. She'd just fallen through the ice without a sound and was swept away as if she'd never been there. By the time I screamed and yelled for help it was already too late.

They searched for her body for weeks but then were forced to give up until spring. The frigid water and the freezing rain that started that night made rescue efforts impossible and she was under the ice somewhere all winter. A fisherman found her body two months later, stuck in the tree roots along one of the banks about ten kilometers downstream.

I now know not to trust river ice; it's unpredictable and the current erodes the ice pack from underneath. If you fall through you'll swept away from the hole and you'll drown in the cold darkness, trapped under the ice, like Heather did.

But the ice on Gravelly Bay seems solid enough tonight: The empty fishing shanties still set up, waiting for the morning's fishermen to arrive, and Delaware's trailer is locked up for the night. Then I notice a light is on and a plume of smoke is rising up from the vent in the trailer's roof. Someone is inside.

I creep up to the trailer, listening for any sound from inside. There's only silence. I try the handle and find it's locked, so I knock. No response. I knock again.

"Who is it?" I hear a terrified voice ask.

"Detective Constable Lucy Gauthier. Please open the door." Nothing happens.

"I'm not going away…You need to open the door now."

Finally I hear the lock click and the door opens a crack. It's Patty. "Come in," she says, her voice resigned.

When I come into the trailer I realize she's been sleeping on the floor, using a winter parka as a blanket. She kicks it to one side and sits at the desk, as if she's been working.

"What are you doing here so late? Are you *living* here?" It's not a residential trailer; it's just for Randy to run the rental business for a few months every winter, then it gets towed away and placed in storage with the fishing shanties and other equipment. No one is supposed to be sleeping there.

She tries to act surprised. "Living here? Of course not! I'm just working late." I burst out laughing at the unlikelihood of that. I'm quite sure Randy has no idea she's even here. No doubt she said goodnight and left work at the end of the day, then when she saw Randy drive off she crept back inside.

"Randy's got customer service issues and reservations all night?" She just looks down at the floor. "You can't stay here, Patty."

"I've got nowhere to go," she whispers.

"Where have you been staying before now?" I feel a prickle of anxiety run down my spine and I realize I already know the answer. "You were at Natalie and Martin Sanger's. In the spare room." Of course Martin would have offered her a room when she arrived in town—a girl with no place to go. That's the kind of people the Sangers were. "How long were you at their place?"

"Just two nights," she whispers. "But I can't go back there."

I know why: She'd been at the house when Natalie was stabbed. Or she was the one who did it. "Did you see what happened to Natalie?"

Patty shakes her head and tears well up in her eyes. "I was still in bed when I heard voices in the kitchen. Then Natalie screamed and…I didn't know what to do. So I hid under the bed."

"Did you see anything?" She shakes her head. "Did you hear anything? Do you know what they wanted?" Her eyes are pools of misery when they meet mine.

"I think they were men…maybe there were two of them? They were shouting, asking her something. She was denying it, saying she didn't understand what they wanted. I couldn't really hear."

"Then I heard her scream and a crash. Then…nothing. I lay there for a long time, praying they wouldn't come in and find me. When I finally came out I saw her lying there, in all that blood. I knew she was dead so just I got my bag and I ran."

"Why didn't you call 911?" She just looks away. "Natalie's in hospital, Patty. She might be okay. But it would have been better if she'd gotten treatment sooner."

"I'm sorry." Patty bursts into tears. "I thought she was dead."

I'm guessing she wanted no involvement with the police, but why wouldn't she have made an emergency call before she left the house? Or at least checked on the woman who'd taken her in and given her shelter? Patty must have been very frightened, and I'm not sure it was just about what happened to Natalie. There's always a reason people choose not to call the police.

I sit down and wait for her to calm down before I ask her any more questions. She has her face buried in her hands and I can see from the roots at her hairline that she dyes her hair; her natural colour is reddish blonde, not dark brown. The chestnut colour doesn't suit her complexion and it occurs to me that she's trying to disguise her appearance. I try to guess at her age. Maybe mid-twenties? She's wearing a t-shirt with the Forks not Knives logo, so I'm guessing she's a vegan. The shirt looks old and well worn, as do her jeans. They aren't new and they could use a wash.

After a few minutes she stops sobbing and takes a few deep ragged breaths, then looks at me her under her lashes.

"Where was Martin when this happened?"

"He was already at work. He always leaves really early, to get started on the holes."

"And after, you just came here, to work?" I'm surprised she didn't keep running, right out of town. "How'd you get here?"

"I walked. I didn't have anywhere else to go. I don't have any money." And when she arrived at the trailer she found Martin was also dead, and soon the place was crawling with police.

"Patty," I begin as gently as I can, not wanting to alarm her. "We're going to need to go down to the station and take your fingerprints, just to exclude you from the inquiry."

"No," she says firmly. "Absolutely not." I'm taken aback. This has never happened to me before.

"Why not?"

"I don't need a reason. I'm not under arrest, am I?" I shake my head. "Then I refuse." This certainly puts a different spin on things. Why is she unwilling to let us take her prints? We're only going to use them to help identify who might have been in the Sanger's kitchen. "I'm protecting my civil liberties," she says. "You have no right to have my fingerprints."

I look at Patty, in her animal rights t-shirt and her eyes flashing with righteous indignation and give up. It's late and I'm really tired.

"I can't let you stay here Patty. It's not safe. But I have a friend who might be able to help you out."

I pull out my phone and call Sophie at the Womyn Collective Farm. Sophie runs her organic flower farm as a shelter for abused women in the region. Patty doesn't exactly fit the profile of the women she takes in since she's not a victim of domestic abuse, but it's a freezing January night and she's got nowhere else to go. Also, as I explain to Sophie, she needs protection. She might be a witness to a crime, though she hasn't yet remembered what she might have seen, or even know if it's important.

As I knew she would, Sophie tells me to bring Patty right over. We lock up the trailer and leave a note for Randy to find in the morning, telling him she might be a bit late since she'll need to find a ride into town. The Womyn farm is out on Concession 7, much too far to walk and there's no bus service that far out of town. But I'm sure one of the Womyn will happily give her a lift in to work.

I notice Patty is carrying only a small child's backpack. "That's all you've got?"

She looks embarrassed and nods, but I don't press her. How is this young woman managing, without a place to stay and evidently without any belongings? She's a little too old to be a runaway.

"Patty," I begin as we drive out into the countryside. "You need to think really carefully now. Try and remember anything you might have heard when the men were shouting at Natalie."

She thinks for a moment, staring out the window as the snow covered fields slide past. Is she replaying this morning in her mind, watching it like a movie, trying to make sure she remembers everything?

"Do you mind if I smoke in here?" she asks. Police policy says she's not allowed to, but what the hell. I don't need an argument.

"Crack a window," I tell her. "Make sure you blow it outside."

She fishes in her pocket and pulls out a crushed package of cigarettes and a lighter. She lights one and inhales deeply. I don't know if she's buying time or simply trying to remember what happened that morning.

"One of them was shouting in another language. I didn't understand what they were saying," she finally says. "I think it might have been Chinese."

SEVEN

Saturday, January 11

I DIDN'T SLEEP well last night. First, because I didn't even get home until one o'clock in the morning after dropping Patty off at the Womyn Collective Farm. Then, when I walked into the house I managed to pick a big fight with Maja. I had rehearsed very carefully on the drive home what I would and wouldn't say to her, if I found her awake. Then I promptly forgot it all. I don't know why I did it; maybe I'm just contrary, but it had been a long day and I was exhausted and I just wanted to go to sleep. Or at least that's what I told myself.

"If you just want to go to sleep, then why aren't you in bed," Maja had reasonably asked when she found me sitting in the living room nursing a large glass of wine.

First I half-lied and told her I was tired and had a big case weighing on my mind. But Maja's no pushover and she's also no fool.

"What's this really about?" she demanded. "We had plans to go to the Festival tonight. With Abby and Chantal."

I didn't have an intelligent response to that and knew I was completely to blame for not communicating with her, but my irritation at her having withheld the story about the cellar murder flared up and I snapped at her.

"How could you not tell me about the body found in the cellar?" Maja's jaw dropped in surprise. "The man who held the women captive?"

"First of all, I have absolutely no idea what you are even talking about," she'd replied, and I immediately knew she was telling the truth. Maja tries to stay off social media and rarely watches the news. It's very likely she hadn't even heard the story yet.

"What *body*? What *cellar*?" She glared at me for a moment before continuing. "Second, even if I did know about some dead body, which I don't because it's obviously not even my case, I have no obligation to tell you the details of my Coroner work. In fact, it's just the opposite! I'm supposed to *not* share information, except through proper channels."

"And third, what gives you the right to be angry about it? What makes you think you're entitled to know everything? Is that what you've been doing all night—sulking? Is that why you stood me up? Grow up Lucy!" With that she'd stormed upstairs to bed and I'd stayed on the couch and drank the rest of the bottle of wine.

Naturally, Vogel notices the minute I walk into the station this morning. "You look like shit Gauthier," he says cheerily.

"Thanks. Helpful. I appreciate you telling me."

We're on our way to the first veterinarian on the Sanger's list, a Dr. Gina Pompeo. She operates out of a clinic in Ridgeway, so we've got a few minutes to review the game plan on the way. Vogel is driving; I don't think my wine hangover will allow me to do more than review our notes. I can barely manage my nausea and headache.

"We need to interview the other volunteers on the rota," Vogel says. "I wonder if they might know something about what was going on with the Sangers."

"Okay...How many are there?"

"Just three. It looks like they each do a couple of shifts a week, but Natalie Sanger and her husband did three."

"And we've got the other two vets."

"Let's split up, get it done faster," Vogel suggests.

"Okay. Just let's get through this first one together, okay? I'm feeling a little fragile."

"That's unbelievable," Dr. Gino Pompeo says in shock when we inform her of the reason for our visit. "Who'd want to kill the Sangers? I can't believe it!"

"What can you tell us about them?"

"They are both lovely people," she said as she ushers us into her office. "Kind, generous, caring. They started the first cat rescue in the area and recruited the other volunteers to help out over the past few years. At first they ran the rescue out of their home downtown by the canal, but then there were complaints from some neighbours, so they had to move out to that bungalow outside town. It's a big lot, away from people so it's better there for them. And for the cats, of course."

"What do they do, exactly?"

"They feed a few feral colonies—in Port Colborne, Niagara Falls and Fort Erie. They set up the TNR program."

"What's that?"

"Trap, Neuter and Release. You can tell if a cat has been TNR'd if the tip of left ear is cut off."

I'm not sure I heard her correctly. Vogel and I exchange a look, thinking of what happened to both of the Sangers. "I'm sorry, did you just say the ear? Why?"

"The tip. Just the pointy bit. It shows volunteers or anyone who might accidentally trap them that they've already been neutered and they can be released back into the colony."

"Aren't they put up for adoption?"

"No," she shakes her head. "Feral cats never make suitable pets. They're wild animals, not just stray cats that have lost their homes. There's a huge difference. The only way a feral cat could be tamed is if we were able to rescue a litter when the kittens are still very young. Then they could be socialized and adopted." I remember the voice message inviting Natalie to help rescue the litter of kittens and hope the rest of the volunteers got to them in time.

"Some local farmers and wineries have taken in colonies and ferals after they'd been neutered. The cats live out in the barns and sheds and they're regularly fed."

"What do the farmers get for that?"

"A team of healthy feline predators who'll look after their rodent and pest populations, for a lot less money than using pesticides. And they're organic," she grins. "The farm relocation program works very well."

"People like the Sangers feed the colonies so they have a chance to survive, and they trap and bring as many as they can into me and the other vets who participate in the program so we can neuter them. That way the feral cat population doesn't keep growing."

"Do you know who'll be taking over the cat rescue, at least for the time being?" I'm holding out hope that Natalie Sanger will survive her injuries.

Dr. Pompeo thinks for a minute. "I need to give this some thought, and talk with the other volunteers. I'm not sure if any of them are up to it or have the space and time."

"There was a woman," she remembers. "A few years ago, who started the program with Natalie Sanger. She took in an entire colony that had been living in an industrial site that was being redeveloped. She brought them all over to her farm. I don't know if she can help, but I'll ask. I'm sure I have her number somewhere."

"So what'll happen to the cats if she can't help? They'll just get abandoned?"

She nods. "Sadly, yes. Like they were before the Sangers started helping them."

I head back to the car wondering what the connection is between the feral cat colony and the Sangers having their ears cut. It's creepy and disturbing. I hope that Natalie Sanger will pull through so she can shed some light on it.

She gives us the addresses of the feral colonies the Sangers were caring for then we split up to interview the other volunteers. Vogel takes the two remaining vets and I head out to meet Cathy Nelson, the woman who'd left the voicemail message on Natalie Sanger's phone.

She lives in a farmhouse on the outskirts of Wainfleet. It's a rambling old place that was probably built when the United Empire Loyalists first came to Canada. It's painted white and blends into the heavy snow so well I can barely see it from the road. I drive right past and have to turn the car around and almost end up in a ditch. My dark glasses certainly don't help my vision but I tell myself they're helping with my hangover. So far my day is not going well.

"I have the Monday and Thursday shifts," Cathy Nelson tells me, once she's over the shock of the news. "I sometimes go alone, or bring along one of my grandkids if they are around. It helps to have someone younger to carry the food bags. They can be heavy."

"What do you do? Just feed them?"

"Yes, and take pictures of new colony members we may notice, or ones that concern us—like maybe if they're injured or pregnant. And if there are any in the traps, we pull the traps into the van, replace them with new ones, and bring the cats into the vet."

"And the colonies where you've placed the traps, that's all recorded? You'd be able to tell where the Sangers had gone on their last volunteer shift?"

"Of course," she says. "We record everything online. I can print it off for you." She heads to the printer, then stops, with a concerned look on her face. "You don't think this has anything to do with the feral cats, do you? I mean…how would that even be possible?"

I do my best to reassure her. "No, we're just trying to piece together a timeline of what was going on before these attacks." I don't need to tell her about the strange way both of the Sangers left ears were cut at the top, just like the feral cats they trapped and had neutered.

By the time I'm ready to leave I have a detailed list of every place the Sangers had stopped on their last night volunteering. I know from our search of the Sanger's house that they didn't seem to go out anywhere, or do much of anything beyond rescue cats and in Martin's case, spend his days on Gravelly Bay waiting for the fish to bite. I'd checked the receipts in Natalie's handbag: grocery store, liquor store, and the bulk pet food store. There were a few overdue library books in her car, ready to be returned. The Sangers were simple retired people on a fixed income, leading quiet lives. Why would anyone want them dead?

It looks to me like Martin had been tortured, possibly trying to force him to reveal information. But what kind of information? PIN codes for their banking? It seems unlikely, given they weren't wealthy people and surely wouldn't have a lot of money in their bank accounts. Is that what the ear cutting was about? Was that part of the torture and it was just a coincidence about the feral cats?

Or had they seen something? Or maybe they knew something and needed to be kept quiet. If not any of those possible scenarios, then that means we have a sick psycho in town, killing a defenseless old man like that for kicks. I'd prefer the torture option if I have a choice. At least that makes sense, in a terrible way.

"Detective, I just thought of something," Cathy Nelson says as I'm heading out the door. "I'm sure you've already done this, but you might want to speak to the young woman who's been staying with the Sangers for the past couple of weeks. I know she went along with them on a few runs. Maybe she noticed something?"

Patty. Who'd told me she didn't even know the Sangers and had only been staying for a couple of nights at their place? Apparently she's been there a lot longer than she let me think. I get in my car and head back out to Gravelly Bay.

Randy has moved the shanty that was near the spot Martin was killed. I expect the hole is already frozen over and with the fresh snow that fell last night, there's no more trace of where the crime was committed. That's not a bad thing. Too many ghouls would be tempted to come around and see the spot.

The gas auger that had been used to make the hole where Martin died was already taken into evidence, and both Randy and Patty are now at work, hand-drilling new holes in the ice for waiting fishing parties.

"That looks like hard work," I say to Patty once I've nervously slipped and slid my way over to her. Thankfully she's fairly close to shore so I just breathe deep and stay focussed on the job at hand.

"It's not so bad. I'm just re-drilling the holes that have iced-over from yesterday. The ice isn't very thick yet." She keeps her head bent, avoiding my eye. She knows there's a reason for my visit and she's nervous.

"How are you today?"

"Okay. Thank you—for getting me to Sophie's." It's clear she has to force herself to say that much. Patty isn't one for conversation either.

"No problem. Glad to help." Sophie has told me Patty is welcome to stay at Womyn Collective as long as she needs to. And, in addition to shelter and food, they'll make sure she gets some new warm clothes. It's not like Patty can go on wearing the same things every day, which she clearly must have been doing. I wonder again what Patty's story is. Why doesn't she have any clothes? Maybe she's an abused wife escaping her husband. She's certainly not your typical runaway.

"I need your help," I begin. It's always better to approach people that way, rather than asking direct questions. It makes them more open and less defensive.

"With what?" She stops drilling and looks up.

"I suspect the Sangers might have seen something on one of their volunteer runs. Something that brought them trouble. Do you have any idea what that might be?"

She brushes it off with a shrug. "I barely knew them. I only stayed there a couple of nights."

"I know that's not true Patty. You've been there for longer, at least a couple of weeks. I know you went on volunteer runs with them."

Patty puts down the hand drill and straightens up. "Cathy Nelson," she says with a sigh. "She told you."

"Yes, she did. And I have no idea why you lied about it."

"I just didn't want to get involved. I thought that if you knew I'd been there more than a couple of nights you'd ask questions…" Her voice trails off. I wonder what questions she doesn't want to answer.

"We want to find out who did this to Martin and Natalie. I'd like your help. No questions, I promise." Reluctantly, she meets my eye and nods. I know I'll be breaking that promise as soon as the first opportunity presents itself.

EIGHT

ON THE WAY back to the station I stop into the Green Bean Cafe—my favourite coffee shop, to grab a hot drink. I need to warm up after spending all day in and out of the car and out on Gravelly Bay. Even though I'm in my winter boots and parka and even have my hat with earflaps on, I'm chilled to the bone.

For the first time in all the years I've been coming to the Green Bean, Phil the owner isn't there. I almost leave, thinking I've somehow come into the wrong coffee shop. There's a dark haired young woman I've never seen before behind the counter, idly pretending to wipe the espresso machine down. But her eye is on the newspaper lying open on the counter in front of her and she's glued to whatever she's reading. She doesn't even notice I've come in and I have to clear my throat to get her attention.

"Sorry," she says, not bothering to smile. "What can I get you?"

Phil always knows my order and for some reason I'm irritated that I have to tell her. Ridiculous, I know, but I'm a creature of habit and this new person is throwing me off.

"Double Americano, please. And leave room for dairy." Phil always leaves me just enough room to add cream—and sugar if I'm in the mood. Today I'm going to need it.

She turns to make my coffee: grinding the beans, filling the filter basket and tamping it down, then as she's waiting for the drip to finish, she goes back to the paper.

"Anything interesting?" I ask. There must be for her to be so consumed by it.

She shakes her head and pushes away the paper then finishes making my coffee. "No, nothing." She rings in the sale and gives me my change.

As I turn to leave I see her head bend over the paper again as if she's studying it. I get a glimpse of the headline: **GRISLY CELLAR MURDER ROCKS REGION.**

I'm not surprised a bit. As DS Agu had predicted, the story exploded across national media and we've been inundated with requests for interviews from reporters and investigative journalists, some trying to connect these recent crimes to those from thirty years ago. Even though there's absolutely no possible connection, it's a great way for them to sell more papers, by appealing to those who missed those murders the first time they made the news. And if the media can make the story even more sensational they'll do it, in order to sell more advertising.

I wonder who that young woman behind the counter is, and as I'm heading to my car I nearly collide with Phil, who's on his way in. He's pushing a handcart loaded with boxes of paper cups, stir sticks, lids and napkins.

"On a supply run?" I ask him, quickly stepping aside so he can pass.

Instead of heading inside he stops for a chat, despite wearing no hat and his coat being unbuttoned. "Yes!" he says with a grin. "For the first time in ages I'm able to get this stuff done during regular business hours, thanks to Elsie."

"Who's Elsie?" I ask stupidly.

Phil laughs and point to my cup. "She made your coffee. She works for me now, part time. How is it, by he way?"

I haven't even tasted it. "Great," I lie. "Not as good as you make it, of course."

"She's a certified barista," he says. "She can even make those nice hearts in the latte foam."

I do my best to look impressed. "How long has she been with you?"

"About three weeks. She just got to town last month."

I wonder why anyone would come to our town in the middle of winter. It's the off-season for tourism and most of the local economy grinds to a halt every year between October and April. The vacation cottages are closed up, the vineyards and fruit farms asleep under the snow and most hiking and biking trails are impassable, apart from the few that are kept open for cross-country skiing or snowshoeing. Whoever this Elsie is, I hope she has a better reason for being here than a part-time job at a coffee shop.

I get back to the station just in time for the briefing. Vogel raises his eyebrow when he sees my coffee. "Where's mine?" he asks.

DS Agu is acting lead on this investigation, and he's now standing in front of the white board, which is covered with the usual crime scene photos, notations and a map. No slide show today.

The briefing room is almost empty, compared with yesterday when the story first broke. From now on the Cellar Man investigation will be handled by a core team headed up by Agu, who'll report directly to the Superintendent. Today in the room there's just Detective Sergeants Agu, DeGroot, Evans and Raleigh and DC Vogel—and me, the newest DC in the Homicide Unit, and the only female.

Agu brings us up to date on the investigation and shares relevant forensic information, such as it is, and there isn't much of it.

"Landry's wife claims she doesn't know anything about the house, or the cellar," he says. "She says she never even knew he owned the property. The farmhouse used to belong to Landry's parents and was left to him in their will when they died. Since Landry had handled all the family finances and business affairs it was news to her. The first she'd heard of it was when she was interviewed."

"How'd she take that?" Evans asks.

"She was angry," Agu says. "But clearly that's not the only secret he'd kept from her all that time." I'm sure she'd have been happier never learning about any of them. The next few weeks and months will be very difficult for her.

"What do we know about his business being burned?" I ask. "Was it arson?"

Agu nods. "Yes. Fire investigators drew that conclusion right away. The initial assumption was that it had something to do with his sudden disappearance."

"Who collects the insurance?" The room erupts in laughter at the irony that the insurance policy is on an insurance broker's office.

"Landry and his wife," Agu laughs. "But I doubt it'll pay out in this case."

"Not surprising," Vogel says. "I mean, the guy's disappeared, his place is torched. It looks like he did it, no?"

"Why would he do it if he doesn't stand to gain from the payout?" I argue. "That theory would make sense if he'd burned it, then disappeared after he got the money."

"Exactly," Agu agrees. "Anyway, Landry's dead. We've had a positive ID on the body." The briefing room falls silent.

"So do we think whoever killed him is the same person who burned down his office two days later?"

"It's a good place to start," Agu says. "And we're still looking for the one that got away." He rubs his eyes, his expression now serious. "She's luckier than she knows." I'm sure she knows that better than anyone.

"FSU has been combing the farmhouse and surrounding property for the past two days, using cadaver dogs on loan from the Provincial Police and the Metro Toronto Police Force. So far they've discovered the remains of four victims in shallow graves at the back of the property. And the search is ongoing."

"We've also located the victim's car." It's tough to think of Landry as the victim here, even though he's dead. All the women he abducted, including the one who got away—they're the only victims as far as I'm concerned. "It was in the police impound in Welland."

A murmur of surprise goes through the room: *We've had his car all along? WTF? The impound?*

"It was tagged and towed last month," Agu continues. "The lot just sent out the mandatory fourteen day notice to Landry's wife." According to police policy, storage lot owners can keep abandoned cars for up to two weeks before they're required to notify the owner.

"The car was towed from the strip mall parking lot across from the train station. It was only because so much snow had piled up on top of it that the car was even noticed." Landry's car might even been in the lot for some time before it was towed and it very probably was. Lots of cars are left in that lot overnight or even over a weekend, despite it being posted. It's an informal car pool stop and since it's near the train station people use it as an overflow parking lot when the station lot is full.

"So we only know the date it was towed?"

Agu nods. "December 18. With the holidays since then the impound lot was slow getting letters out. And they missed a few workdays, thanks to Christmas, Boxing Day and New Years' Day. Odds are the car was parked there at least a week before it was noticed, in order for that much snow to pile up on it. So, I'll say it would have been dumped the first week of December, which tallies with our time of death." He turns to DS Evans. "Check the snowfall records, see if we can get narrow it down."

Vogel speaks up. "So, our girl kills Landry and escapes, grabs his keys and drives into town, heading for the highway…"

"Why didn't she drive to us?" I interrupt. "Come straight to the police?"

"Good question," Vogel agrees. "She's on the run already? In some kind of trouble? In hiding? There's a bench warrant out for her arrest?"

"No," Agu says. "None of the prints from either the chair leg or the car are on file. So whatever it is that was keeping her from coming in to report it to us, it's not because she's in trouble with the police." He turns back to the white board. "We do know she ran out of gas because the tank is empty. She leaves the car here." He points on the map to the spot where the car had been found. "And she...disappears."

"No CCTV footage of the lot?"

"No...not in that area. There's only one camera at the train station and one at the strip mall entrance."

"Landry's bank records show he withdrew twelve hundred dollars in cash on December 6. We've never found his wallet, but we can assume she took the money and tossed the wallet into a trashcan somewhere. She hasn't used any of his credit cards. She's either too smart or afraid to get caught. Both, probably."

"Knowing how much cash she had will help us determine how long she could survive. Or how far she could run."

"Why not just fill up Landry's car and keep going? She could have put gas into it but she chose instead to abandon the car. Why? Did she think it would be traced?"

"Maybe she had to make a hard choice. There wasn't enough there to put gas in and survive for a while, so she left the car."

I'm skeptical. "I don't know....A thousand dollars can last quite a while, if you're careful." I'm having a hard time accepting that she'd just abandon the car where she did. If it were me, I'd have driven as far away as I could from that cellar and from what happened to me there. "Maybe she's from the area? Or was coming here when she was abducted in the first place."

"And then what? She just went home or wherever and didn't say anything?" Agu shakes his head. "I don't see that."

"Maybe she hopped on a train?" Vogel speculates. "Or stuck out her thumb and hitched a ride?"

"People aren't that willing to pick up hitchhikers these days."

"Maybe not a guy…but a woman? Alone? I bet there are a few guys who'd take a chance."

"No way," I interrupt. "There's no chance she'd willing be to put herself into that situation, given what she'd just escaped from." There's a murmur of agreement throughout the room.

Agu points to the map on the white board. "A lot of cars pull into that lot," he says. "It's near the train but also just before the border crossing. Last chance to use the washroom, grab a coffee before they wait in the line to clear customs. Maybe she snuck onto one of those vehicles? Like, into a trailer or the back of a truck? Got herself a lift across the border?"

"That's risky. That would take a lot of brass. Easy to get caught."

"I'd say taking risks is one thing she's proven she can do," I say. "She took a big chance attacking Landry and getting away. If she hadn't done that she'd have ended up like the rest of his victims."

"However, there's not much point in our pursuing that line of inquiry," Agu says, putting up his hand. "If she's crossed the border into the US there's no chance we'll ever see her again. We need to stay focussed on her either taking a train or still being somewhere in town. DeGroot—you follow up with the train station. Check their CCTV and see if anything shows up." I don't envy DeGroot that job. The odds of him noticing anything out of the ordinary about a woman buying a ticket and boarding a train aren't good. "She'd be alone and without any luggage or handbag. That might help narrow it down."

Agu continues. "If she's still in town, the question is why. It's possible she's from the area. Or, she was coming here for a visit, maybe to see family? Or to work?"

"What work?" DeGroot is shaking his head. "At this time of year?" He has a point. Most of our employment is in agriculture and that's pretty much stopped until spring.

"She could be here for the Icewine harvest," I suggest. "That brings in a lot of workers, for a short period anyway. Or maybe she's a working for one of the cannabis growers? They have crops year 'round."

Agu looks skeptical. "Maybe. I can't see many other options that would bring people here in early January. Gauthier, I need you to check missing persons. See if any women in the region went missing in the right time frame."

"Sir, I'm not sure where we'd even begin," I reply after a moment. I don't look forward to the tedious job of searching through those records, especially without more to go on. "We don't even know how long he had her down there. Was it a month? A year?" The room falls silent, contemplating the horror of what happened to this woman.

"Let's go back six months," he instructs me. "As a start." Agu then turns to Vogel. "Assuming she wanted to stay here, in town, she'd need a place to sleep. Check cheap hotels for that time frame, see if anyone fits the description. There's also a YMCA emergency shelter for women in Niagara Falls, and one in St. Catharines. Check them both out."

I raise my hand. I can't shake my earlier question about why she hadn't come to us for help. "Sir, how would she know about the emergency shelters, unless she was from around here? Logically, her first call should have been to the police, and we'd have directed her to one of them. But she didn't make that call. Why?"

"Maybe she doesn't trust the police," someone says.

"Maybe with good reason."

"Any theories?"

"Not really, no," I have to admit and Agu goes back to handing out assignments.

I have no problem believing she wouldn't trust the police, even though I am one. In my personal experience many are jerks and a few have also been corrupt. It's not unlikely there are even more of those out there.

If she'd chosen not to go to the police once she'd escaped that cellar, then she had a good reason and my stomach tightens as an idea occurs to me. What if Landry hadn't worked alone? Maybe he brought other men down to his cellar. Maybe one of them was a police officer. That would explain why she didn't come in to us, but there's no way I'm going to share it with the rest of team.

NINE

I'VE SPENT THAT last few hours systematically going through all of the missing persons reports for the last six months, looking for any possible women who might be our Cellar Man escapee. It's painstaking and slow and I'd much rather be out in the car interviewing people or doing pretty much anything else, even traffic duty. This record searching is tedious and frustrating, and even though I understand it's potentially valuable I hate doing it. I especially hate it because I get so much of it, being the newest member of the team and the lowest in the pecking order. I try not to let the fact that I'm a female factor into it, though on some days it's painfully obvious to me.

Suddenly Vogel appears by my side, and it's like the sun coming out from behind a cloud. He clears his throat to get my attention and I look up from my computer to see him fully dressed in a winter parka, thick gloves and a hat with earflaps. Then he stamps his feet and I look down to see he's wearing heavy winter boots.

"C'mon," he says. "Suit up Gauthier. We've got another body."

I grab for my boots and follow him, my adrenaline rush pulsing through my veins so intensely I forget my coat and hat and have to turn back to get them.

We drive out into the Twenty Valley, windshield wipers slapping back and forth against the driving snow. It's been dark for three or four hours already and the temperature has dropped even further as the sun went down. Row after row of vines stretches into the darkness as we pass hundreds of acres of frozen vineyards, driving toward a faint light glowing on the horizon, like an alien landing on a frozen moonscape.

When Vogel turns off the main road and through the gates of Ambrosia Winery we reach the source of the mysterious glow: at the end of the lane is an ambulance and two patrol cars, their lights flashing blue and red. There are also all the lights from the barn, as well as the headlights from a tall grape harvester lighting up the farmyard like daylight.

A crowd of people is milling around, all dressed in warm winter gear. They are an unlikely assortment of millennials in thrift store fashion and middle- aged people in expensive goose down parkas, all chatting happily as they drink from steaming mugs of mulled wine. I recognize them right away as volunteer grape pickers, at Ambrosia Winery for the experience of harvesting Icewine grapes. Maja and I did this same thing last year, at another winery on the other side of the valley. We'd come across a brochure that promised a gourmet meal along with an educational evening learning about Icewine production and we couldn't sign up fast enough, despite the price, which put a big dent in our budget for the month. It turned out to be one of those *seemed like a great idea at the time* adventures that we'll never do again, even if they paid us.

The winery where we picked is one of the more established Icewine producers in the region and they provided an excellent meal with fellow oenophiles, sommeliers and vintners discussing Icewine growing and fermentation. We had a tour of the winery, saw the pressing and bottling, and then we were led out into the vineyard to help with the harvest. It was a freezing cold night like tonight, and we picked the frozen marbles until our hands were raw, pulling them from the vines and tossing them into bins that were collected by the winery labourers and taken away to be pressed. One by one the paying participants fell off and went home, their hands and fingers numb from the cold but Maja and I kept on to the bitter end, finally finishing our night as the sun rose. We were the last to leave, only because both of us are too stubborn to give up on anything.

My throat closes up and tears spring to my eyes as I remember that night. I feel terrible that I haven't made a move to patch up our fight yet. The last time Maja and I broke up it was entirely my fault: my being so emotionally unavailable, my doubts and anxiety, and mostly my stupid stubbornness. Haven't I learned anything? I know I have to call Maja the minute I get a chance to, to make things okay between us again before I screw up as badly as I did last year. I quickly wipe my eyes before Vogel notices and climb out of the car, following him toward the cluster of police officers and the forensic team.

"She's just over here," one of the Constables says, motioning for us to follow him into the barn. We slip under the police tape and head toward the hydraulic grape presses at the back of the barn.

Dr. Vijay Singh, the Coroner on call, is already on the scene. From the way he's dressed it looks as though we've disturbed a special night out. He's wearing a formal suit under a long camel winter coat and his fine leather dress shoes under his booties make my feet feel cold just looking at him. He's bent over, peering into a large stainless steel tank that's part of the grape press.

"Good evening DC Gauthier, DC Vogel," he says as he pulls off his examination gloves. "I'm just about done here."

"What is it?" I ask, trying to get a look over his shoulder. I'm looking at the press, half afraid to hear the answer. If she was crushed in there it's going to be messy.

"A young woman," he says. "Head trauma looks to be the cause of death. She's been dead a while, based on liver temperature." He straightens and stands to one side so Vogel and I can look at the crime scene. "Thankfully, the machine wasn't operating. I think she was just placed in there. Maybe to hide the body."

"How long is *a while?*"

Dr. Singh shakes his head. "It's very cold. I wouldn't like to say." He shrugs. "Two or three hours, maybe. I really need to take a closer look at the body before I can give you a more definitive Time of Death."

I lean in next to him to get a better look.

The victim is a young Asian woman, wearing a pink puffy coat and matching snowboarding pants. Based on her warm boots and gloves I'd say she was planning on spending the night out in the cold.

I notice the top half of her left ear is missing and I point it out to Vogel. "There's no blood anywhere," I say, to no one in particular.

"That cut would have been done post mortem," Singh says. "But again, I'll be able to give you more information after a closer look."

"What the hell is she doing out here?" Vogel asks, looking around the barn. "It's freezing!"

"She's here for the harvest," I say, putting the pieces together. "Like all the rest of them." I gesture toward the group of people in front of the winery. Vogel looks skeptical. "The Icewine harvest."

Dr. Singh glances at his watch then motions for the ambulance attendants to remove the body, allowing the FSU team to get to work. "I have to go," he says as he heads toward his car. "I'm already late. It's my twenty fifth wedding anniversary."

As soon as the Coroner leaves, the winery owner comes over and introduces himself as Kurt Schröder. He gives us a big smile, like a politician or an entertainer and grips my hand in a tight handshake. He's only in his early forties I'd say, but his face is weathered from a lifetime spent outdoors and he walks with a slight stoop, as if he's an older man.

"I don't know what the protocol is for this sort of thing," he begins as if he's uncomfortable speaking to us. But underneath his words I sense a calculation, as if he's to figure out how to play us to get what he wants. "But I'm on a tight deadline with this harvest. And I've got all these people out to help…When can we get to work?"

Vogel immediately gets his back up. "Sir, you'll just need to wait. And please stand back. This is a crime scene."

"I'm aware of that," Schröder snaps back. It's clear he's got a temper and isn't used to being told what to do. "I'm the one that called you in the first place."

"You found the body, Sir?" I insert myself between him and Vogel. "Do you know her?"

Schröder shakes his head. "My wife found her. I've never seen her before. She must have come out with the rest of the volunteers and guests." He shifts impatiently then looks again at his watch. "Look, I really need your help here," he says. "If we don't start the harvest I'm going to lose my volunteers." He indicates a few of them already starting to walk away, heading toward their vehicles. "Without them, I'm screwed. I need to start picking."

He's also going to need his grape press. "I'm afraid you won't be able to use this," I tell him, in case he has other ideas. "It's part of the crime scene."

He looks disgusted at the idea. "That's my old press," he says. "It's basically scrap." He points across the barn to a new machine, standing next to a second set of open doors. "That's what we'll be using tonight—assuming you let me get on with the harvest."

I do a quick assessment of the situation before I respond. "Have any of your volunteers been into the barn? Did any of them see anything?"

He shakes his head. "No. They were all out front or inside the winery, keeping warm and waiting for us to get started. I came back to open the doors to make sure the barn gets cold enough inside." I can tell he's told this story a few times already. "I saw my wife standing there, frozen in shock. I went over and saw the dead woman. Then I called the police."

I flash on an image of what might have happened to our victim if she'd been dumped into the new press instead: her body crushed beyond recognition in the hydraulic press.

"What's wrong with this old grape press?" Vogel asks.

"It can't handle frozen grapes. The hydraulic presses we need for Icewine use about two hundred pounds per square inch—ten times the pressure you need for regular grapes."

"Can you please tell us why your wife would have been looking into this grape press tonight, Mr. Schröder? I mean, given that you aren't going to be using it?"

I watch as he struggles to come up with an answer and fails. "I don't know! I guess she was just…checking everything over, before we start the harvest." He rakes his hand through his hair. "Honestly, we've both been so worked up and anxious. There's so much riding on these few days every year. Neither of us can sit still…"

He shrugs. "So we just keep going around and around, checking everything over and over. It's a bit crazy, I admit." I get it. Maybe he and his wife have similar OCD and anxiety issues to mine.

It sounds like an honest answer so I decide to cut them some slack. Most people can't account for their actions during the day; nobody ever imagines they're going to need an alibi or to account for their whereabouts as they go about their business. I'd be more suspicious of someone who remembered everything they did, why they did it, and where they were on any given day. They're the crazy ones, the ones you need to keep an eye on.

"Where is your wife now Mr. Schröder? We'll need to talk to her."

"The other police officers already did that," he says. "When they first arrived. Can't it wait until tomorrow? She's just managed to calm down and pull herself together."

"Fine." We aren't going to get anything from her if she's upset anyway. We can come back in the morning. "Do you have the names and contact information for all your volunteers?" I know he'll have it for insurance purposes, but want to confirm before it's too late to get it. I'd hate to have them all start to leave in frustration, before we have any way of tracking them down.

He nods. "I'll get it for you right away....if you please just let me start the harvest now." He smiles, trying to get us onside.

"Where are you picking?"

"Over by the creek," he says, pointing away from the barn. "About five hundred yards away."

I make the decision. "Okay, go ahead."

Schröder nods his thanks and leaves. We watch as he waves his arms and gets the attention of the pickers. Then he gives them instructions and the group sets off together toward the far end of the vineyard. Each couple carries an empty plastic bin between them to hold the grapes they harvest. At the end of each row of grapes is a larger bin that they'll empty theirs into once they're full. Then a small tractor will empty those into larger, one-tonne bins that finally are tipped into the press. Everything is done as quickly as possible to make sure the grapes remain frozen until their juice is extracted.

Vogel stands there, looking annoyed with me for taking charge of the situation. "What was that all about," he demands. "You just let them go?"

"If he misses the harvest tonight, he'll lose all those volunteers, and it's likely to affect his income for the season. This Icewine harvest is a huge deal to the farmers." I look at Vogel and shrug. "I didn't think it would help to make him antagonistic. Anyway, we have the list of volunteers who are here tonight. We can talk to them at some other time. Let them have their fun."

"*Fun!?*" He laughs. "You call that fun? Who the hell would do that on a Saturday night in January?"

"We did. Maja and I, last year." I feel another pang as I remember that beautiful night, with the full moon glowing in the sky over the snow-covered fields. I wish we could be there together now, even in this bitter cold, instead of being in the middle of an argument.

"There were about fifty of us volunteers, along with all the winery staff who are dragooned into participating every year. We kept warm by passing a flask of whisky around and the farmer kept bringing us hot cider and snacks. It was a lot of fun." I don't mention how cold and numb our hands and feet were by the end of the night.

Vogel looks skeptical and stamps his feet. "At night? Why? I'd rather be drinking that wine, at home, in front of a warm fire."

"It's always done at night, when it's coldest. They need to make sure the grapes don't melt," I explain. "The grapes for Icewine have to be harvested and pressed at eight degrees below Celsius, or colder. If the sun gets on them, they might start to melt, which would dilute the juice."

"Why pick by hand? Can't they do it with that machine?" Vogel points to the brand new grape harvester idling nearby. It's a bright yellow rig, raised at least six feet in the center between the pairs of wheels to allow it to be driven above the rows of grape vines. The lights on top of the cab and between the huge black wheels brilliantly illuminate everything within twenty feet.

I shrug. "In some vineyards in Germany it's illegal to harvest Icewine mechanically. Maybe he's going to use that to do some of the larger fields and have some harvested by hand? That way he can still sell the tourist experience and manage to get his crop in too."

We stand aside as the forensic team finishes up and packs their equipment. The grape press has been photographed from every angle and swabs and samples taken from all over. Now it's being sealed with plastic and police tape, to make sure it's as protected as it can be until the investigation is complete.

"What do you mean, *sell the experience*?"

"I can tell you that we paid two hundred dollars each for the privilege of picking by hand." Vogel's jaw drops. "But we had a really nice meal, paired with delicious wine, as part of the deal," I laugh. "And it was totally worth it, by the way. Sort of."

Having said that, I look around the barn of Ambrosia Winery and conclude this operation is nowhere near as well run or successful as the one where we'd picked. The equipment looks old and not very well maintained and everything just feels shabby, apart from the brand new hydraulic press and the harvester.

I wonder if the Schröders are struggling financially, and if they are, how'd they managed to buy the new equipment. Probably took out a big loan, like every small business. Not every winery makes money, not even with Icewine. Or maybe they are just new at this; it must take years to become established and build a name for your winery. Still, they must be doing all right if they were even able to borrow enough to buy new equipment for this harvest.

Kurt Schröder appears out of the darkness and hands over a copy of the picker list. "This is everyone who showed up tonight, including staff," he says. "All of them and my team will be out in the fields for the next few hours, but they'll all be back here to help with the pressing later, if you want to wait to talk with them."

He looks at the grape press and the barn area marked off with police tape. "Is there any way I can disguise this? Like maybe park a vehicle in front of it or drape some tarps over it all?" He laughs nervously when he sees our raised eyebrows and stony expressions. "It's just that these people have paid a lot of money—a hundred and fifty dollars each—for a dinner and this Icewine harvest experience. If I have to make them work in the barn next to a crime scene..." He shakes his head.

"People might ask for their money back?" Vogel says.

"Worse. I'm sure there'll be complaints online, on Yelp or whatever. I'm trying to grow my business here and I really don't need the bad publicity."

I'm trying to wrap my mind around the kind of publicity he'll get when the news gets out that there was a murder at his winery, but don't say anything. I meet Vogel's eye and shrug.

"That should be okay," Vogel says. Schröder thanks him profusely and runs over to grab some tarps and barrels, placing them around the police tape to try and disguise the scene. Then he gets into an old Ford pick up and drives it into the barn, parking right in front of the old grape press. Within a few minutes he's done the best he can. If you didn't know there'd been a body found in here, you probably wouldn't notice a thing. I do briefly wonder what he'd told the group of pickers while they were waiting out front. It would have been tough for them not to notice the patrol cars and ambulance with all the flashing lights and police activity, but it's not my problem.

He props open the barn doors wide near the new grape press and is heading out to the harvester when I call him back.

"How long did you say it'd be before the pickers are back?" Vogel asks. I can tell he's not keen to wait around, and I don't blame him.

"Five or six hours," Schröder says. "But I'm sure not everyone will last the entire time. It's not easy work." No it isn't, I remember clearly. But when they're done they'll each get a nice gift bag, complete with a couple of delicious bottles of Icewine, to take away as a memento.

Schröder puts the harvester into gear and roars away in the other direction. We watch as he goes down the first row and the machine begins shaking the frozen grapes from the vines. Even from this distance we can hear the metallic pings ricocheting like bullets as they hit the bins. In the far distance I can see the lights from several other harvesters, travelling up and down other wineries' fields. The first night of the harvest has clearly begun.

"I'm not going to wait around here for five hours," says Vogel. "It's as cold in this barn as it is outside."

"It's supposed to be. I bet they'd do it outside if they could. The grapes need to stay frozen solid through the entire process. When they're pressed, the ice and grape skins get left behind in the press, and this intense, aromatic, flavourful and concentrated juice is extracted. But there's not very much of it—only about fifteen percent of what you'd get from regular wine. That's why Icewine is so expensive."

Vogel raises his eyebrows. "How expensive?"

"About a hundred dollars for a small bottle."

He whistles in amazement. "Picking in the freezing cold to

squeeze just a few drops, and it's really expensive too? Is it even worth it?"

"Have you never tasted Icewine?" I stare at him in astonishment. "Vogel! It's amazing. It's nectar of the Gods! *It is worth it?*"

I glance down at the list Kurt Schröder handed gave us. Our victim is Asian, so I quickly scan for any names that might fit. Nothing. So, either she gave a false name, or she wasn't one of the registered volunteers. One of the names catches my eye.

"Take a look at this," I point out a name on the list to Vogel.

"Patty Smith?" he says. "Who's that?"

"She's the one who works at Randy's Ice Fishing Rentals. The one who was staying at the Sangers."

"She's volunteering here?"

"I doubt she can afford the ticket. Maybe he's paying her to pick. Working the harvest is one of the only jobs going at this time of year."

"Do you suppose that's why she came to town? To pick grapes?"

"It's possible I suppose. If she arrived a few weeks ago, waiting for the temperatures to be right to start. Got some work with Randy Delaware while she's waiting."

Vogel is quiet for a moment, thinking it over. "There's something else we haven't considered. What if this Patty Smith is the missing woman, from the cellar?"

I hadn't considered that possibility, but the timing is right. "We definitely need to have another talk with her," I agree. "I'm sure she's not telling us everything. One thing she said when I drove her to Womyn has me thinking." Vogel pauses to listen. "She said she thought she heard people talking in Chinese, on the morning when Natalie Sanger was stabbed."

Vogel nods. "So maybe our new victim had something to do with that. And with the murder of Martin Sanger."

TEN

Sunday, January 12

IT'S SEVEN O'CLOCK and I'm lying in bed, still exhausted after my sleep, if that's what I can call it. Vogel and I finished up at Ambrosia by around eleven and I came straight home to talk to Maja and apologize, but she wasn't here. And she didn't leave a note. I guessed she'd decided to go to the Icewine Festival without me and probably ended up staying with Abby and Chantal.

At eight o'clock I'm showered and dressed when I get a call from the hospital. The doctors have decided to bring Natalie Sanger out of her medically induced coma. The intracranial pressure is reduced enough that there's no more risk of further brain injury and they are taking her off both the medication and the ventilator. They say within an hour she'll be conscious. I call Vogel to meet me there so we're both on hand to question her if she's well enough.

The doctor insists on being present in the room, to ensure she remains stable while we talk with her, which is fine with us. Natalie Sanger is the victim, not a suspect, and we want to keep her as comfortable as possible.

She's lying on the bed and her head and left ear are heavily bandaged. She's hooked up to several monitors and looks peaceful, as if she's asleep.

"Mrs. Sanger?" the doctor says. "How are you feeling?" Natalie Sanger's eyes open and she searches the room, her eyes first taking in the doctor then coming to rest on Vogel and me. She nods.

"I'm okay," she whispers, her voice hoarse. The doctor gives her an ice chip to help her dry mouth.

"These are police detectives. They are here to ask you some questions about what happened." Natalie's eyes widen; her pupils dilate as she starts to breathe rapidly and tries to sit up. "It's okay," the doctor says with a concerned glance at us. "You're safe."

She lies back in the bed, wincing from the exertion. Then she mumbles something and I lean in closer to hear.

"The cats," she says. "Need to look after the cats."

"Don't worry about the cats," I tell her. "The other volunteers are caring for them. They're fine." She sighs in relief and lies back on the pillow.

"What do you remember from that morning Mrs. Sanger?" Vogel starts the questioning. She closes her eyes and says nothing.

"Do you remember getting up? Making coffee?" I ask. Her eyes open after a moment and she nods.

"I got up to see Martin off," she whispers. "We had coffee, like always. Then he went to work." She doesn't know her husband is dead and I'm not going to tell her. Natalie Sanger is barely alive herself and telling her the truth won't help her recovery.

"Do you remember what time that was?"

She shakes her head. "It was still dark. Maybe six or seven o'clock?" Her eyes open wider and she looks around the room again. "Martin?" she says. "Where's my husband?"

"He's on his way," I lie.

"And then what happened after he'd gone?"

Her brow furrows in concentration as she tries to remember. Then there's a panicky look in her eyes.

"Do you remember what happened then?" I ask again.

She shakes her head. "No. I don't."

I know she's lying. "Are you sure? Did you see the people who attacked you?"

"I told you I don't remember anything." She's starting to become agitated. "I didn't see anyone."

The doctor shakes her head as she studies the monitor. "I think you need to leave now," she says, frowning. Vogel and I do as we're told.

"We're not going to get anything out of her," Vogel says. "Not until she's feeling stronger."

"Maybe then she'll stop lying and tell us what really happened that morning."

"You're right. She is lying, but why? They don't have any money. Nothing was stolen from their place."

"Another good reason for us to talk to Patty Smith again. I'm sure there's more than she's saying." Both times I've spoken to her she's been defensive, saying as little as possible, trying to stay out of the situation. Maybe the third time will be the charm.

Vogel and I head back out to Ambrosia Winery. I try to call Maja again, but there's no answer. She's probably at work by now, possibly with a patient. I can't leave a message with Vogel sitting right next to me, so I send her a quick text.

I'm sorry. I'm an idiot. I love you.

Once we're into the countryside the roads are frozen with ice and snow, so Vogel has to reduce his speed. We drive past empty white fields and orchards filled with the eerily beautiful black skeletons of fruit trees. Under the gloomy overcast skies everything is reduced to white and black. It feels peaceful and quiet, as if the earth is drawing in and nature is at rest.

"I hate winter," Vogel sighs. "I just booked a trip to Cuba, in February."

"You'll still have to come back to the cold after your week in the sun."

"Yeah," he sighs. "Or maybe it'll all be over by the time I get home." He glances at my skeptical expression. "A man can dream, Gauthier."

He turns off the road and in the daylight I can see the hundreds of rows of vines, laid out perpendicular to the lane. Row after row is still hung with grapes and the vines are all covered with heavy plastic netting. Something catches my eye: a black object hanging on the end of the row.

"Stop, the car! What's that?" I peer through the falling snow and see it's a dead bird, its carcass hanging from the wires on the end post. It feels like a premonition and a chill runs through me.

"There's another one over there," Vogel points out as he starts to drive again. I count another eight dead birds before we arrive at the end of the lane. When I climb out of the car I hear a shotgun echoing in the distance.

Kurt Schröder meets us outside the barn. He looks like hell. Or like a man who hasn't slept in over twenty-four hours.

"What's with the nets?" Vogel asks.

"Starlings," Schröder mutters. "They'll devour every grape if we don't net the vines. They'll feast on everything and I can lose tons of grapes. Literally. Tons."

Another shotgun blast erupts, closer this time. "And the shooting? Is that your team?"

Schröder nods. "Trying to scare them off. I have a guy patrolling every day. It's like a horror movie, thousands of them flying around and what they don't eat they'll peck at and destroy, just for the hell of it."

"Speaking of horror movies," I say, pointing toward the vines lining the laneway. "What about all the dead birds?"

"Scares them away," he says with a shrug. "Or so I'm told by the old timers."

"Sounds like a tough way to make a living Mr. Schröder," Vogel says. "Freezing cold, fighting off ravenous birds."

"You don't know the half of it," he laughs. "If it's not the fickle temperature or the greedy birds, it's insects or deer or rodents or hail storms or sleet or high winds that blow the grapes right off the vines."

I look around the fields while he's chatting with Vogel. The harvest is paused for now, but will resume tonight and every night it remains cold enough until the grapes are all off the vines. The volunteers have gone home to bed but I can see the winery crew still working near the grape press. It can take hours of pressure to extract a few drops of juice if the grapes are really frozen hard, so I guess it's taking a long time.

"You aren't picking now?" Vogel asks.

"It's too warm."

"You call this warm? It freezing!"

Schröder shakes his head. "The temperature rose to six below this morning when the sun came up. That's at least two degrees too warm for picking. So, we'll take another run at it overnight—assuming it gets cold enough. The forecast predicts it'll go down to ten below, so we should be fine."

"What about the presses?" I ask. "If it's too warm to pick, isn't it too warm to press?"

"We're okay. We just finished up in time," he says. "Now we're just cleaning up for the next round. Took just under ten hours to press this batch, thanks to our new machine." He turns to the new grape press and grins with pride.

As both Vogel and I make appropriately impressed noises about the shiny new press I notice there's a small excavator just outside the read barn doors. It looks like Schröder is building something.

"Are you expanding the barn?" I ask, indicating the construction area.

Schröder nods. "We need more space. I'm planning a sort of entertaining area, for guests to relax in front of a fire, sample wine, maybe eat something."

"Tough time of year to be doing construction," Vogel says. "Are you pouring a concrete foundation?"

"Yeah. We've had to stop for now until it warms up a bit. But once the harvest is done I can get back to work on it. I'll tent it and heat the space if it's too cold. As long as we make sure there are additives in the concrete it'll set up fine."

"So many capital investments," Vogel says. "New press, new harvester, extension on the barn. You must be doing okay."

"We're doing great," Schröder says, clapping his hands together. "Very excited for the future of Ambrosia Winery." He stops talking and we stand in awkward silence for a few minutes. I notice a movement out of the corner of my eye and look up to see a pair of yellow eyes staring down at me from one of the barn rafters. A large long-haired tabby is perched there, watching us carefully. His left ear is cut. I glance around and see there are several more cats hiding around the barn and there's a feeding station in one corner by the door. Several cats linger nearby, waiting for the food bowls to be filled.

"What can I do for you, Detectives?" he finally gets around to asking.

"We'd like to speak to your wife, and some of the other crew who are working here today. Assuming they were here last night as well."

"They were. It's all hands on deck during Icewine harvest." He directs us over to the workers. "I'm going in to get some sleep if that's okay. I'll send my wife out. We're taking it in shifts." He checks his watch. "I've been counting the minutes until I can go to bed, believe me."

Kurt Schröder turns to head back inside, walking past two of the cats. They dart out of his way and he kicks at one who's come too close. Ambrosia Winery must be participating in the feral relocation program Dr. Pompeo had told me about. I suppose they are better off here, being sheltered and fed regularly, even if Kurt isn't kind to them.

Vogel and I approach the five people who are working by the press. Two look like they are cleaning out the skins and stems from the machine and two others are shovelling the waste into bins to go into compost. One young woman is standing around idly, bantering with the men who are hard at work. I'm not sure if she's a member of the crew or if she's just visiting and providing moral support. When I get closer I recognize her as the new employee at the Phil's coffee shop.

"Hi," I say. "Aren't you from the Green Bean Cafe? Elsie?"

She looks over and eyes Vogel and me suspiciously. "Yeah. Elsie Duggan."

"Working here too?" Vogel asks.

She shrugs. "Sort of."

"Wine lover?"

"Not especially," she laughs. "I need the money." I don't miss Vogel giving me a look.

"Were you working here last night?" Vogel asks, flipping open his notebook.

She's wary and her eyes narrow and shift between Vogel and me. "Yes, why?" I tilt my head in the direction of the still-camouflaged crime scene. "Right," she mumbles. "Sorry."

"What can you tell us about what happened?" I'm opening my notebook and pulling out the photo of the victim to show her.

"Nothing. I never saw her."

"You didn't even look at the photo."

"Are you kidding me?" She rolls her eyes. "Asian woman? Pink coat and pants, right? It's all we've been talking about all night! Pretty sure I'd remember."

Vogel and I speak with the four other workers and get the same response: none of them saw the dead woman; none of them know anything. For what it's worth, I believe them. They would have been out in the fields preparing the bins and removing the netting so the volunteers could pick the grapes more easily. It's unlikely any of the picking crew would have seen our victim. She'd have been dead before everyone got out into the fields.

When we're finishing up with them Schröder's wife comes into the barn, clutching a mug of black coffee. Her eyes are puffy and she looks still half-asleep. I can't tell if she's avoiding us, ignoring us or is so focussed she doesn't even notice us. She heads straight over to the feeding station and opens a few large cans of cat food then dumps them into the dishes. As she's working the cats come close to her, waiting patiently as she prepares their meal. She tears open a bag of kibble and pours it out, then reaches over and manages to pet one of the cats on the head.

"They let you pet them ?" I ask when she eventually comes over.

"Not really," she says, not meeting my eye. She seems introverted and uncomfortable and my heart goes out in empathy. I recognize and can relate to anyone with social anxiety. When I'm not in costume and playing the role of police detective, I barely know how to function in public. But when I'm wearing my uniform, everything makes sense. "They aren't very trusting. But they know I feed them every day. That counts for something. I'm Renee Schröder," she says extending her hand, almost mechanically, as if doing so is unfamiliar to her. "How can I help you?"

"Can you tell us what you saw last night?" Vogel answers. "Walk us through it?" I'm sure of one thing: this woman is frightened. She's also clearly exhausted and no doubt in some shock. Finding a dead woman at your winery can't be good for morale or business. I tip my head at Vogel, indicating he should take a walk and leave me with Renee Schröder. I'm sure she'll feel more comfortable talking one on one, without his six-foot shadow looming over her. He shrugs, wanders over to the other side of the barn and gets out his phone. I can feel her relax in relief when Vogel is gone.

"I was restless and worried," she begins in a quiet voice, looking down at her feet. It's probably torture for her to look at our faces, but there's no need for her to do that. "About the harvest, and about how the night would go. It was the first time we'd opened the farm up for anything, the first time we had paying volunteers here. It was a lot of pressure on us, making sure the dinner was good and that everything was going to plan. Let alone the weather and the usual worries about the temperature and the harvest." She rubs her eyes. "Honestly, I'm not even sure why we decided to do it at all."

I imagine it would be for the money: at least hundred and fifty dollars per guest, less the expenses of whatever the restaurant meal cost. "Exposure? Publicity?" I suggest instead.

"Yeah, you're right," she rolls her eyes. "That's exactly what Kurt said. It'll help grow *awareness of our brand*." She sounds cynical.

"I guess it's pretty competitive," I say. "Lots of small wineries getting into Icewine?" I'm trying to make general conversation, just to help put her at her ease. The longer she spends chatting in a non-threatening way, the more relaxed she'll be. Not that she'll ever truly relax, I know. But maybe speaking with us won't be such a punishment.

"You have no idea!" she whispers. "It's insane. The rivalry, the squabbles."

"What kind of rivalry?"

"Over awards, mostly. Competitions. But some go way back, to when their grandfathers owned the land. How it got divided up, blah blah blah."

"Any wineries in particular?"

Renee looks worried. "No...not really."

"*No*, or *not really*?"

"I suppose we've always had this...*competition* with Left Foot winery," she admits. "But it's not a huge deal, really."

"Left Foot? Why them specifically?"

It's obvious Renee wishes she hadn't said anything. "It used to be owned by Kurt's family for ages," she says. "His brother operates it now." I wonder if Kurt's being in competition with his brother is significant in any way.

I also wonder what it's like to have a sibling. I'm an only child and it seems to me that even having a competitive relationship with a brother or sister is better than having none at all, but I could be wrong. I feel a pang of something, maybe even jealousy, as I'm talking with Renee. Kurt had grown up on a family winery. I'm alone. No heritage and no family. At least not one I'll ever speak of.

"How did that come about?"

"When his mother died, Kurt wasn't interested in the winery and his brother was, so he bought out Kurt's share. Kurt was young, was travelling, playing in bands. He even worked on a cruise ship for a few years." She manages a smile, thinking of her husband. "He was a talented musician." I nod. Call me a cynic but I'm sure there's no shortage of *talented musicians* who toured in rock bands in their youth. I'm sure the smooth Kurt blew back into town and swept shy Renee off her feet and she's been in love with him ever since. She seems to idolize him, which is rare in couples who've been married a while. It usually doesn't take too long for reality to rub the shine off love.

"Then he changed his mind? About wine?"

Renee nods. "He came home and realized wine was what he'd grown up with, and that he had a real passion for it. And of course he has all the skill and experience he needs to run a successful winery."

"Surely he doesn't do it all himself?" I'm irritated by her excess modesty. I mean, I get women supporting their partners, but surely she's got to deserve some credit for running Ambrosia Winery.

Renee laughs, sounding embarrassed. "Kurt runs the winery, does all the administration and the books. I've been trying to take that over from him, to help out. I've got a good head for numbers."

"How's that working out?"

"Not great, to be honest," she admits quietly. "He's having a hard time handing it over to me."

"Old fashioned, I suppose. Did you buy this place together?"

"It was in my family," she says. "We've grown fruit here since my great grandparents' day. They grew peaches, nectarines, and plums—stone fruit. They left it to me." I look around. As far as I can see there's only grapes.

"So you and Kurt started competing with his brother, tearing out the old trees and giving it all over to grapes." She nods but her expression is sad. I think I get it. Kurt wanted to expand the wine operation, at the expense of the fruit trees, at the cost of her heritage.

"Have you ever been married, Detective?" I shake my head. "Kurt had a dream. I had some land." She shrugs. "We're trying to make it work."

"Life's a compromise."

She laughs. "Well, marriage sure is!" "

"But you're okay with it, right?"

"When my parents and great-grandparents farmed here, there wasn't much of a local wine industry. It really only started up in the last thirty years or so. I like to think they'd have embraced it, if it existed in their day."

"I'm sure you're right," I say. "Farmers are very practical people." I'm not sure I mean it, but I'm hoping to make her feel better about the hard choices she's had to make. Then I change the subject.

"Where is Kurt's brother's place?" I've never been out to Left Foot but I know it's somewhere nearby in the Twenty Valley. I also know it's a very successful winery, often winning awards for their products. Looking around the ramshackle Ambrosia yard I can't help but wonder how Kurt feels, having to compete with his brother, who's now running the winery that could have been his if he'd made different choices in life. I don't know what that would feel like, but it's not a stretch for me to imagine it would be a bitter experience.

"It's just down the road." Renee points south, across the vineyard. I see a black plume of smoke rising into the sky and can hear the grinding of a shredder. Equipment is moving along the ridge as they are digging up fruit trees, and grinding them up.

"What's going on there?" asks Vogel, who has wandered back over, probably bored once he'd finished up on his phone.

"We're tearing out a hundred acres of peach and nectarine trees,"

Renee mumbles, immediately retreating into her shell. "Going to plant Vidal Blanc and Riesling."

"Why?" I glare at Vogel and he flinches. Then he strolls away again, this time toward the car.

"There's more money in wine, especially Icewine."

I watch the destruction, listening to the whine of the chainsaws. "That's sad."

She gives me a look and I can tell she agrees with me. "Well, they were about twenty five years old, if it makes you feel better. They weren't producing as much and they needed to be replaced anyway." She sighs. "Not sure it helps me to know that though, to be honest."

"No more scent of peach blossom on the air every spring," I say, shaking my head. "No more food for bees…it's a loss."

"Yes. It is." I hear her voice breaking, but when I glance up at her she's pulled herself together and masks whatever emotion she might have just felt.

I pull out the photo of the victim and show it to her. "Do you recognize this woman?"

She barely glances at the photo then she shudders and pulls her coat tight around her. "No. I didn't know her last night and I still don't know her."

I thank her and head over to the car, where Vogel is waiting.

"What's her problem?" Vogel asks. "Is she autistic? On the spectrum?"

"Vogel!" I hiss at him to keep his voice down. Not that Renee Schröder can hear us. She's heading back into the barn to check on the cats. "Anyway, I don't think so. I think she's just got social anxiety."

"She's odd. Definitely not the warm and friendly type, that's for sure." No, she isn't, I have to agree. But she's not cold or unfriendly. She's just another introvert, like me.

"Hey, are you guys going downtown?" A voice calls out. "I could really use a lift." It's Elsie Duggan. She's standing and grinning at us, with her thumb stuck out as if hitchhiking.

"Sure," Vogel says. "Get in." He holds open the back door and she slides in. "Where to?"

She gives us an address downtown on Victoria Street and Vogel starts driving.

"How long have you been in town, Ms. Duggan?" I ask. "Phil said you've been working for him for a three weeks. Since last month."

Elsie takes her time answering. "I got here in December," she finally says, but doesn't add anything more. Interviewing her is going to be slow work. She doesn't seem the chatty type. Or maybe she's not the cooperating with police type.

"Are you enjoying working for Phil, over at the Green Bean?"

She shrugs and looks out the window.

"What brings you to town?" Vogel asks, giving me a sharp look. I know where he's going with that line of inquiry. He's thinking of the Cellar Man's last victim. Any woman new in town is of interest to him as a possible suspect.

"I just kind of…ended up here, I guess."

"Do you have family here?"

"Nope." Talking to Elsie Duggan is like pulling teeth.

We turn onto Victoria Street, into one of the older more established areas of town. She tells us to slow down. "It's just this house here, on the left. The big stone one."

The house she lives in is one of the original mansions, built by the town's founders. Most of the large houses built around the same time have long ago been carved up into rental units. But this one seems to be still a single family home, in good repair. Whoever lives here has a lot of money. So if it's not Elsie's family home, who's she staying with?

"Thanks for the ride," she says as she climbs out of the car and runs up to the side entrance. I watch as she gets out a key and goes in the door.

Is Elsie Duggan being evasive? Why didn't she volunteer any information about herself?

"Ms. Duggan didn't seem particularly eager to chat. Or to give us any information at all."

"She doesn't owe us an explanation Vogel. She's not a suspect." I don't know why I'm defending her.

Vogel sighs in frustration. "You know what I'm thinking."

"I do know, and I don't see how it's going to help us. Are we supposed to look at every woman who's new in town as one of Cellar Man's victims? As the one that got away?"

ELEVEN

WE'RE BACK IN the station in time for the team briefing. DS Agu stands in front of the white board, which has been divided into our three current cases. Taking up almost half is the Landry case, or Cellar Man as most of us now refer to it. The remaining half of the space is divided between the Sanger case and our new mystery Asian woman. There are photos of the victims and of the crime scenes, as well as relevant documents and notations of evidence and important information we record as we build the cases. Agu will have to bring in another board soon because we're running out of room.

"What can you tell us about this new victim? The murder at Ambrosia Winery." Agu looks over at Vogel and I for a volunteer.

"Not very much at this point, Sir," Vogel begins, reading from his notes. "There was no ID on the body. No fingerprint match to anything we have on file…"

Agu holds up his hand, interrupting him and addressing everyone in the room. "That's including Cellar Man crime scene, so she's not our missing victim." He nods for Vogel to continue.

"There's no evidence of sexual assault. It appears she was just hit over the head and dumped into the wine press, though we're still waiting for the final report from the Coroner. Her winter coat and boots looks newly purchased and are barely worn."

"So," I stand and take over from Vogel. "We're thinking that possibly she was a tourist, someone new to our winter climate. Maybe she came here to participate in Icewine Festival. Her name isn't on volunteer list provided to us by the winery owner Kurt Schröder."

"We still need to interview all of the volunteers and paid guests from the winery," I continue. "To see if anyone remembers her. It's a long list, maybe fifty names on it so it'll take a while."

Agu nods. "You'll need help then. Raleigh, you're with them. Evans and DeGroot stay on the Landry investigation." Raleigh nods in agreement and I can't help notice how bad he looks. His eyes are red and sunken and his face is creased with lines. He looks ill and I wonder how much help he's going to be, especially if he books off sick.

"Speaking of which," Agu continues, addressing DeGroot. "What do you have from the train station? Any progress on a mystery woman boarding a train?"

DeGroot shakes his head. "Nothing yet, Sir."

"Okay, keep on it." Agu takes a deep breath. "As you are all painfully aware, the Landry case is front page news and that's putting us all under additional pressure and scrutiny. And you also know why." We all do: The shadow of the Leslie Mahaffy/Kristen French case is always looming over us.

"Here's what we know so far," DS Agu continues. "FSU have found the remains of seven dead women, in various stages of decomposition. The FSCC has all of the evidence and are investigating. We'll have more information in a few days." It makes sense that every piece of evidence will be sent to the Forensic Services and Coroner's Complex in Toronto. DS Agu will want to ensure there are no mistakes made, not like all those years ago.

"The investigation of the house is ongoing, as is the research into Landry's finances and personal life. His wife is being kept in isolation—primarily to protect her from the media. We'll be interviewing her again when we are able."

Vogel raises his hand. "Is she in danger, Sir?"

Agu shakes his head. "I don't think so. We're just trying to protect her and her family as best we can, until the noise dies down a bit. What about the Sanger case?" Agu asks, with a glance at the clock. "Anything new there?"

I look to Vogel and he takes his turn. "Natalie Sanger regained consciousness early this morning. Gauthier and I interviewed her briefly, before we were chased out by the doctor," he smirks. "It wasn't very helpful. She says has no memory of the morning she was attacked…"

"But we don't believe her, Sir," I interrupt. "It was evident to us that she's hiding something, or is unwilling to tell us what she did recall." I shrug. "Maybe she knows who did it. Or why."

"There is one unusual connection," Vogel says. Agu's eyebrows rise in curiosity and I wish he hadn't spoken. "There's a name on the Ambrosia winery list—Patty Smith." It's instinctive, illogical and unjustifiable, but I just don't feel like Patty is a suspect.

"Is that the same young woman who worked with Martin Sanger at the ice fishing shack?" Agu turns to study the white board and finds Patty's name there.

"And who was staying at their house," Vogel adds, bringing Agu up to speed.

"So who is she?" Agu demands. "How long has she been in town?"

"A few weeks," I say, dreading what that timing will hint at. As I predicted, Agu glances at the Landry board. A few weeks could tie in with the missing woman who escaped Cellar Man.

"What do we know about her?"

"Not much." "Nothing." Vogel and I say at the same time. Agu rolls his eyes.

"Get her prints to use as elimination," he orders.

I take a deep breath. This isn't going to be pretty. "Sir, she's not willing to provide them." Legally we can't compel Patty Smith to give us her fingerprints unless she is charged with a criminal offence. If she doesn't want to cooperate, that's her right.

"Why not? What's she hiding?" I hear the murmur of suspicion rumble through the briefing room. Like most cops, they're immediately suspicious if someone won't help us in our inquiries.

"She says she's protecting her civil liberties." Even though it's damn inconvenient for our investigation, I see Patty's point. I wouldn't give the police anything I wasn't legally required to. Not all of us can be trusted, and I speak from personal experience.

I know I'm stepping out onto thin ice but can't help myself. "Sir, speaking hypothetically, even if we find she is connected to Cellar Man, and we found her prints on the chair leg, would we seriously consider arresting her for killing him?" I look around the room at my fellow officers. I don't mention the torture and suffering she'd endured before she managed to escape. "It seems like someone did the world a favour by killing James Landry. She'd deserve a medal, not a criminal record."

"That's not the way it works Gauthier, and you know it," Agu snaps. "Stop messing around and get those prints."

"Sir, we've already got all the prints from the Sanger's house," Vogel says. "None of them are a match to anything on file—or to the Landry case. So, either Patty Smith was very careful when she stayed at the Sanger's and never touched anything…"

"Which is highly unlikely, Sir," I chime in.

"Or," Vogel finishes his thought. "She has no record and she is just a…*conscientious objector.*"

"A *civil libertarian,*" I echo.

"Don't you mean a *pain in the ass?*" Agu says.

I think back to when I first met Patty the day Martin Sanger was found dead. She was wearing gloves while she was outside smoking. And Friday night when I found her in the trailer, before I took her out to Sophie's, again she was wearing gloves. Was it that cold in the trailer? Or was she avoiding leaving fingerprints? I feel a prickle of anxiety and I wonder if maybe she is hiding something after all.

Once the briefing is over I head home for dinner. I need to see Maja, to apologize and to make this whole mess up to her, or at least to make a start. I stop by our favourite Thai restaurant on the way and order all of her favourites: Green Curry Chicken, Coconut Rice, Pad Thai and Mango Salad and I set the table and put a bottle of wine in to chill while I wait for her to come home. The clinic closes at five o'clock on a Sunday, so she should be home soon and I wait as patiently as I can. I'm not good at being patient.

Maja's been avoiding my calls all day, and barely replied to my worried texts when she didn't come home last night.

Stayed over at Abby and Chantal's. Too much wine.

It wasn't much, but it was better than nothing and I'd teared up in relief when that text arrived.

At quarter past five she comes in the front door and I can feel her hesitate on the threshold, as if she doesn't even want to come inside. Is it that bad? Is it worse than I realize? I'm so out of my depth most of the time with personal relationships maybe I don't really understand how upset she is. I know she's angry. I know it's my fault. I just wish I could figure out what I should be doing before I always seem to make the wrong choice.

"Something smells good," she says when she finally comes into the living room.

"I got Thai. Your favourites." Maja takes a deep breath and looks at me, waiting. I fling my arms around her. "I'm sorry. Really sorry."

"Why?" She looks at me, a half smile playing on her lips. She's testing me to make sure I'm not just trying to buy her off with dinner.

"For sulking like a baby and expecting you to share medical information with me. It's not right and I know it. I just get carried away…" She looks at me and shakes her head. "And for missing the Festival last night. I know you were looking forward to it."

Maja shrugs it off. "We went anyway. Had a great time." Then she takes pity on me and smiles. "But you were missed."

"I love you," I say. "Even though I forget to say it. Or my actions maybe don't show it."

"I love you too," Maja says and I well up with tears. "Let's eat. I'm starving."

I put out all the dishes on the table and open the wine, but only pour myself a small glass.

"You're going to work tonight," Maja says, sounding disappointed as she helps herself to the Pad Thai.

"Just for a couple of hours. Vogel and I are staking out some cats."

TWELVE

AT JUST AFTER six o'clock we pick Patty up at the trailer on Gravelly Bay. As we pull into the parking lot the strings of fairy lights go out, officially closing the ice fishing rentals for the day, though I expect everyone on the ice has been home for hours by now. I knock on the door and step inside, and find Patty eating a slice of pizza. There's a box open on the table, with just a few crusts left in it, and a fresh cigarette burning in the ashtray.

"I'm starving," she says. "I just had to grab a quick bite. I haven't eaten all day." I wonder how she got the pizza. Santini's—the restaurant on the box, is on the other side of town and they don't deliver. Then I realize the pizza must be left over from one of the ice fishing parties and Patty is eating their scraps. My heart goes out to her, but I know mentioning it will only humiliate her.

"I'll see you in the car," I say. "Let's go."

Five minutes later she joins us, first locking the door to the trailer and checking it twice. Then she climbs into the back seat, barely acknowledging Vogel. It's clear she doesn't want to be here, or to help us in any way, which I find irritating. Sure, she may distrust police. She may even be afraid, given whatever her personal circumstances might be. But surely she wants to help find whoever did this to Martin and Natalie Sanger. They were kind people who helped her out. Doesn't that count for something?

"I'm busy tonight," is what she'd said when I asked for her help.

"Really? Doing what?" I'd snapped.

"I'm working," she shot back. "At the winery."

"We'll make sure you get there in time to start, okay?" Grudgingly, she'd agreed, and I'm sure it was only because I'd promised we'd drive her out to Ambrosia. God knows how she'd have gotten out there if we didn't take her.

"Where to first?" Vogel asks once she's in the backseat, keeping his voice light. He's good at charming people, trying to make sure everyone gets along. He always says *You'll catch more flies with honey than vinegar.* I'm sure he's right, but most days I struggle to be sweet.

Patty shrugs. "You're driving." She's acting like a sulky adolescent.

"Okay then," I say. "We're going to load up at the Sangers' first. You can tell us what we need, right?"

Patty doesn't reply.

I turn to look at her. "You know Patty, you could make this a lot easier on all of us. I don't feel like working this hard getting you to talk. It's been a long day, I'm tired and it's late." To her credit, she looks ashamed. Vogel starts the car and we drive out to the Sangers' place.

"So what do we do first?" I ask Patty after Vogel has loaded the SUV with a couple of empty cages and a large bag of cat kibble. She doesn't say anything but points to the map we've taken from the Sangers' fridge.

"Head for the marine salvage yard by the canal," I tell Vogel. "It's off Lake Road."

"That's one of the feral colonies?" I turn to ask Patty, but she's staring out the window ignoring me.

Vogel drives along Lakeshore Road and crosses the Main Street Bridge over the canal, then turns north toward the salvage yard. At this time of night the place is deserted. It's an industrial area, and most of the businesses are closed at five during the week and shut up tight on weekends. Cranes and conveyors line the canal, next to two story high piles of sand and gravel the Town uses to spread on the roads all winter. We turn into the road alongside the salvage yard and drive up a few hundred feet until Patty tells us to stop the car.

"It's just over there," she points out the window to a gap in the fence. I hesitate, unwilling to open the door or leave the warmth of the vehicle. It's really cold again tonight and there's still more snow in the forecast.

"Where are the cats?" Vogel asks. "I don't see any."

"You won't," Patty says. "They hide from humans. If you do see one it's probably sick or injured." She opens the door and climbs out, carrying an old bath towel under her arm. "Let's go."

I open the back door, hoist the sack of cat kibble onto my good shoulder and follow her into the darkness, feeling an uncomfortable strain in my left shoulder. Patty walks along the gravel road and ducks through a gap in a chain link fence, then holds it open so I can get through. Vogel follows behind. I regret picking up the bag; it's a lot further than I expected and I should have let Vogel or Patty carry it. I hope it doesn't set back my recovery. One of them can get it the next time.

Tucked under a corrugated metal overhang are three large empty plastic tubs. "Those get filled with cat food," Patty instructs me. While I'm doing that, she fills some other bowls with water from a tap in the side of the shed wall.

"Won't those freeze in this weather?" Vogel asks.

Patty shrugs. "Yes. But until then they'll have fresh water."

"What do they drink then? Do they eat snow?"

"Yes," she says. "But it's not enough to keep them hydrated and it lowers their core temperature. Sometimes they'll drink from puddles, but around here…" Patty looks around, "…any puddles could be contaminated with antifreeze or gasoline. Or worse."

Up against the wall are at least twenty picnic coolers, stacked two rows high. Each has a circular hole cut out of the side.

"What are those for?"

"They're shelters," Patty explains. "Martin made them." There's genius behind them—the Styrofoam cooler will keep the cats inside warm on a cold night, the same way they'd keep beer cool in the summer sun.

"He bought all these coolers? That's expensive, especially when you add in the cost of food and vets." I wonder how the Sangers managed to pay for it all.

"I guess so," Patty shrugs. "There's piles of them at each of the colonies. He put dry straw into them. They'll keep the cats warm even when it's really cold."

"Where are they?" Vogel asks again, looking around. "Are you sure there are any cats here?"

Patty holds her finger to her lips and takes Vogel by the arm, spinning him around so he's facing into the scrapyard. "Look under the vehicles," she whispers. In the shadows there are dozens of pairs of gleaming yellow eyes, watching us, unblinking.

"Now we need to check the traps. When it's this cold Natalie always checked them three or four times a day. I'd hate to have one of the cats freeze to death in there before we can save them."

She leads us around the corner to a secluded spot under the eaves of the shed. There's a trap set inside a large cardboard box and Patty approaches it cautiously, crouching and peering inside. She turns and gives us the thumbs up sign, then slowly slides the cage out of the box, covers it with the towel and leaves it at our feet. Then she heads out in the opposite direction with another towel. She ducks around a corner out of sight. After a moment she returns, carrying an empty cage.

"I think maybe we shouldn't reset the traps tonight," she says. "Without Natalie around, I don't know who's going to look after them. She always organized everything."

"That makes good sense," I agree. "Let's just bring in all the cages and however many cats are trapped in them. Over the next few days the rest of the volunteers can regroup and figure out how best to proceed."

We put the trapped cat into the back, first covering the cage with a blanket, then drive to the next colony and repeat. This time we don't have any luck and both cages are returned empty.

"Are all the colonies in these out of the way kind of places?" I ask Patty, not anticipating a reply. "They're so far off the beaten path."

"We want to keep them as far away from humans as possible," she says to my surprise. "It's safer."

"What do you mean? Wouldn't more people be willing to feed them, to help out, if they knew…"

Patty's harsh laugh cuts me off. "People are assholes! More likely they'd try and kill them."

"Kill them?"

"Yeah," she nods. "Last year someone poisoned a lot of cats at one of the colonies. Natalie told me about it. That's why we don't let the public know where they are."

I can't argue with her since I know Patty is right about people; that's been my experience anyway.

The last colony is a twenty-minute drive away in a light industrial area. It's very close to the highway, next to a couple of warehouses.

"What is this place?" I ask when we pull into the lot. There are hundreds of metal shipping containers stacked behind a chain link fence.

"It's a shipping and freight forwarding yard," Vogel says.

"Shipping what?"

"Anything and everything. Wherever it needs to go. By air or sea." Vogel points above the door. "At least that's what their sign says."

This time Vogel carries the bag of cat food and we repeat what we've done at the first two colonies. But we're in luck; we've captured two cats in traps and we efficiently load them into the back of the SUV. "We're getting pretty good at this," Vogel says. Patty doesn't laugh.

"So that's it?" I say once we're all back in the warm car. "Once the three colonies are checked, it's done?"

Patty nods. "Natalie used to take any trapped cats home and keep them in her basement until she got them to the vet. They need to be kept in isolation, in case they're sick."

"Fine. We'll take these guys to the Sangers' tonight and I'll call the vet tomorrow morning." I think for a minute. "So, what we've just done, that's exactly what the Sangers did every time they did their volunteer shifts? This was business as usual?"

"Yes, exactly. Sometimes we'd catch cats, sometimes not. But the rest was always the same—feed them and fill the water bowls, then leave."

"Did you ever see anyone? Any people still working at the sites?"

"Sometimes I guess," she shrugs. "But mostly there was nobody around. The businesses were closed at night. I never really paid attention."

"Think Patty. Did anything unusual happen? Ever?"

She looks nervous and I wonder again if she's hiding something. "No," she shakes her head. "Nothing unusual happened. Not that I saw." I wonder if maybe nothing *unusual* happened because whatever it may have been happened regularly. Maybe something like a meeting. I also wonder if there's any way we'll ever find out what it could have been.

We climb into the car and head first back to the Sangers, so we can unload the cages and cats. Then we'll drive Patty up to Ambrosia so she can do another shift at the harvest. I take a quick glance at her clothes. The coat and boots she's wearing don't look warm enough for a night harvesting grapes at ten below Celsius. At least she's got a hat, I note as I she nervously twists the wooly cap in her hands.

We drive for a few minutes through the dark countryside in silence. Outside of town there's very little artificial light from streetlights or shop signs. But the moon is full and it's reflecting off the white snow and bouncing back the illumination from the headlights.

"What is it about these colonies?" I say to Vogel after a few moments' thought. "Is there anything that the Sangers might have seen or heard when they were out there?"

"Something they were killed for?" Vogel says. "I don't know Gauthier. It seems like a stretch. I didn't see anything, did you?"

"Vogel, someone tortured and drowned Martin Sanger. Then they stabbed Natalie Sanger…" I'm cut off by a cry from the backseat. *Shit.* I'd forgotten Patty was back there.

"I'm sorry Patty," I mumble. I should have kept my mouth shut. Still, maybe Patty needs a harsh reminder of what happened to the Sangers, in case she's hiding something from us. Putting a scare into her might make her more willing to share her secrets.

THIRTEEN

Monday, January 13

JUST AFTER THREE o'clock in the morning I'm awoken by my phone ringing. It's one of the Constables on night shift telling me Natalie Sanger is dead.

"What do you mean, dead?" I whisper, trying not to wake Maja, as if the loud intrusive ringtone wouldn't have already woken the dead. "She didn't make it?" Even as I ask the question fighting my way out of a wine soaked sleep I realize it makes no sense. Nobody would be calling me if she'd died of natural causes.

"Somebody killed her."

"I'm on my way," I say and as my feet hit the floor I'm already wide-awake. Whoever had stabbed Natalie Sanger in her kitchen had gone into her room at the hospital and finished the job.

I'm in the security office of the hospital, staring at the bank of video monitors when Vogel joins me. It had taken me three tries to track him down. After our night out cat wrangling in the cold he'd gone to a local bar and found a young woman to warm him up.

"How'd she die?" he asks as he pulls up a chair next to me, managing to jostle my arm so I spill coffee onto the keyboard.

"Looks like she was smothered. Someone held a pillow over her face at between two and three o'clock this morning."

"Wasn't she being watched?" Protocol requires a constable be posted outside her room, since she was the victim of an assault.

I shake my head. "No. I'm not sure what happened there. Agu is raising hell."

"What's this?" he asks, indicating the video stream on my monitor.

"The CCTV footage from earlier tonight. There are cameras at each of the main hospital entrances, four in total. Get comfortable, we've got a lot to look over."

Our local hospital isn't large; it has only around five hundred beds and limited critical care and specialized treatment facilities. It's a bit run down and none of the security systems are up to date, but at least there is some CCTV coverage.

Vogel and I watch hours of footage on fast-forward, seeing hundreds of people coming and going, including staff, paramedics and other first responders.

"After visiting hours are over at eight o'clock all the doors are locked, apart from this one and the door by the main entrance."

"Unless someone came in earlier and managed to prop open one of the other doors. I used to work part-time at the hospital when I was a teenager," Vogel says. I stop the DVD and turn to pay attention to what he's saying. "The kitchen access was always open at five o'clock in the morning to let the staff in. We were supposed to all enter past the security guard at the main entrance but that would mean we had to walk all the way around to the front of the building. So the first one in always propped open the back door."

"So you're telling me I'm wasting my time here? That anyone can get in, anytime?" Vogel shrugs. "That's reassuring."

I pull out the DVD for the rear doors and insert the disc with footage of the main entrance. Luckily last night was quiet and from seven o'clock to just after nine when the visitors should have all left the building only a few dozen people come in and leave.

"Immediate family members and new parents aren't always required to leave by the posted hours," Vogel says. "If someone's really ill or dying the nurses don't always enforce the rules. How could they? It'd be inhumane."

"Good point. So we need to look at the footage after hours too."

I turn back to the monitor and restart the video. At 21:38 a familiar figure enters through the sliding doors and I freeze the DVD. It's a woman with shoulder length black hair, tucked under a black toque.

"Recognize her?"

Vogel starts in surprise. "That's Elsie Duggan. What's she doing there?"

"No idea. But it's hours before Natalie was killed, so there may be no connection."

"She could have gotten in, hidden somewhere for a few hours then left out another door after she murdered Natalie."

"What, through another helpfully propped open door?"

Vogel shakes his head. "Not necessarily open. Most of the exits aren't even alarmed. Getting out is easy."

"Awesome." This is going to be much harder than I imagined.

Vogel pulls out the DVD and inserts the one from the Emergency entrance. "This one is the busiest door," he says. "People come and go twenty four hours a day."

"Start it at eight o'clock," I suggest. "When the other entry doors are locked. If we don't see anything we can always look back at earlier times."

Vogel starts the DVD and we watch, drinking coffee and staring at the screens as the timer ticks along. Every now and then one of us pauses the DVD and leans in closer to the monitor.

"That person looks familiar," Vogel says. Then we roll back the video feed and take another look, before deciding they don't after all. Finally, at 02:57 I see someone I definitely recognize.

"Stop it. Right there, look." Her head is down and she's looking away from the camera, but it's definitely Patty Smith. She's walking out the Emergency doors, leaving the hospital.

Vogel sits back in his chair. "How is that possible? I thought she was working last night. Didn't we drop her at Ambrosia Winery at around eight o'clock?"

I nod. "We certainly did. I'd say we need to have a talk with her."

"And with Elsie Duggan too," he says. "Funny though how neither of these young women ever have much to say to us, no matter what we ask."

Our first stop is at the Green Bean Cafe, because it's close by and because I need another coffee. It's a Monday morning and the place is jammed with the typical early morning crowd: students on their way to school, office workers and construction workers needing a caffeine fix to prime themselves for the day, and freelancers using the tables as their remote offices. Both Phil and Elsie are busy behind the counter.

Vogel and I wait our turn in line and as we draw closer Elsie notices us. She looks nervous but carries on making lattes and cappuccinos until we get to the counter.

"Americano?" Phil asks when he sees me.

"Make it two, please. And we need to speak with Elsie." Phil looks anxious and he turns to make the coffees as Vogel and I find a quiet table and take a seat.

Elsie delivers our hot drinks and flounces into a chair next to Vogel.

"What do you want?" she asks. "I've already told you everything I know about that woman who died at Ambrosia."

I pull out my cell phone and start the video of her that we've copied from the CCTV footage. "Can you please tell us what you were doing at the hospital last night?"

Elsie watches my phone screen for a moment, then looks up and throws up her hands. "I was visiting someone. Is that a problem?"

"Who were you visiting?"

She looks at us suspiciously. "Why do you want to know? How is it your concern?" Vogel catches my eye and I know what he's thinking: *Here we go again, never answering a direct question.*

"It's our *concern* because someone was murdered at the hospital last night."

Elsie considers what I said for a moment then shrugs. "I didn't do it."

"That's good to hear," Vogel says. "Now can you please tell us who you were visiting last night, after visiting hours were over?"

She thinks for a moment then sighs heavily. "I was visiting Lenore Campbell. I'm her caregiver."

I almost laugh out loud at the thought of Elsie Duggan looking after anyone, with her lazy, careless attitude. "You're a *caregiver*," Vogel says. "Since when?"

She chooses to disregard his sarcasm. "The last two or three weeks or so. I live in."

I'm processing what she's said and comparing it against what I know of Elsie Duggan. She works part time for Phil, and she needed money so she took a job at the Icewine harvest. She's been in town only a few weeks, has no family here, but is also apparently a live-in caregiver for someone named Lenore Campbell, who from the look of the home where we'd dropped Elsie, is a wealthy woman.

"I'm surprised you weren't at the harvest again last night. I thought you said you needed the money."

She laughs. "Yeah, I need money, but not that bad. Working in the cold all night, for minimum wage? No thanks! There are lots of easier ways to make money."

As Vogel and I leave I wonder what those might be.

We're back at the station in plenty of time for the briefing.

"There's a delay on the findings for our Ambrosia victim," Agu says. "Dr. Singh is sending the body into Forensic Services and Coroners' Complex in Toronto for a full autopsy."

I raise my hand. "What exactly is the problem, Sir?" It's obvious if she was frozen they'll need to wait before doing any post-mortem exams. But they've had thirty-six hours already, since she was first found on Saturday night. Wouldn't she have thawed out by now?

"He's uncertain about time of death, because of the cold temperatures the body was exposed to. Initially he thought she'd been dead a few hours, but now that's open to question. He doesn't feel confident in saying when she died."

"Her body appeared to be partially frozen when she was found, but some of her internal organs were completely frozen, which makes no sense. He doesn't want to under or overestimate her time of death."

"He did share that the top of her left ear was cut off, but it would have been done post-mortem since there was no blood at the wound site. He also suspects that the cut might have happened some time after death, even as much as a week, given the frost damage to the ear."

"A week?" I repeat in surprise. "So when did she die?"

Agu throws up his hands. "It opens up the investigation quite a bit. It's unlikely she'd have been in that grape press all this time, so now we'll need to find where she was killed, where her body had been stored all that time, how and when it was left at Ambrosia."

"And who she is."

FOURTEEN

LENORE CAMPBELL IS in a private room with a view of the lake. Before Vogel and I came in to meet her, we'd had a quiet chat with the nurse on duty, who'd rolled her eyes as soon as she heard the name.

"Is she a difficult patient?" I asked, given her reaction. I hoped the nurse would be unprofessional enough to share her opinion.

"She's okay, really," she laughs. "But *her son*! He's. The. Worst. Ever."

"What's she in the hospital for?"

"Broke her hip in a fall. But she's had surgery and is on the mend. She should be discharged in a day or so."

Lenore Campbell is lying in her bed, an open box of chocolate truffles next to her. On her bedside table is a vase of fresh flowers, and there are several more on a table across the room. She's a remarkably beautiful elderly woman; her sharp cheekbones could cut glass and her large eyes are still bright blue. She's wearing full makeup, including false eyelashes and it looks as though her hair has just been styled.

She sees us come in and sizes us up in an instant. "Who died?" she barks.

"We're not here about a death Mrs. Campbell."

"Too bad," she says drily. "Thought it might be my son."

I'm not sure how to respond to that, but I don't think she's joking.

"You're not fond of him?" Vogel asks.

She just tosses her head.

"I'm Detective Constable Lucy Gauthier, and this is Detective Constable Andrew Vogel. We'd like to ask you a few questions about Elsie Duggan."

Lenore Campbell lies back in her bed, an intrigued expression on her face. "Elsie? *My* Elsie? Now what can I tell you, Detectives? Please have a seat," she extends her hand in an exaggerated, playful way.

"We understand she works for you?"

She nods, clearly intrigued. "She does indeed."

"For how long?"

"Since about a month ago."

"What does she do exactly?"

"She amuses me." I find that hard to believe. Elsie barely says a word. How can she *amuse* anyone?

"Pardon?" Vogel asks. "In what way?"

"Elsie keeps me company. Tells me stories. Takes me on drives. She's a paid companion."

"How did you find her?"

"My son posted an ad somewhere," she says, waving her hand.

"You didn't go through an agency?"

"No. They only have foreigners. Coloured people." I take a deep breath and count to ten. Vogel takes over the questioning because he's not confident about what I'll say to her now.

"At first she was just a daily, hired for two or three days a week. But Elsie is clever, she quickly figured out a way to get more work. Now she lives in."

"What do you mean?"

"She knew exactly how to play on an old woman's sympathies, which is not easy since I'm very mean. I'm difficult to get along with—just ask my son, he'll tell you all about it," she smirks. "That's why Elsie was hired. He's tired of me. Just doesn't want to deal with his mother anymore." I'm intrigued by Lenore Campbell and tempted to ask a few questions to learn more about her. But that's not why we've come.

"You say she lives in?"

"She said she was looking for an apartment, because her house-mate was moving on. I have this big old house and I'm rattling around alone in it most of the time. So I offered her a place to stay."

"That's generous of you," Vogel says. "She's practically a stranger to you."

"Honey," she gives me a sharp look. "Elsie's no stranger. It's like I'm looking at myself in a mirror, sixty years ago. She's a delight!"

"She's like you? How is that, exactly?"

Lenore Campbell laughs until tears stream down her cheeks. "She's a chameleon. A hustler, and an opportunist. I love that girl to bits."

We find Patty sitting outside the ice fishing trailer, cigarette in hand. She starts crying when we tell her Natalie Sanger is dead and takes a while to calm down. Then she seems frightened and her defiance is gone, but she's still not talking. She stubs out her smoke and heads back inside to the warmth of the trailer.

"Patty, you've got to tell us the truth," Vogel begins as we follow her in. "We've got you on CCTV." He slides the photo of her leaving the hospital, with its time stamp prominently stating across the table.

"Okay," she sighs. "I was there."

"Why?"

"I was visiting Natalie."

"Patty, hospital visiting hours are over at eight o'clock. This photo was taken at just before three o'clock in the morning."

"It's the earliest I could get there. You know I was working all night! The harvest didn't end until after two o'clock."

I know we'd driven her to Ambrosia, and left her there at around eight. "How did you get back from the winery?"

"One of the crew dropped me off." That will be simple enough to check.

"Natalie was in a medically induced coma. How is it that you thought you'd be able to visit her?"

"I've read that talking to people in comas is helpful. I thought… it might make her come around."

Vogel shakes his head, clearly not believing her. "Patty, a medically induced coma is caused by sedatives, by medication the doctor has in the IV drip," he explains. "You could talk to her for a year and it wouldn't bring her out of it as long as she's sedated."

Patty ducks her head, embarrassed. "I didn't know that."

"And then what happened?" I ask. "Did you see Natalie?"

"No. There was a cop sitting outside her room. I just left."

"Then what did you do?" She's nervously chewing her nails and looking down at the floor. "Patty? What did you do after you left Natalie's room?"

"I never went into her room!" she corrects him. "I told you. There was a cop there." Her eyes narrow and she glares at Vogel. She knows he's trying to trap her.

"Okay," Vogel says, holding up his hands to calm her. "The hallway outside her room then."

"I was looking for a place to crash," she finally admits. "I had no way of getting back to Womyn that night. It was so cold outside…"

"Where did you go?"

She's reluctant to say anything for a minute, probably weighing out the risk of telling us the truth. "I went down to the basement," she finally says. "Where the kitchens and service area is. I thought maybe I could get into the laundry area or something…I hoped they wouldn't be locked."

"Then what happened?"

"I got chased out by some maintenance guy. He came in

and caught me trying to get some sleep in one of the linen storage closets."

"What did he look like?" Vogel and I exchange a look. We're going to need to corroborate this.

"I didn't really see him. I just ran." It shouldn't be too difficult to find out what maintenance staff were on shift that night. We can find the guy and have him corroborate Patty's story.

George Campbell's office is on Main Street, in an old storefront between a gluten-free bakeshop and a shop that sells sheet music. There are two signs on the door outside: One for Campbell Global Logistics and the other for Campbell Insurance Brokers, and neither of his companies seem to be in high demand, given the abandoned feeling of lobby. The reception area is empty, the furniture looks worn, and I bet the magazines are months out of date. George Campbell's receptionist shows us into him a few minutes after we arrive without an appointment. Clearly he's not busy.

George Campbell in the flesh is an unimpressive specimen, even as far as middle-aged, overweight and balding men go. He's either got a cheap spray tan or he's using a bronzer that's the wrong shade for his skin tone, and I'm pretty sure he's wearing a hairpiece—an inexpensive one. He should have spent a bit more if he had any hope of convincing people it's natural.

"Elsie?! What's happened?" He gets worked up when we state our business, his upper lip beads with perspiration. "What's she done?"

"Nothing we're aware of, Mr. Campbell. Why would you think she's done something?"

He purses his lips and looks at us over his reading glasses. "I've been waiting for you to show up. It was only a matter of time."

"You don't approve of Ms. Duggan?"

He snorts in disgust. "*Approve?* I should say not. From the second I hired her I knew there'd be trouble."

"I'm sorry…then why did you hire her?"

He glares at us. "Have you met my mother?" It's a rhetorical question and I ignore it.

"Why don't you tell us the story, from the beginning?"

Campbell sighs deeply. "My mother has needed some help around the house for some time, but was too stubborn to accept it. Then she lost her driver's license and needed a driver, to take her to appointments, or to play bridge, or to get groceries. So I posted some notices, looking for a companion, offering to pay twenty dollars an hour."

"That seems like a good wage."

"I thought so," he says with a self-satisfied nod. "I wanted to ensure we found someone of quality. With credentials."

"And does she have credentials?"

He snorts in disdain. "No. But she managed to charm my mother. Now she's got her wrapped around her little finger." I look at Vogel and he shrugs. Neither of us seems to have picked up on Elsie's charm. How she'd managed to get in with Lenore Campbell so quickly is mystifying.

"After a week or so, my mother offered Elsie room and board. It seemed like a good idea. I thought we'd been clever and had got her cheap." He shrugs. "A live-in helper, days off to be negotiated, for only twenty dollars an hour? I was going to negotiate her fee down because of the room and board. Now I wonder if that was her plan all along."

"What do you know about Elsie Duggan?"

"Nothing. Nothing at all."

"Forgive me, but it seems a bit careless, letting her into your home, giving her a key, when you so clearly dislike and distrust her…"

"It's not my home," he interrupts. "It's my mother's. She's mentally competent, or so I'm told. Certainly knows her own mind. What am I supposed to do?"

"Why is your mother in hospital, Mr. Campbell?"

"She had a fall last week." He looks at us, his eyes narrow as if he's making a point. "Down the stairs. Broke her hip."

"How did that happen?"

"Apparently she tripped over some carpet at the top of the stairs." It feels like he's trying to say something.

"*Apparently?*" Campbell gives me a look over his glasses, indicating there's more to the story. "You think something else caused her fall?"

He shakes his head. "Nothing I can prove." So, it's clear he thinks someone pushed the old woman. Is he implying Elsie Duggan did it? What would be her motive? I dismiss the idea immediately. George Campbell is just a nasty bitter man, jealous that his mother likes Elsie better than she does her own son. I don't blame her one bit; he's a creep.

"Those fractures take a while to heal, especially in the elderly," Vogel says diplomatically shifting the tone of the conversation.

"Yes," Campbell replies drily. "Lucky for us, Elsie is on hand to help out."

I take it from his tone that Elsie Duggan has a job for life, and he doesn't like it one bit. I wonder if we should be investigating this fall down the stairs. But without a formal complaint or evidence of deliberate intent to harm Lenore Campbell it's unlikely we'd get far. Besides, it may just be spite; George Campbell's making no secret of his dislike for his mother's companion.

Vogel and I thank him for his time and get up to leave.

"What is it you do here, Mr. Campbell?" I ask on my way out.

"We offer custom global supply chain solutions. You know, freight forwarding, consolidation, deconsolidation, distribution, warehousing, logistics."

I smile and nod then follow Vogel out. "Do you have any idea of what he just said?"

"Not a clue." I'm relieved it's not just me. As we pass out through the shabby reception area I'm sure that whatever it is that George Campbell does it doesn't seem to be in high demand.

FIFTEEN

I SIGN OUT for my lunch break and go see Doreen up at Pelham Woods retirement home. I try to see her once a week out of kindness and because she's a great source of information since she's lived in town for all of her eighty-something years. She knows everyone and everything, and what she doesn't she'll ferret out through her network of old friends and acquaintances.

When I find her I immediately regret coming all the way out here to visit; she's miserable and cranky and she's taking it out on whoever happens to be there, in this case, me. It doesn't take a genius to figure out why.

"What's the problem? Haven't you been able smoke as much you'd like?" This past week of intense cold has made it impossible for her to sit outside, where she likes to relax and have a chat with her fellow nicotine addicts. The most she's been able to manage is to bundle up and dash outside for as long as she can stand the temperatures to get her fix.

"Think you're smart, eh?"

"I am a Detective, Doreen."

She laughs, which starts her into a coughing fit that sounds a lot like a backing up garbage disposal. "And I'm in trouble with the management," she admits when she's able to catch her breath.

"Again?"

"They caught me smoking in my unit," she grumbles.

"Again?" This is not the first time, and I'm confident it won't be the last.

"They threatened to evict me."

"Again?" I laugh.

She shrugs. It's unlikely they'll even try to make good on their threat. The rents are too high and they have too many vacancies at Pelham Woods to lose a paying customer. But they have to make it look like they're in charge. More fools them. Nobody can control Doreen McAlpine. She's like a force of nature.

"Maybe step out onto your balcony next time. Or at least hang out the window."

She glares at me. "I did! That's how they saw me. Petty bureaucrats."

Thanks to the cases piling up at work it's been a little over a week since I've seen Doreen. She understands, and even though she's bored to tears at the nursing home at least she knows that when I do make it out to visit I'll have some stories to share. As far as Doreen goes, I never withhold anything. Sure, it's unprofessional, but so far she's helped me more with information than any paid informant ever could.

I've only known Doreen for just over a year, but you could say we go way back, thanks to a family connection I'm never going to share with anyone. The only person who knows the story is Maja, and I haven't even brought her out to meet Doreen yet. I will, soon. I've just been working up to it.

Doreen's in her eighties but will probably live forever, since she's pickled from the whiskey she drinks and well-smoked from the pack a day she goes through. She swears like a sailor and dresses like she doesn't own a mirror. But she grows on you.

I pass her a paper cup of takeaway coffee and sit down next to her in the conservatory of the nursing home. She's bundled up in her winter coat and is facing into the weak sun that's trying to filter through the clouds. I'm already too warm even without my coat, but she seems comfortable.

"I'm always cold these days," she says, reading my mind. "Is it my imagination or is winter getting longer every year?"

"The cold snap is supposed to end soon. Some low pressure system is coming up from the US," I say unhelpfully. I know it's not the actual weather that's getting her down. It's being old and bored and living in a nursing home surrounded by people with whom she has nothing in common except their advanced age. One of her two oldest friends was murdered last year. The other is living two floors up in the dementia wing here at Pelham Woods and she no longer even remembers Doreen. Life can't be easy when you outlive all your friends.

"So," Doreen says, picking up the coffee and turning to me. "Cheer me up, Lucy. Who's dead?" Nothing like a fresh corpse to make an old lady feel alive.

"You already heard about Martin Sanger, right?"

She nods. "He drowned, right? Ice fishing?"

"He *was* drowned, by someone else." Doreen's eyebrows rise in interest. "And his wife was stabbed in their home. She wouldn't give us a description of her attacker. Then someone smothered her with a pillow in her hospital room sometime around two thirty this morning."

She shakes her head in amazement. "Wasn't she in some kind of protective custody or whatever it is you people do?"

"There was an officer assigned to watch her room. He'd stepped away for a minute to use the bathroom. Came back and she was dead. Never saw a thing."

"Someone has balls the size of church bells to pull that off."

"We're thinking it was someone who is familiar with hospital procedures, who might know their way around…"

"Like me?" Doreen was a nurse for over thirty years at the local hospital. That's one reason I thought I'd come and have a visit.

"Don't worry," I laugh. "You're not a suspect."

"That's a shame. I could use a little excitement."

"When did you retire?"

"Over ten years ago. When I turned seventy two." I've never been quite sure how old she is, and there's something about Doreen that made me reluctant to ask. She could be a hundred for all I know.

"Isn't retirement age sixty-five?"

"There's no legal mandatory retirement age and I liked my job. What else would I do? Sit at home? Learn to knit?" She laughs, sounding like a chainsaw. "But once my arthritis got bad I didn't really have a choice, since I could barely walk." She gives her walker a little shove with her shoe.

"So, what do you think?" I get back to the subject. "How easy would it be to sneak into the hospital after hours, find a patient's room, kill her and get away with it."

Doreen laughs again. "As easy as taking candy from a baby. The security cameras don't work half the time. The doors are supposed to be locked when visiting hours are over but they usually aren't because staff need to pop out and get some fresh air on their breaks." She gives me a look. "Speaking of fresh air, I could really use some."

"Okay, zip up your coat." I get one of the loaner wheelchairs and sit Doreen into it, then push it outside through the conservatory doors. She can still walk, but she's so slow these days we'd both freeze to death before she got what she really wants: a cigarette.

Doreen lights up and inhales deeply, savouring every moment. I notice a few angry faces at the window, watching her smoke within less than the legally required twenty feet of the exit. But I'm sure the prominent police badge on my winter coat is enough to make them think twice before they complain.

Once Doreen has smoked two cigarettes I wheel her back inside and help her back into the armchair in the sunny conservatory. Her face is red from the cold but she looks much brighter than when I first arrived. She gives me a sly look, knowing I've got another question for her.

"What can you tell me about Lenore Campbell?" Doreen has lived in town for her whole life; there's nothing and no one that passes her notice.

Her face comes to life and she's grinning with delight. "*Her*! Oh yeah, she's a piece of work." I nod. "Is she involved in this?"

"Not her, I don't think…

"Too bad," Doreen interrupts. She cackles and shakes her head, I assume thinking of some karmic payback for Lenore Campbell. "She used to work across the border, back in the day. Lenore was a beauty, real movie star material, you know? Tall, leggy, busty like Jane Russell."

"Who?"

Doreen rolls her eyes. "Google her. She was the biggest movie star of the day." She holds her hands out in front of her chest. "And I mean *biggest*."

"What do you mean she worked across the border? Where?"

"In Buffalo," Doreen shrugs. "In some clubs. For gangsters."

"What kind of *clubs*?"

"I guess they'd call them Gentlemen's Clubs, back then."

I raise my eyebrows. "Was she a sex worker? A prostitute?"

"No…I don't think so. Nothing that hard. Maybe an escort? An exotic dancer? Or a cigarette girl? I wasn't ever sure."

"I guess it would have been legal to work in the US back then, without papers."

"I'm not exactly sure what she did was *legal*," Doreen cackles. "It was something shady, for sure." She shakes her head, reminiscing. "We all just came and went back then, over to Buffalo or Niagara Falls for dancing and drinks. No passports, none of this bullshit Border Services Agency crap like now."

"When was this?"

"Back in the fifties I guess. Maybe the early sixties? She'd be about my age, or a little older. Maybe eighty-five now?" That sounds about right. And the ballsy, brassy woman I'd met in the hospital certainly fit with the line of work Doreen mentioned.

"Lenore ended up marrying Arthur Campbell, descendent of one of the town's first families," Doreen continues. "His father was a lawyer, and his grandfather, too. At least one of them was an MPP. Maybe even MP, I don't recall. The family had all sorts of businesses—trucking, real estate, and a couple of small hotels. They even ran a big insurance business, I think." She gives me a sly look and laughs again. "Well…you can imagine the stink when Arthur ends up married to this hussy from a nightclub over the border! His family went nuts. I'm pretty sure they tried to buy her off, but she wasn't going anywhere. She knew a good deal when she had one."

"But I will say, the minute she came to town she cleaned up really well. Did charity work, played bridge, had a son…I think…" her brow furrows in thought.

"Yes, George. I met him."

Doreen drifts off in thought for a moment. "Her husband died in hospital. He was one of my patients at the time, on the ward."

"What did he die of?"

She gives me a sly look, then cackles. "The clap."

"Are you serious?"

Doreen nods. "Untreated syphilis. Probably got it from his wife. Technically, he died of an aortic aneurysm." She pats her pocket for her cigarettes, which I now know is a sign that she's got a story to tell. Then she remembers she's back inside and can't smoke. "*Shit,*" she swears in frustration.

"We thought at the time it was just regular old heart disease. But I looked at his chart—there it was: Cardiovascular syphilis led to an aortic aneurysm. By the time he was hospitalized it was too late to help him much. His heart was already too badly damaged. He died a week later."

She gives me another sly look. "So, what's the story with Lenore Campbell? Why are you fishing around about her?"

"I don't know yet…but it may be that someone was trying to bump her off." I can't quite let go of the idea George Campbell hinted at: that Elsie might have been responsible for Lenore falling down the stairs, even though I have no idea what her motive might have been. From we've been told she barely knew Lenore before she came to town.

Doreen claps her hands in delight. "Surprised it's taken this long. Promise you'll keep me posted on that story. I can't wait for the next installment."

"Yeah, I don't know what's going on there," I say. "Maybe nothing. But there's some connection to a young woman she's got working for her and Ambrosia Winery." As I say it I wonder if it's true. Is there a connection between Elsie and Ambrosia—apart from the obvious one that she worked there?

"Where that body was found? I just heard about it this morning." She shakes her head. "Poor Kurt and Renee."

"You know the Schröders?"

"Oh sure! They both used to work at the hospital. I think that's where they met, actually. She was a nurse, like me. A good one, too."

"And Kurt? What did he do?"

Doreen smiles. "As little as possible," she laughs.

As I pull into the station parking lot Vogel is just on his way to his car. "Agu's looking everywhere for you," he says when I roll down my window. "He seems pissed."

"What about?" I'm not really alarmed. DS Agu always seems pissed.

Vogel shrugs. "Where have you been?"

"I needed to get some air," I evade. "Took a drive." Vogel raises a skeptical eyebrow but doesn't press.

"I found out something interesting." He glances over his shoulder then gets into my car. I park, but don't turn off the engine. I want to keep the heater running.

"I found out a little bit more about the Schröders." I tell him what I've learned: Renee was a good person; a hard worker and a caring nurse; Kurt was work shy and into shortcuts, which definitely fit in with my impression of him. He looked like a burnout, a party guy who drank too much and lived too hard when he was young. "He's not too smart, I think."

"Who told you? Where'd you get that information?" I'm reluctant to tell Vogel.

"Doreen McAlpine."

He looks puzzled. "McAlpine. Isn't that the old lady who was involved in the Pelham Woods thing last year, when DC Decker died?

I nod and leave it at that. The other connection I have with Doreen is nothing I want to share with Vogel.

SIXTEEN

AS SOON AS I step into the station I'm pulled up by DS Agu. "Gauthier, I've been looking all over for you. I need you to come with me." *God forbid I take a lunch break*, I mutter to myself.

"Pardon me?" He snaps.

"Nothing, Sir." I don't say another word and I follow him and DS Evans out the door and into a patrol car.

Evans drives out of the parking lot, heading across the Canal Bridge toward the newer part of town, with Agu beside him in the passenger seat. I'd hate to be in his position now and having to drive Agu around and feel his scrutiny. My anxiety would spike so hard I'd probably have an accident.

DS Agu is the most intimidating person I've ever met. He's intelligent, impatient, decisive and in my experience, almost always right. *Not every time, though* I smirk. There have been a couple of occasions where I've bested him, not that it's a competition.

"Where are we going, Sir?"

"To interview Mrs. Landry. I need the woman's touch on this." I almost laugh out loud.

"Sir? Seriously?"

"Yes," he turns to glare at me. "I will feel better with a woman detective present during this interview. So, please do your best to act like one," he orders in his deep Darth Vader voice. Then his face creases into one of his rare smiles so I know he's joking. I hope.

I settle back for the ride, looking for the upside. At least I'll get some insight into the Cellar Man investigation. Since I'm not on that team, all I ever learn is what's being shared in the briefings, which isn't enough to satisfy my curiosity.

"We haven't interviewed her thoroughly yet. It was only three days ago that we got a positive identification of James Landry, and his wife has been in shock. I don't know how much she's actually managed to process of what's happened, or of what he'd been doing all these years."

"You don't think she knew about it, do you?" Neither Agu nor Evans responds, but I know it's the elephant in the room. How could the wife not have known? Was she part of it all?

"I hope she hasn't been reading the papers," Evans says. Not only will that upset her if she's innocent, it will taint her knowledge of events. What she genuinely might have known or even just suspected will be mixed up with what she's heard in the media and with what she's imagined while she's been trying to understand it all.

"I know the media have been hounding her at home," Agu says. "She's had to move to her daughter's place. It'll take them a while to track her down there. The daughter's married name is Smith." He chuckles. Even if the media did their research and found her daughter's marriage announcement there are a lot of Smiths in the area.

The door is opened immediately by a thin woman with a drawn face. I assume it's the daughter but she doesn't introduce herself. She shows us into the living room then she discreetly leaves. I wonder if it's to allow us privacy or to protect herself from the horror of what her father has done.

"Good afternoon Mrs. Landry," Agu begins.

She holds up her hand. "Please. I will no longer use that name. It's Hauptman. Mary Hauptman." DC Evans makes a note of that in his book. "Please, sit down," she offers. While we make ourselves comfortable she continues talking in a low monotone. "I'm told my house has had graffiti spray painted all over it."

"I'm sorry. It's true," Agu says. "There has been some vandalism." The Landry family home had been painted with obscenities and two of the windows smashed. Someone had set fire to the Christmas tree that was still standing in the front room, but luckily the fire department had put it out before the entire house went up. I imagine she'd left the tree up as some kind of a symbol of hope that her husband was coming home soon since she'd reported him missing. I can't imagine it was a very nice Christmas for the Landry family, not knowing what had happened to him. Still, that would be better than actually knowing what he's done.

We've had to post a patrol car in front to discourage any more vandals. People have become unhinged over the Cellar Man story. It's torn open old wounds that had barely started to heal.

"How can I get my things out of there? How can I sell it?" She's shaking her head. "I can never go back there. Never."

She's right. What her husband did is so far beyond any normal moral code it's impossible for people to forget it or get over it or understand it in any way. She'll need to hire a service to take care of it all for her—the emptying of the contents, the moving, and the sale. And I'm sure she'll take a big loss on the house. Who wants to buy the house of a serial rapist and murderer? Nobody—except possibly another one.

"I know this will be difficult for you, Mary," Agu begins. "More than what you're already going through. But I need you to identify some objects from the... farmhouse." It's the first time I've heard Agu hesitate. He must be finding this hard, though I doubt anyone who didn't know him would ever notice.

Mary Hauptman looks at him, a look of dread on her face. "What now?" she asks. "What could possibly be more difficult?"

DS Evans pulls out a large manilla envelope and hands it to Agu, who then removes a stack of photographs from it and lays them on the table. They are photos taken of some physical evidence found at the crime scene: clothing, jewellery, makeup and books.

"I need you to tell me if you recognize any of these things," he says, sliding some of the photos across to her.

She doesn't look at them. "From that terrible place? Why would I know any of them? "

"We have to ask."

The first several images are of clothing—one silky and one woolen scarf, then one of a baseball cap, and one of a wooly hat. Mary Hauptman shakes her head but can't bring herself to look at the image.

"You'll need to look at the picture please," Agu urges her. Reluctantly she turns her head and stares at the image of the scarves. Then she shakes her head.

The next is a book of nature photos. Again, she shakes her head.

Then Agu shows her photographs of a silver bracelet and an antique cameo brooch and she recoils in horror. "That's my bracelet!" she whispers. "And my mother's brooch. She left it to me." Her bottom lip starts to quiver as she realizes what it means. "I thought I'd lost them ages ago."

"There are more, Ms. Hauptman," Agu says.

She's shaking her head in disbelief. "What are these? Gifts he gave them? Stolen from me?"

"Some things may have originally belonged to the...victims." Or they may be things he bought them, with money he took from the family joint account, or his business accounts. Agu doesn't need to share that with Mary Hauptman.

After giving her a minute to compose herself, he goes through the rest of the images: several more pieces of jewellery, none particularly valuable, and none of them belonging to Mary Hauptman.

By the time we're done she is writhing in shame and rage, her face a mask of revulsion.

"This was going on for years and I had no idea. My own

husband…I let him touch me. It's disgusting." There's nothing we can possibly say that will make it any better. I reach across and place my hand on her arm. Small comfort, but it's all I can offer.

"I want to scrub myself with bleach," she wails. "I feel so dirty. And the times he hugged and kissed me and our daughter, and our grandchildren! Like a normal person. But he was a monster. How is this even possibly real?"

"None of this is your fault," Agu says, but his words are meaningless.

It's not her fault, but she'll be blamed somehow. Just like with the vandalism on her house, somebody always has to pay. And who better than the wife? The whispers will grow louder until they are shouts. Or more graffiti will be sprayed on her home, or people will spit on her in the street. *How couldn't she know what he was up to? Did she just turn a blind eye? Was she involved? Did she help him lure the women?* Mary Hauptman may change her name but she'll never escape the cloud of shame and suspicion that will follow her the rest of her life.

Once I'm back at the station Vogel appears next to my desk, grinning like the Cheshire cat. "So, I just checked out Elsie Duggan," he laughs. "There's no criminal record and no driver's license on file."

I'm baffled. "But they hired her to drive…"

Vogel shrugs. "I don't imagine they actually checked. Probably just asked her if she knew how to drive." Vogel chuckles.

"So…either she's driving Lenore Campbell around without a license, which I suppose doesn't surprise me…"

"…Or she's using a false name," Vogel suggests with a grin.

"Thanks. That's really helpful."

DS Raleigh joins us, a sheaf of papers in his hand. He's been following up with the rest of the volunteers from Ambrosia, systematically calling them all and asking what they may or may not have noticed the night the woman was killed at the winery. It's painstaking, repetitive and slow work, but it's the best way we have to get things done.

"Have you found anything?" Vogel asks him.

"I need to talk with you both, privately," he says, careful to keep his voice down. Vogel and I follow him into an interview room and close the door. Raleigh still looks exhausted. There are deep lines around his mouth and his eyes are red rimmed. He slumps into a chair and drops his head into his hands. Vogel and I exchange a glance as Raleigh starts to talk.

"About two months ago I was working a late shift, on patrol. I was tired and really needed a coffee, so I pulled into a coffee shop. There was a girl there." He rakes his hand through his hair and meets my eye. Adrenaline starts pumping through me and my heart starts to race. I'm not going to like where this is going. "She came up to me and told me she needed a ride to the women's shelter. Said she'd lost her money and asked if I could help her out."

Raleigh stops for a moment, gathering his thoughts before continuing. "James Landry was there, getting a coffee. He offered to help out, to give her a lift to where she needed to go." I glance over at Vogel. His eyes are narrow and he looks disgusted with Raleigh, his lips curled in distaste. "I was tired. I just needed a coffee, a break."

"I knew Landry," Raleigh continues, his voice shaky. "He seemed like a decent guy. He sold me my house insurance, for God's sake! So I told her to go with him. I said that it would be all right. She got into that car with Landry…I never gave it another thought."

"When I found out Cellar Man's name, when it was in all the papers I realized…I knew…what I'd done that night. I sent that young woman to him. I pimped for him." He's close to tears. I can see he feels terrible about what he did, but I feel no pity for him.

"You didn't know that's what would happen," I say, but my words are empty.

"No, but I'm responsible. She came to me for help. And I let her down. If I'd driven her to the shelter, then…"

"She'd have been safe, but he'd just have found another victim anyway," says Vogel. "At least this young woman, whoever she is, was strong enough to end it. She deserves a medal, if we ever catch up with her."

I'm not letting him off the hook. Raleigh needs to face disciplinary hearing for what he did. "You need to tell this to Agu."

"I know. I just wanted to tell you first."

I understand now why she didn't come to the police when she escaped. She'd asked us for help before it happened and we let her down. If we'd done our job she would never have been trapped in Landry's cellar.

"So based on the timing, this young woman would have been his last victim. And she would have been trapped down there about a month." My stomach turns over at the thought of what she'd gone through in that time before she'd escaped. "She'd be the one who ended it, the one who got away. So, where'd she go?"

"What did she look like?" Vogel asks.

Raleigh thinks for a moment. "She was wearing a wooly hat. Dark hair, I think…a lot of makeup. Pretty." He's thinking… "Freckles. Blue eyes. Medium height. Wearing jeans and a short jacket—definitely not warm enough for this weather. Vans or Converse or some kind of sneakers, not winter boots. I noticed that at the time and we chatted about it. She said where she had just come from it wasn't this cold. Maybe she'd come from B.C.? She had this big knapsack with her, like she'd been travelling to get here." I'm sure that knapsack would have been lost when Landry abducted her. Whatever worldly possessions she'd brought with her were gone.

"Oh…I remember something. She said the cold was *good* and she hoped it would get really freezing soon. That it would *help the grapes*. I have no idea what that meant."

I do. I understand immediately.

"She was talking about Icewine. The grapes need to freeze before they can be picked."

"Maybe she came out here for the harvest," Vogel says.

"Lots of people show up to pick." Raleigh looks confused. "If she was young, she could have been a student, here to learn about Icewine making. If this woman had come to town, hoping to find work at a vineyard, maybe she continued with her plan? She'd still need to make money."

"Let's check out all the wineries that make Icewine. There are lots more than Ambrosia and they're all harvesting now." If she'd come to town to pick, then she might be on some winery's list. That's the next logical step in that investigation.

"But what about the Ambrosia Winery list?" Vogel asks. "Have you called everyone on it yet?" I know we've been calling that list looking for information about the victim found in the wine press at Ambrosia. Now he's going to have to call again and ask about the one that got away.

Raleigh sighs and rubs his eyes. He's obviously exhausted. "Most of them. I haven't been able to trace a couple of the names yet. Either they didn't give us an address, or their printing was illegible, but I'm still working on it. Most I've spoken to are middle-aged wine lovers and some are viticulture students from the college. They came out that night as part of an Icewine Festival package the Schröders sold them through the school: dinner, wine pairings and the opportunity to pick Icewine, at a student discount.

"Did any of them mention seeing the woman in the pink outfit?"

Raleigh nods, looking at his notes. "Almost all of them. She was very friendly, chatting them up about the weather, the grapes, how much she loves Icewine."

"Did she introduce herself? Anyone remember her name?"

He shakes his head. "Doesn't seem to have been that kind of a crowd. She would have been at the dinner in the restaurant before as well, but nobody really remembers her there. Everyone was together in a private room, at two long harvest tables. But most people were paying attention to the speakers at the front, watching the presentation about Icewine.

"Okay, thanks," I say. "Keep after those guests. Maybe we can figure out who she was." I turn to leave but Raleigh holds me back.

"I've been looking for her," he mumbles. "Ever since…you know." He's talking about the other woman, the one he put into James Landry's car that night. If he'd been putting in overtime trying to find her that would explain why he looks so tired and ill.

"No, I don't know." I'm not letting him off easily. I know I'll never again be able to trust Raleigh's judgement, not after what he did that night.

"Ever since the news broke about Landry, about what he did with those women. I've been to a few of the other wineries around already. On my own, unofficially."

"Do you have a list of those?" He nods, handing it over. No point in us replicating work he's already done. I know he's been working this hard to save himself and cover his ass. I must have been tough for him, torn between hoping the woman had escaped so he wouldn't have to bear that guilt for the rest of his life, and hoping she was dead so the story would never come out. Poor Raleigh. My heart bleeds.

SEVENTEEN

Tuesday, January 14

THE SNOW SQUEAKS and crunches under my boots as I walk toward the group standing behind the police tape. It's so cold again this morning my nostrils stick together when I try to breathe through my nose. So I hold my scarf over my mouth and breathe in that way.

I'm the last to arrive and they've already set up a tent to shield the scene from passersby and protect the evidence. Vogel is there, stamping his feet as he chats with one of the FSU team, their breath forming clouds in the frosty air. As I approach Maja steps out of the tent, her expression serious. She catches my eye and shakes her head almost imperceptibly. She's telling me I won't like what's inside.

I take a deep breath and duck into the tent with Vogel right behind me, breathing down my neck. When I see the body I stumble and might have fallen to the ground had he not been there, with his hands out to catch me.

"I'm sorry," he mumbles. "I didn't get the chance to warn you."

It's Renee Schröder. She's been strung up at the end of a row of grape vines, her body held in place by the netting. Blood streams down her face and her eyes are missing.

"Who would do this?" I whisper.

"Birds," Maja says. I hadn't noticed she'd come back into the tent. "Starlings, I'm guessing, based on the huge flocks of them in the trees outside."

"When was she found? And by who?"

"One of the workers, Ramon Figueroa," Vogel says. "He was driving up the lane to start work and saw her hanging there. We've got him in one of the patrol cars now, to stay warm. He's…upset."

"I can imagine." How horrifying. It's a sight I'm sure will haunt him for a long time. "When do you suppose she died?" I ask Maja.

"Hard to say," she shrugs. "In this cold, exposed to the elements like she is, her body would have cooled quickly. Liver temperature suggests she's been dead around six hours. Oh, and you should know," she says as she carefully lifts a strand of Renee Schröder's bloody hair up off her face. "A piece of her left ear has been cut off. Just like Martin Sanger."

"Okay, thanks." I duck out of the tent as quickly as I can. I've seen more than enough. Vogel is right behind me and I'm sure he's thinking the same thing.

"Does the husband know yet?"

Vogel shakes his head. "I don't think so. Figueroa called from his cell phone and waited in his car in the lane until we arrived. I haven't seen any sign of activity from the house."

I nod then we walk together up the laneway to the house. Vogel's been waiting for me to arrive, as he should. Nobody wants to inform a man his wife's been found murdered, let alone without back up. We'll be sure to withhold the details of how she died when we tell him.

I have to knock on the door a few times before Kurt Schröder answers, rubbing the sleep out of his eyes.

"Sorry," he mumbles. The reek of alcohol on his breath knocks me back a step. "Late night. What can I do for you?" He stumbles over his own feet and grabs the doorframe to steady himself.

Neither Vogel nor I say anything, probably because neither of us wants to be the one to break the terrible news.

"Is there something wrong?" Schröder asks. Then he looks past us, over our shoulders, and sees the emergency vehicles down the lane. His face goes white. "What happened?"

"May we come inside Mr. Schröder?"

After we give him the news he sits at the kitchen table in stunned silence, trying to process the information. I'm sure it's even more difficult to do in his inebriated condition. The kitchen is a complete mess of empty pizza boxes, beer and wine bottles, dirty glasses and plates. I find a bottle of whiskey on the counter that has still some in it and pour him a shot. Not sure if the hair of the dog is a good idea, but it's the only one I've got. When I lean in to hand it to him I notice he smells like a distillery and I have no doubt he's still drunk. From the state of the room it looks as though they were at it all night.

"When did you last see your wife, Mr. Schröder?"

He shakes his head, as if trying to clear his mind. "Last night. After we'd finished the harvest. We all had a drink. A lot of drinks." He rubs his eyes and tries to focus. "We were celebrating."

"What time did you finish *celebrating*? Can you give us a time?"

"Four? Five, maybe?" He guesses. "I think I passed out."

"Was your wife with you during that time?"

"Of course! She was here…"He looks off into the middle distance. "I saw her…I remember she paid the pizza guy."

"Who was here with you?"

"Staff. The core team."

"No volunteers?"

"No. That's only for the weekend nights. It was just a way for us to make a bit of extra money." I wonder if it was worth it. From what Renee had said it seemed like a lot of extra work and worry. I can't imagine it would have been easy for her to do, given her personality. Talking to groups, giving tours of the winery and entertaining in their new barn extension sounds like torture for an introvert like her.

"Can you give us a list of their names?" I'm hoping some of them were more sober and will be able to remember last night.

I tear out a piece of paper from my notebook and slide it across the table to him with my pen. He stares at it for a minute, as if unsure what he's supposed to do with them. "The names, Mr. Schröder. Please write down the names of who was here last night." He closes his eyes and sways in his chair. Vogel puts his hand on Schröder's shoulder to steady him while he prints like a child writing lines in detention. This is not a great way to start.

Once we get what we can from him we order him to bed to sleep it off then head back out to speak with Ramon Figueroa. Maybe he'll have better recall. I ask a Constable to wait with Schröder until he wakes up, and sobers up, so we can have a more informative interview.

We find Ramon Figueroa staying warm and comfortable in the back of a patrol car. So comfortable that he's fallen asleep.

"Mr. Figueroa?" I say, loudly into his ear. It's the third time I've said his name and I'm becoming frustrated. I turn to Vogel who's laughing at my irritation.

"He's as drunk as Schröder. Now he's passed out? And he drove to work in this condition?! I'm going to breathalyze him, then he's going to jail."

Finally Figueroa wakes up with a shout. "*Que*?!" He stares at Vogel and me, wide-eyed.

"Mr. Figueroa," I snap at him. "We need to speak to you. Now."

He stares at me for a moment. "I'm sorry," he says. "I no hear you. I'm deaf." I shake my head. I guess it's going to be that kind of day.

Vogel steps in and takes over. To my surprise he begins to use ASL and signs to Figueroa as he speaks. "We're sorry to alarm you, Sir. We need to ask you some questions. How are you feeling?" Figueroa watches Vogel's lips as he speaks.

"I'm okay, thank you," he grins in happy surprise finding someone he can communicate with. "I read lips."

"What time did you leave the winery last night?"

"I go home after the harvest end. Maybe two o'clock?"

"You didn't stay for the celebration?"

"No. Too tired, man. I clean out grape press. Kurt insist I join the party for one drink, so I do. Then I go home to bed."

"Who was there last night?"

"Everyone! We were all drinking and dancing. Kurt was really celebrating. So happy. I've never seen him like that before."

"What do you mean?"

Figueroa mimes drinking and weaving around with a silly look on his face. So Kurt was drunk. "And did you see Renee Schröder at the celebration?"

He nods.

"How long have you worked here at Ambrosia Mr. Figueroa?"

"Since Kurt and Renee buy it. Fifteen years."

"Is it a good place to work? Do you enjoy it here?" I ask, and Vogel signs my words.

Figueroa nods again.

"Are they doing well? Is Ambrosia successful?" He hesitates then nods and shrugs at the same time. "So, not so well? Are they struggling?"

"A couple of times they pay me late."

"You think they have money troubles?"

"They both had to keep their old jobs after they bought the winery."

"That's tough. They must both be tired."

Figueroa shrugs. "Sure. Especially now with Icewine harvest. But now we rest up. Prune vines, get ready for spring. It's a good time." His glance flicks back to the tent and he shivers as if he's felt a chill.

"Did they get along? Was it a happy marriage?" Figueroa doesn't look at me. A long moment of silence passes, which speaks volumes. "What did they argue about? Money?"

"Sure, like me and my wife," Figueroa is trying to downplay the arguments.

"Same for everybody," I say. "Hard times."

"I think maybe it was something about the taxes," he says. "The government."

"They owed money?"

He nods. "Kurt make some mistake, maybe? It was trouble for them. Renee was saying she wanted to take over doing the books. Kurt was angry." That doesn't surprise me. Kurt's ego must have taken a hit if he'd screwed up on Ambrosia's tax filings, then another one when Renee wanted to take over from him. It's something we need to look into right away.

"That's it?" Nothing else?"

"About the vines. And the trees."

"The fruit trees?" He nods. "Renee didn't want to tear them out to plant grapes?" He nods again and his eyes flick to meet mine.

"She love the trees," Figueroa says.

I remember very well how sad Renee had been when we spoke. Maybe she resented it more than she'd let on, despite her talk about compromise. Did Kurt bully her into going along with him? It wouldn't surprise me.

"Can you remember the last time you saw Renee Schröder?"

He thinks for a moment. "She was outside, talking on her phone when I leave." We need to find Renee Schröder's phone and see who she was talking to last night.

His gaze drifts over to the tent and I know he's thinking about the horror he saw this morning. Then he drags his sleeve across his eyes. "I wave goodbye to her."

We release him and let him go home to get some sleep. There'll be no work done at Ambrosia Winery today.

EIGHTEEN

WE'RE WAITING FOR DS Agu to begin the briefing. He's already half an hour late. DeGroot is peeking out through the glass door, filling us in on the reason for the delay.

"He's talking to two guys in suits," he reports. "I recognize one of them—it's DS Sampson, from the Fraud Unit. I don't know the other one—he's some Asian guy. Shit, here they come."

He rushes back into the room and sits in a chair, trying to look casual.

Agu holds open the door and admits the two men, who stand next to him at the front of the room in front of the white board.

"Good Afternoon," Agu says. "Sorry for the delay. I'd like to introduce you to DS Sampson, from the Niagara Region Central Fraud Unit and Sergeant Xiao Chen, from the RCMP's Anti-Fraud Center. They've identified our victim from Saturday night at Ambrosia Winery."

"Her name is Mei Zhen Lai." Sergeant Xiao Chen steps forward. "She was a Special Investigator with the Hong Kong Customs and Excise Department, working with the RCMP on an operation to trace a counterfeit wine distribution network in the area." DS Evans steps up behind Agu and starts to add the information to our white board, printing the victim's name next to her photograph. He's become our team's unofficial recorder, since he has the most legible handwriting of us all.

"Did you say counterfeit *wine*, Sir?"

"Yes. Specifically Icewine." DS Agu nods for Sergeant Chen to continue. "China is the single largest market in the world for Icewine—around two million bottles consumed last year. Canada exports more than fifteen million dollars of Icewine annually to China, through legitimate channels. However, about fifty percent of Icewine being sold in that same market is counterfeit. Fake Icewine is an epidemic."

DS Sampson takes over from him. "There's been a suggestion that several Canadian producers are complicit in the fraud. They've been selling bulk, unbottled Icewine to be repackaged in China."

"What do you mean by *repackaged*? Fake labels?"

"The original bulk Icewine is diluted and mixed with water and sugar," Chen explains. "Or it's reduced to thicken it, and colouring and flavouring is added, which can create a potential health catastrophe if hazardous chemicals are added. There's a lot of historical precedent of wineries using illegal additives to enhance the flavour and aroma of their wines."

"The last thing we want is a repeat of the 1985 Austrian antifreeze scandal," Sampson interrupts. "Some wineries adulterated their wines with diethylene glycol—antifreeze—to make them thicker and sweeter."

Vogel leans in to whisper in my ear. "Did you say nectar of the Gods? Sounds delicious."

"Sometimes the wine sold in China doesn't even have a drop of Icewine in it. It's something else entirely that's been bottled with a fake labels. A lot of the time the labels are of non-existent wineries, or have crude spelling mistakes on them. But," he shrugs, "if your end purchaser doesn't speak English they aren't going to notice."

"It's been difficult to trace and prosecute the counterfeiters because the Chinese have a legitimate product of Canada—there's usually some small percentage of Canadian Icewine in the bottle. They have invoices, customs declarations, and all the required paperwork to show they are legitimately importing genuine Canadian Icewine and just bottling and distributing it in China. That makes it difficult for either of our governments to act."

DS Agu steps in to take over. "Our victim Ms. Lai was working with the Chinese government to audit and trace Icewine shipments from Canada. She'd been investigating the wineries in the region, posing as a tourist and wine lover."

"They'll be providing us with all of the intelligence that Ms. Lai has gathered so far," Agu says. "What wineries she's visited, who she's spoken to. But I can tell you it isn't much yet. She only arrived in Canada two weeks ago." So that explains her brand new, barely worn winter clothing.

"We now have to assume whoever killed her did so because they found out she was an undercover operative on this counterfeit wine case. We've found that her hotel room was searched. "

"A break-in?" Agu shakes his head.

"No. Whoever killed her must have taken her keycard and gone in afterwards. We're checking the security records to find out when that individual entered the room."

"Is there CCTV footage of the hotel?"

"Yes, and once we've determined the time her room was entered," Agu looks at me impatiently. "We'll check the cameras for those time frames." I try to stay quiet, but can't resist.

"Wasn't her laptop stolen from her room, when it was searched? Isn't that weird?"

Agu shakes his head. "It wasn't stolen because it wasn't in her room," he says. "We found it in her rental car, in the trunk. We assume whoever it was didn't know which car it was, or where it was parked. Luckily."

I can't help wonder why it took so long to discover Mei Lai was missing. "Sir, why didn't the hotel report her being missing? Didn't the maid notice the bed wasn't slept in, that there weren't any dirty towels in the shower?"

"There was a Do Not Disturb sign hung on her door," Agu shrugs. "They were probably just happy her credit card was pre-approved and the daily charges were adding up."

There's a knock on the door and a Constable hands DS Agu some paperwork. He scans it quickly then passes it off to Sergeant Chen and DS Sampson to read. From their expressions it's not good news.

"This is the Coroner's report on our victim Mei Zhen Lai," he says. "It appears she was dead at least seven days before her body was discovered on Saturday night." He turns to DC Evans at the white board. "That puts her Time of Death at January 3rd."

A murmur of confusion and disbelief rumbles through the room. "The date was arrived at by analysis of her stomach contents, matched against what we know was her last meal, based on her receipts and records."

"How could that happen, Sir?" Evans asks. "When she was found, Dr. Singh said liver temperature indicated she'd been dead only a few hours."

Agu nods. "Evidently Ms. Lai was killed by blunt force trauma as we already know. Her body was then frozen. It was in the process of thawing out when she was discovered."

Sergeant Chen steps up. "We now need to revisit the time-line, since she died eight days before we originally thought." Several people in the room groan. That's hours and hours of work now wasted. We have to start over.

"We need to find out where she was and who she was with in the week before January 3rd, when we now know she died. We have receipts from her files—restaurants, coffee shops she visited during that window. I want to know who she met with. Check CCTV footage, talk to anyone who may have seen her."

"But Sir," I raise my hand, about to state the obvious. "Ms. Lai was seen, on the night her body was discovered at Ambrosia. We have several witness statements corroborating it."

Agu raises a skeptical eyebrow. "Was she? The Coroner's report says different."

Agu is right. There's no way the forensic evidence is incorrect. So that means all of the people who claim they spoke to the woman in pink at the Icewine harvest are lying, which makes no sense at all. Why would almost fifty people lie about seeing a woman who wasn't there?

DS Agu thanks Sampson and Chen and escorts them out of the briefing room.

Agu comes back in and closes the door. "Before we continue I want to let you know that James Landry's wife, Mary Hauptman as she prefers to be called now, has been taken to hospital. She attempted suicide this morning." So much for my gentle female touch. Poor woman. She must have felt she couldn't live with the shame of being Cellar Man's wife.

DeGroot make the sign of the cross when he hears the news. It always surprises me when I come across a religious person on the police force, especially one in the Homicide Unit. I can't see how anyone could believe in God, given what we're exposed to on a daily basis, and the Cellar Man case just underscores that for me.

DS Agu continues the briefing. "Also, FSU has found her DNA at the crime scene." A murmur goes through the room, and Agu holds up his hand for silence. "It was on a scarf found at the scene."

"Where exactly was it found?"

"On the floor near the bed," Agu points at the photo of the crime scene on the white board. A scarf is clearly visible a few feet away from the body of James Landry.

I raise my hand. "Sir, we know Landry gave things to his victims—some of things he stole from his wife. Isn't that the likeliest explanation for her DNA being on it? If it was her scarf, what would we expect?"

Agu nods. "Except that, as you'll recall, when we visited her and asked her to identify the photographs from the crime scene she didn't say she recognized the scarf. The jewellery, yes. Not the scarf." I know where Agu is going with this and I don't like it.

"There are only two reasons the scarf would be there," he continues. "Either Landry gave it to one of the victims and she didn't recognize it, or his wife was present in the cellar at some point."

"Sir, why would she be there? It's impossible for me to imagine…"

"Imagination isn't going to help us solve this case Gauthier. The evidence is indisputable."

"Why would she be there? You seriously think it's conceivable that Landry's wife is a participant in what went on in the cellar?"

"Not a participant, but maybe a bystander. Maybe willing to pretend nothing was going on, despite her suspicions?" I can't believe what I'm hearing. There's no way that the woman I met is capable of participating in something so evil.

"That would be a tough thing to do," Vogel says.

"Do we even know how old that scarf is? Is it five years old? Brand new?"

"It looks barely worn," he says. "I'd say it's either new…"

"Or was taken from his wife shortly after she bought it." Agu nods, conceding the point.

It's revolting enough thinking that Landry stole his wife's things to give to these poor women he victimized. But the alternative, that Mary Hauptman had been on the scene, that she knew what was going on in that cellar, is far worse.

"Moving on," Agu says, moving over to the section of the white board dedicated to the Ambrosia Winery murder. So far nothing about the new murder has been added. "What do we have from that, Gauthier?"

I stand and deliver. "The victim is Renee Schröder. She owns the winery with her husband Kurt. She was killed the same way as Ms. Lai—blunt force trauma. The top of her left ear was also cut off. But instead of her body being hidden somewhere, as Ms. Lai's was inside a grape press, she was strung up for anyone to see, in the netted grape wines next to the entrance lane."

"So looks like whoever did it is either getting bolder…"

"Or maybe it's a warning," Raleigh interrupts. "Some kind of a message."

"It's not a stretch to connect the two Ambrosia Winery murders," Agu says, dismissing Raleigh's speculation. "And it's also not a stretch to connect them both to this Icewine fraud issue. We need to follow up there."

"We will, Sir. When the husband sobers up. We weren't able to get anything out of him this morning."

"This is the fourth murder in less than a week," Agu continues. "Apart from the death of Cellar Man and his victims, that is." He points to the photos of the Sangers. "These other two: Martin and Natalie Sanger—could they be connected to the Ambrosia Winery killings?"

"I don't see how, Sir," Vogel says. "The Sangers weren't in that circle. Not wine people."

"Sir," I raise my hand. "The Sangers and Renee Schröder all had their ears cut. Just the top of the left ear, as did Ms. Lai. And, there is one other connection." I'm hesitant to say it. Agu looks at me, waiting for whatever I have to share. Raleigh is watching me as well. He's afraid I'm going to drop him in it with Agu. "Patty Smith."

Agu shakes his head and glances at the white board, looking for some information on her.

"She's the young woman, who was staying at the Sangers' for a while. She's also working at Ambrosia for the Icewine harvest. So she's a link between them all."

"The *civil libertarian*?" Agu's eyes narrow in suspicion. I nod.

"We now have her on CCTV as being in the hospital the night Natalie Sanger was killed," Vogel adds.

"Is she a suspect? Have you questioned her?"

"Not yet, Sir. Everything seems a bit circumstantial, possibly just coincidence."

"I don't believe in coincidences. Bring her back in." He glares at me. "And this time make sure you get her prints."

NINETEEN

VOGEL TRACKS PATTY down at the ice fishing trailer and brings her in for questioning. Predictably, she was unwilling to come in, but Vogel was able to either convince or intimidate her into cooperating; I'm not sure which and I don't much care, as long as it satisfies DS Agu.

I have no rational reasons for believing her when she told us what happened at the hospital. In all honesty, it's far too coincidental that Patty just happens to be around when each of the murders have happened: She was at the ice fishing shack shortly after Martin Sanger's body was discovered. She says she was hiding under the bed when Natalie was first attacked and was in the hospital the night she was killed. She was at Ambrosia the night Mei Zhen Lai's body was found. The only death she doesn't appear to be connected to—yet—is that of Renee Schröder. Like Agu, I don't believe in coincidences, and it really is impossible to believe she's not somehow involved. And yet, I just don't feel she is. Maybe my intuition is broken.

I watch through the window as she's being fingerprinted. Vogel must have done a great job of convincing her to forgo her civil liberties. I imagine having her on camera at the scene of a murder carries some weight.

When they are done and the fingerprint technician leaves I join

Patty and Vogel in the interview room, and bring her a cup of coffee to placate her, at least as much as a hot beverage in a paper cup can do.

"This will help warm you up," I say. "You must be cold sitting in that trailer all day."

"It's not so bad. Temperature's going up overnight," she says, wiping the last of the ink from her fingertips. "Randy says the January thaw is coming. Thanks though," she adds, to my surprise. Her manners seem to be improving.

"We just need those prints to eliminate you from the inquiry," I say. "You understand that, right? You're not under arrest." She nods.

"There's been another murder," I say, watching for a reaction. There is one, as you'd expect: shock, horror, confusion and fear. The last one interests me the most.

"Who? When?" It's unlikely she could have heard anything yet, being stuck in that trailer all day. We'd only managed to get Renee Shröder's body into the morgue a couple of hours ago. She'd been frozen into the grape wines and they had a job of cutting her out.

"Renee Schröder. She was found dead at the winery this morning."

Patty stares at us in horror, mouth agape, frozen with her coffee cup poised to take a sip. She puts the cup back on the table, her hands trembling. She blinks back tears and hugs herself and I wonder if that's to disguise the now-uncontrollable shaking of her hands.

"How?" She whispers. "Who would do that?"

"We're not able to tell you how," Vogel says, flipping open his notebook. "And I'm sorry to say we don't know who. Yet." The threat is unmistakeable.

"Were you at the harvest last night, Patty?"

She nods. "For a while."

"How long?"

"A few hours. There wasn't much left to pick," she says. "We'd done most of it the first two nights, so it was just ten or fifteen rows to do."

"When did you leave?"

"They sent most of us home at around one thirty. The regular crew were still working, getting in the last few bins, running the grape press."

"You didn't stay until the pressing was done? Clean everything up, like usual?"

"No, just the core team stayed—the full time employees. They let the rest of us go early, probably to save money."

"Did you see Renee Schröder last night?"

"Yes. She was working in the fields with us the whole time."

"Picking?"

Patty nods. "And taking in the bins to the press. She brought us out hot cider a couple of times."

"How'd she seem? Upset? Worried?"

Patty makes a face. "Tired, I guess. Picking is hard work. Intense." She thinks for a minute. "She wasn't ever much of a talker. But she said something weird like *You never really know the truth*, or *You never really know someone*. Something like that."

"Any idea what she was referring to?"

She shrugs. "No. I just assumed it was a marriage thing. People argue. It's stressful trying to build a winery."

"How do you know so much about wineries?"

"I don't," she's quick to deflect. "I just assumed."

I'm not sure I believe her, but can't think of any reason she'd lie to me. "Where did you go after that?"

"Home—to Womyn, where I'm staying." I know we can check that easily enough. Sophie has security cameras all over the Womyn Collective, as a deterrent to prevent abusive husbands from finding their wives at the shelter.

"How did you get there?" It's only a couple of kilometers away as the crow flies, but that late on a cold night it wouldn't be easy to walk it.

"One of the regular crew drove us all home. The deaf guy, Ramon—he left when we did."

I hear a commotion out in the hall. A loud male voice is shouting and others are trying to get him under control. I note a look of terror that passes over Patty's face when she hears it. She clearly recognizes the voice.

"Excuse us," I say to Patty and rush out with Vogel to find out what's going on.

It's Kurt Schröder. He's standing in the middle of our lobby, demanding to see whoever is in charge.

"Believe me Mr. Schröder, you do not want to see the person *in charge*," I say to him. "He'll toss you behind bars for causing a disturbance, without giving it a second's thought." Schröder looks in my general direction, swaying and unsteady on his feet. He grabs onto a chair in the lobby to stop the room from spinning.

"Is he still drunk?" Vogel asks. "How did he get here?"

"I don't want to know." But I'd bet he drove his truck. I turn to the clerk at the front desk. "What's he want?"

"He's demanding to know what's going on, why no-one will tell him anything." Kurt Schröder has slumped into a chair, his head between his knees. I pray he's not going to throw up.

"Find someone to drive him home," I tell the clerk. "And take his keys."

I walk over to Schröder and bend so he can hear me speaking slowly and clearly into his ear. "Mr. Schröder, out of compassion for your loss I'm not going to charge you with DUI. Do not make me regret this. Go home and sober up. We'll be around to see you later."

When we return to the interview room, Patty has retreated to her usual posture: arms crossed, head bowed, clearly unwilling to cooperate. I know she's frightened but she has clammed up.

"You don't like Kurt Schröder?" I take a guess. Patty shrugs. "Wasn't he a good boss to work for?" Another shrug.

"I liked Renee. She was good person." I note that Kurt is excluded from that assessment.

"How were they, as a couple?"

"I mind my business," she mutters. "No idea what she saw in him."

"Did they seem to get along?" Vogel asks. "Did you ever see them arguing?"

Patty looks frustrated. "I was only there for a few days at harvest. How would I know?"

"I don't know, Patty. It seems to me you'd have a lot of time to chat during those long nights picking. I know my girlfriend and I did. Hours in the cold—and we only managed to do it one night."

"There was some argument," Patty reluctantly admits. "Something about the land where the fruit trees are."

"The ones they're tearing out? The old peach trees?"

"I guess so. Renee didn't want to do it. She wanted to keep them but Kurt was insisting they needed to grow more Vidal Blanc. He kept going on about money. How they needed more money. I guess there's a lot more to be made in Icewine."

We let Patty go back to work, then head into another briefing. We offer to have a patrol car drive her and she says she'd prefer to walk back to Gravelly Bay.

"I'll grab a coffee on the way," she says but I'm pretty sure she doesn't want to be seen getting out of a police car.

We're a bit late coming in and DS Agu is standing with Sampson and Chen in front of the white board. It's not a huge deal, since neither Vogel nor I are assigned to the case, but it's always good to stay on top of all the Homicide Unit's investigations. And it's never a good idea to let Agu notice your absence. Unfortunately for us he notices us slipping in the back.

"Good of you to show up," he says, giving us a pointed look. So much for a discreet entrance.

"We've now accessed all of Mei Zhen Lai's files," he continues, "From her laptop, which was found in her rental car. Her cell phone has not been found and I would imagine it has been destroyed by her killer, so whatever data we might have been able to retrieve from it is lost."

Agu begins a slide show, with photos of any evidence the investigating team thinks pertinent to share. Chen steps forward and describes what we're looking at on the screen.

"This is the list of wineries she was investigating. You'll note it's quite long—there are forty-three names on it, including all wineries in the Niagara region that produce Icewine. We don't know which of these she has visited the day she was killed." There's going to be a lot of legwork for the team, checking all of those out.

"This spreadsheet and the interview notes," Chen flashes through several screens, "will bring you up to speed. Mei Zhen Lai was a thorough and meticulous note-taker. All of her findings will have been recorded."

"However, the spreadsheet was not updated on the day she died. Presumably she would have normally done that at the end of her workday. So, whatever she did, whoever she spoke to on the last day of her life is not in these notes."

"We know she left the hotel shortly after eight o'clock the morning of January 3 and her body was found at Ambrosia Winery at ten forty-five on January 11. In between those times we have no information. Her rental car was left in the hotel parking lot.

"These are an assortment of business cards we found in her files." Chen clicks past a dozen cards for wineries, specialty wine importers, sommeliers and shipping companies.

"Her investigation began in China last year, after several foreign wine companies—in France and Canada, filed complaints. A Chinese wine company was convicted of making and selling wine with counterfeit labels of foreign wines.

"That initial investigation revealed how the fraud operates: someone in the area is importing bulk wine from Chile and Uruguay and bottling it here in Canada—possibly mixing it with Icewine, or another local sweet late harvest wine. Then they are putting on an approved VQA designation sticker and label and exporting it to Asia.

"Her notes indicate that in the last month alone, ninety pallets of Icewine, filling five forty-foot shipping containers were sent out by truck to B.C., where they were then to be loaded onto a cargo ship and sent to the port of Guangzhou in China. That single shipment is just one of many just like it, quite apart from shipments from legitimate wineries in the Niagara region. It adds up to thousands of bottles and millions of dollars.

"The counterfeiters aren't worried about repeat business or the quality of the wine. But they are going to a great deal of trouble to copy the real packaging to make the product labels look as legitimate as possible."

"How are they doing that, Sir?"

"Copying them from real bottles, printing off thousands of labels, including VQA stickers and quality control tags, and applying them here before the shipments go out."

"We just don't know which winery it is. Or they are, since there may be more than one."

"Okay," Agu says, taking over. "DeGroot and Evans, you take the list of wineries. Raleigh, you've got the business cards." Agu turns to Vogel and me. "You two, come with me."

He leads the way into his office and I can feel the eyes of the rest of the Homicide Unit following us. I get the feeling we're in big trouble, but I can't figure out what we might have done wrong.

"I can't spare anyone to go through this," Agu says as he shuts the door to his office. "I need to focus on Mei Zhen Lai now, with DS Sampson and Sergeant Chen." He exhales in exhaustion. "Two high profile cases at once is stretching our resources very thin. The Landry case is a huge attention-grabber with the public, but the murder of a special investigator from Hong Kong, who was looking into fraud in one of our region's most important economic engines..." He shakes his head. "We have to wrap this up quickly, before the media gets hold of it. Right now she's just some tourist who died at a winery. And that's all I ever want the public to know." He glares at us, making his point.

"Sir," both Vogel and I say at the same time.

Agu hands us a folder. "This is what FSU found in Landry's car," he says. "I've had to pull DeGroot and Evans off that investigation. It's yours now."

"But what about the Sanger case, Sir? And Renee Schröder?"

"Sanger is a lower priority. And Schröder is being investigated alongside Mei Zhen Lai. Same location," he shrugs. "Probably related. Need to make efficient use of our time."

I take the folder from Agu and Vogel and I sit down at my desk. Disappointed as I am, I understand why the Sangers have been pushed down the line. They're not rich or famous or influential in our town, and they've got no family to put pressure on us to solve the case. So, we'll have to take our time, and come back to it when the high-profile cases are wrapped up. We have no choice, not with all the bodies piling up.

Vogel perches on the desk next to me. It's been empty since DC Decker died last year and we use it as a common dumping ground for files on their way back to storage, old newspapers and empty coffee mugs.

"Okay, so Landry disappears," I say. "He was reported missing by his wife on December 10." Vogel nods. "And his office is burned to the ground on December 12— a couple of days later." Another nod. "Co-incidence?"

"No way," he says. "I'd say our one that got away did it. For revenge." Vogel's getting excited by his theory. "She had Landry's car. She knew his name and address from the registration papers in the car."

"I don't see it," I argue. "She escapes. She takes his car. Then she hangs around town for a couple of days, finds his office somehow and burns it down? Then why not burn his house down too? That's the address she'd have found on his vehicle registration—not the office. She'd have to do some research to find that out."

"Our girl is not lazy or dumb," Vogel says. "She's a survivor. She'd have no problem finding it out."

"Seriously Vogel, that makes sense to you? As a revenge? Burning his office down?" I shake my head. "It doesn't fit."

Vogel shrugs. "The guy's already dead. She's killed him. What else could she do to avenge herself?"

"You'd think if anything she'd burn down the farmhouse," I argue. "Or, if she was in too much of a hurry to get away, then maybe Landry's home, when she'd calmed down and given it some thought. I get that there's no way she'd ever want to go back to the farmhouse." I think for a minute. "Hell, she might have run away in such a blind panic she wouldn't even have been able to find her way back there. Especially if she's not from around here."

Vogel starts to go through the Landry file. There are pages of notes, copies of fingerprint evidence, and reports from forensics and he turns them over one by one. Then he freezes and a smile spreads across his face. He slides the folder over to me. It's a photograph of a business card for George Campbell Insurance Broker, front and back. On the back a phone number is scrawled in pen. I pick up the phone and punch in the number. It rings four times then goes to voicemail.

"This is George Campbell. I'm unable to take your call at the moment. Please leave a message and I'll return it as soon as possible."

I put down the phone and take the photograph from him.

"There could be a perfectly innocent reason for James Landry to have this card," I say, but neither Vogel nor I believe a word of it. My heart is racing with excitement. "But, think about this for a second. George Campbell hired Elsie Duggan to look after his mother. Elsie Duggan, who just mysteriously appeared in town a few weeks ago, completely from nowhere, as far as we know. Elsie Duggan, who we have on CCTV at the hospital the night Natalie Sanger was killed. Strange number of coincidences, don't you think?"

"What are you saying? Elsie Duggan is the missing girl from Landry's farm? And she went from there to working for Campbell? How does that scan?"

"Maybe it doesn't," I sigh. "You're probably right. I'm grasping at straws here. It does seem pretty far fetched, and in any case, what's the connection?"

"It doesn't have to be connected to anything, Gauthier." He's trying to be the voice of reason. "James Landry had a regular life, apart from what he got up to at the farm. He went about his business, had a family. This card could just be part of that. He was an insurance guy, right? I'm sure he had clients, people he sold insurance to."

"Agreed. Campbell could have sold insurance to Landry. We already know he sold it to Raleigh."

"I guess we need to head over there and talk with him again."

Campbell is surprised to see us, and it's obvious he's not pleased about our showing up in his office a second time. As usual, the place is empty and the receptionist barely glances up when we walk past her right in.

"Good afternoon Mr. Campbell. We have a few more questions for you."

He looks nervous, but invites us to sit down.

"Can you please tell us how you know Mr. James Landry?" Campbell's eyes widen when he hears the name. He can't have missed all of the news stories about the Cellar Man.

"I don't know him!" he says.

Vogel slides the photo of the card across the desk so he can see it. "We found this in James Landry's personal effects," he says. "Your personal cell phone number is printed on the back. Now do you know him?"

George Campbell flushes red and beads of sweat form on his upper lip and forehead.

"I was his insurance agent," he says. "He needed coverage for his business…"

"And maybe for his house?" I interrupt. "What about the farm?" Campbell refuses to look at us. "You knew about the farm, didn't you?" He shakes his head.

"No?" Vogel says. "So, when we look through Landry's records we won't find an insurance policy for the farm?"

Campbell finally looks up at us. "I may have written up a policy for him, when he first inherited it. I'd have to check with my receptionist."

"And you've never been there yourself?"

"Certainly not," he says. "There would have been no need for me to visit. I would have just sent an appraiser over, years ago."

"So, then I guess you have no explanation for how your fingerprints were found at the scene." The red flush disappears from Campbell's face and he goes pale.

"I may have...I don't recall..." Then George Campbell faints to the floor.

His receptionist rushes in. "Mr. Campbell? Are you all right?" She grabs a bottle of water from his desk and tries to get him to drink.

"Should we call an ambulance?" I ask, but I'm not very keen about doing so. It'll mean we have to stick around.

"No need," she says. "This happens, on occasion." Vogel and I exchange a glance and start to back out of the office.

"Okay then," Vogel says. "We'll just leave you to it." I glance over my shoulder and see her cradling George Campbell, whose hairpiece has gone askew. She's holding the bottle of water to his lips and it looks like she's nursing a large ugly baby.

"What did that just prove?" Vogel asks once we're back in the car. "You lied. We don't have his fingerprints at the farm."

"No, but now we know he's definitely been there." I just don't know why.

TWENTY

"SO, HAVE YOU recovered from this morning yet?" Maja says as she hands me a glass of wine when I get in from work. She's only half-joking.

"Honestly, I'm not sure I'll ever get over seeing that." The gruesome image of Renee Schröder's mutilated face, eyes missing, is something I know will haunt me. I take a big drink to chase it away. "This is delicious," I say. "What is it?"

"It's a local VQA Riesling. Maybe a little sweet?" She takes another sip and wrinkles her nose.

"It's perfect." I slump onto the couch next to her. "How was your day?"

"Definitely an anticlimax after this morning," she says. "The usual viruses and sprains and bronchial infections. You?"

"It was kind of interesting, really. Turns out the victim from Saturday night at Ambrosia Winery is from Hong Kong. She was working with the RCMP and our Fraud team on a counterfeit Icewine racket. Can you believe it?" My reward is her look of astonishment and rapt attention as I share the details of what I learned today.

"So you think this Chinese woman…"

"Mei Zhen Lai."

"…Was killed because she was onto something to do with Ice-wine fraud? Something at Ambrosia?"

"Or, someone is trying to make it look like Ambrosia is involved. They might have recognized this Mei Zhen Lai and killed her at Ambrosia to throw suspicion onto the Schröders."

Maja shudders. "So then who killed Renee Schröder? And why in that horrible way?"

"Maybe it's a message?"

"From who? Like a Chinese gang or something?"

I laugh. "I don't think we can blame a Chinese gang for the birds doing that to her eyes. But stringing her up? Sure, why not?"

"Maybe whoever did it is familiar enough with the bird problem they'd know that could happen. Eyeball look a lot like frozen grapes I guess…" She pats my leg and gets up. "Let's eat. I'm hungry."

My stomach does a little flip. Maja's a doctor and a Coroner so this sort of thing just rolls off her. But even though I've seen more than a few dead bodies in my life I don't think I'll ever get used to it.

"I didn't feel like cooking today," Maja says. "So I just bought a prepared lasagna on the way home. It should be warmed through by now. Do you want to make the salad or set the table?"

I choose salad and set to pulling things out of the fridge while Maja lays out the cutlery and dishes. We make a great team. I'm better with her than I am alone; better than I've ever been in my life and I'm grateful every day for her love. Unfortunately I often forget to let her know it.

Since she's moved in with me my anxiety disorder is mostly under control, and I feel better than I have in ages. I haven't had to take as much of my rescue medication for months now. My visits to my therapist are still weekly but they're easier, somehow. Probably because I have less need to lie about how I'm really doing.

I used to spend most of my appointments acting like I was better, and that I wasn't medicating with alcohol and intense work-outs. I couldn't even tell you why; it's just a default I revert to, pretending I'm okay and everything is fine when my world is spinning out of control. I'm sure it's because of my childhood and how the everyday violence escalated into bloodshed and horror. It doesn't take a psychiatrist to figure that out. Who wouldn't want to pretend everything is fine, when the truth is far from it.

I'm very careful to not ask Maja any questions over dinner about Renee Schröder's autopsy. I'm no genius but I can learn from experience. I don't want to say or do anything to upset Maja, like I did last time.

"I don't suppose you have any questions about the postmortem?" Maja asks after a moment of quiet. My heads snaps up. Is this a trick? "It's okay," she laughs. "I over-reacted last time. Here's the deal I'm proposing: if it's my case, you can ask whatever questions you want to. But if it's not mine, then you have to wait until either you get formal results from the Coroner or the forensic pathologist. Or I share it with you—because I choose to. But no expectations, okay?" She reaches across the table to hold my hand and reassure me we're still okay. "So, any questions?" She repeats with a smile.

"I have all of the questions. Please."

"In the end I just did the post-mortem exam," Maja laughs. "I didn't feel the need to send her in for a full autopsy. There was no question about the cause of death, despite the unusual presentation of the body."

"And?…"

"We found wine, grape residue, and traces of diesel fuel on her body. From filling one of the tanks on the farm I assume. Really nothing at all out of the ordinary. She'd eaten pizza and had a beer shortly before death."

"She'd have been killed elsewhere and then taken down the lane," I think aloud. "Either carried by someone strong, or on one of the little tractors they use to pick up the bins of grapes. Then she was strung up."

"It would definitely take some strength to do—she was

a well-muscled farm woman, weighed around a hundred and sixty pounds."

"So, either a strong man or maybe a couple of people, working together?"

"Or someone with some ingenuity. People can be pretty resourceful if they have to be. Have you found the murder weapon?" she asks me. I shake my head. "I can tell you it was a large irregularly shaped object, like a rock or even a big icicle. If you ever find it I can do a match to the head wound. But without it, I can only guess."

"FSU have combed the entire Ambrosia vineyard and the lane where she was found. Turned up nothing. There are tons of tracks and footsteps all over the place, from farm vehicles and people and cars coming and going. Nothing usable. And of course no fingerprints—everyone's wearing gloves because it's so cold out."

After dinner Maja goes to have a hot bath while I clean up the kitchen and start the dishwasher. Then I pour myself another glass of wine and sit down with my laptop to review my notes.

I suspect the Schröder and Lai cases will soon be out of Agu's hands. Given its international scope it'll be considered too high profile for our department to deal with. Still, until that happens, we need to gather as much information as we can before we hand it off to whatever level of police investigation takes it over. I'm guessing it'll be federal—the RCMP, with our local support.

I turn to my notes on the Sanger case, despite Agu having asked me to push it onto the back burner and to focus on the Landry investigation. I know there has to be some connection between the Sangers and the deaths at Ambrosia, given the fact that the victims all had their ears cut. I just need to figure out what it is.

I have another drink of wine while I review the file. First, Martin Sanger: No progress. We know he was drowned. He was tortured first. Ear cut. Bruising on his neck indicates he was forced down into hole—as if we didn't already know that. Second, Natalie Sanger: No progress, no idea who stabbed her in the kitchen, or who smothered her in hospital. Ear cut.

What's the motive for both their deaths? There's none that I can see. I've gone through their bank accounts. They have no money. They're living on pension income and have no savings. They spend most of what they earn on the cats, buying the food and even though vets subsidize the costs of any procedures and treatments there are still some fees they have to cover. And now there are also the many cooler shelters Martin Sanger has provided for each colony. I wonder how are they managing to pay for it all?

Two cash deposits of five thousand dollars have gone into their account over the last two weeks, but I have no idea where that money would have come from. A lottery win? An inheritance?

People are tortured generally to extract information. So what did Martin Sanger know? Was it something worth dying for? According to what Patty Smith said, on the morning Natalie Sanger was stabbed, someone was demanding she tell them something—apparently something she didn't know, and for which she was stabbed. What would that be?

What could the connection be between the Sanger murders and what happened at Ambrosia Winery, apart from their ears being cut? It seems impossible that there is one, on the face of it. Who are the Sangers, really? Martin was by all accounts a nice guy who drove the Zamboni in a Santa suit, and Natalie rescued feral cats. Hardly the type to be involved in an international counterfeit wine fraud. Then I remember something and my heart starts to beat faster. I'd completely forgotten about it. Patty had said she'd heard the men who attacked Natalie were speaking in Chinese.

Maybe there's some connection I just can't see yet, between the Sangers and the counterfeit wine. But what could it be, apart from both Sangers and Mei Zhen Lai having their ears cut? The fact that it was done to both Lai and Renee makes sense inasmuch as there's the Icewine connection between them. But the Sangers? Nothing comes to mind.

Or, maybe there's no connection at all, and the ear cutting is just the work of a random weirdo, and I'm trying to connect dots that just don't connect. No, that makes even less sense.

What I need to do is figure out how the Sangers connect to both Renee Schroder and Mei Zhen Lai. There's got to be more to the Sangers than we know and there's only one way to find out. I grab my coat and car keys and head for the door.

"I'm just going out for a bit," I shout up the stairs to Maja. "I'll be back in an hour."

First I drive back to the Sangers house but there's no reason for me to go inside. My plan is to retrace our route from the night we'd fed the feral cats, to see if I notice anything that I missed the first time. They did the same things, went to the same places, at the same times on the same days every week. What if they'd seen something one night? Something that they'd decided to try and profit from—at five thousand dollars a payment. It would explain those two mysterious cash deposits into their bank account.

I go first to the marine salvage yard, this time intending to pay closer attention to the surroundings. I drive into the same entrance Patty took us through and follow the gravel road through the site. But rather than parking I drive deeper into the site, exploring what I can of its layout, in case I notice something. It's massive and spreads across acres along the entrance to the Welland Canal. Lining the road on either side are orderly piles of scrap, likely meant for recycling, as well as the stripped out empty hulls of large fiberglass sailboats and powerboats, stacked like cordwood waiting to be ripped up and sent to landfills.

This salvage yard sustainably recycles boats of all sizes, from pleasure craft to full-sized Great Lakes freighters once they've reached the end of their working lives. Anything that can be salvaged, like engines, propane tanks and metal hulls, is removed and recycled.

It's a busy yard, especially in summer. But tonight there's nobody around and I suspect this isn't a spot the Sangers would have seen anything suspicious.

I have some trouble remembering how to find the spot Patty led us into when we fed the cats. When I finally crawl through the fence it's clear someone has recently been here. The food dishes are full and the water in the bowls hasn't yet frozen over.

I stand and look around, spinning slowly in a circle and see nothing. I'm surrounded by piles of scrap metal, wrecked boats and in the distance are the heaps of sand and gravel at the municipal gravel and sand storage depot. The only people coming here would be snowplow operators and sanders, filling up before they hit the roads after another snowfall. Could the Sangers have seen something here? Something they shouldn't have?

I climb back out through the fence and head over to the second colony, by the shopping mall in Welland. That's even less illuminating since there's nothing around there but parking lots and chain stores, backing onto a residential district. There's a small pedestrian shopping area along the river, lined with cafes and shops and a few cats, no doubt on their way over to the colony for the feeding.

Finally I end up by the highway in a light industrial area. I glance at the dashboard clock and realize I've already been out more than an hour, so I have to move quickly. I don't want to worry Maja.

Just as it was the first time I visited, the warehousing and freight-forwarding yard is full of shipping containers. The now-familiar stacks of coolers and bowls of cat food and water are tucked in beside the entrance to the yard, just this side of the entry fence.

Without Patty and Vogel for company the place feels lonely and deserted. It's dark and quiet, and I'm sure the cold has made the cats stay in their shelters. That's why I don't see even one near the food bowls. As I round a shadowy corner I stumble over something and almost fall. I shine my flashlight down and see a dead tabby cat, lying in a pool of blood. A predator like a coyote would have eaten the cat, not left it so I know even before I crouch to inspect the body that the killer was human. The cat's been shot. I shine my flashlight around the area and see three more cats, all shot dead. My blood boils and I remember what Patty had said about people killing them. I guess the word is out about the location of this feral colony.

I keep walking past the feeding station toward the shipping yard's entrance. The wide double gates are open and I can walk in as far as the main office, but beyond that there's another set of gates and a ten-foot tall metal fence topped with razor wire. There aren't any lights on in the office and I have no desire to scale the fence, especially after a glance through it tells me there are only more and more shipping containers back there, lined up in rows and piled on top of one another. Nothing to see there. This expedition looks like it was a waste of my time.

I'm going to have to call the vet and the volunteers on the rota to let them know about the dead cats. I don't know how they are going to manage to stop whoever did this. Maybe they could set up some security cameras, with the permission of the freight yard. That, along with some threatening signs might make the creep think twice before coming around to shoot more cats.

I'm heading back to my car when I glance up at the sign above the office door. I don't know why I hadn't noticed it before. Now that is interesting.

FREIGHT CONSOLIDATION, INTERNATIONAL SHIPPING,
BY AIR OR SEA
CUSTOMS BROKERAGE, GLOBAL SUPPLY CHAIN SOLUTIONS
CAMPBELL GLOBAL LOGISTICS

I hear a flat dull plink sound, as if penny is being dropped down a deep well. It's followed by another then suddenly I feel a searing pain and I instinctively run for cover. I've been shot.

Maja meets me in the Emergency room, finding me lying on a gurney, with a large wad of gauze on my left butt cheek.

"Not quite how I thought our evening would end." She shakes her head and sits down next to me. "How do you feel?"

I'd called her from the car as I drove myself to the hospital. Once I realized I'd been shot I ran to safety, and a quick check assured me the injuries weren't that serious. Still, I was bleeding heavily and knew enough not ignore that.

"I'm fine. Bored. Lonely. They gave me something for the pain."

"Bored and lonely is good," Maja laughs. "The last thing anyone ever wants is to be the center of attention in an Emergency Ward. If the triage nurse leaves you to wait, you aren't dying anytime soon." She reaches for the chart hanging on the end of the gurney and scans it, then goes out to speak with the medical team. It's great having a girlfriend who speaks doctor. She'll be able to translate all the medical jargon and get me out of here quicker, I hope.

In a few minutes she's back. "Looks like two entry wounds in your gluteal muscles, not sure how deep they've penetrated. Small projectile—likely a small caliber bullet. They're going to do an x-ray, possibly a CT scan if it's warranted, to find the location before they extract." A small caliber bullet, probably a 22. And I barely heard a thing, so the shooter must have used a noise suppressor. That doesn't make a lot of sense, to shoot cats in a deserted shipping yard.

I groan in exasperation. "Such drama. Can't they just dig them out? They can't be that deep!"

Maja glares at me. "No, they can't. And, speaking of drama, if you hadn't gone down there—alone—in the middle of the night we wouldn't even be here." I don't have a response to that.

Two hours later they do the extraction under a local anaesthetic, and the doctor presents me with two spent Hornet pellets. That tells me the shooter used an air rifle, and was probably within thirty to fifty meters of me. I'm not about to head out to the scrapyard again tonight, but plan on making a visit tomorrow in daylight. Part of me isn't sure I should even bother. There is any number of spots in the shipping yard the shooter could have hidden.

"They're typically used for hunting," the doctor says. "Lead with brass points. Good penetrating power."

"You don't have to tell me."

"It's lucky you had your coat on," he continues, ignoring me. "The pellets weren't able to go very deep. Just minor damage." He applies a gauze pad and tape to my butt cheek.

"Is it possible to trace the bullets?" Maja asks.

"Pellets," I correct her. "No way. They're from an air rifle. You can buy them and the ammunition anywhere."

"Any you never heard anything?"

"Air guns are practically silent. They use springs or compressed air to fire the projectiles. No explosive charge like with other guns." I think back to the flat *plink* sounds I heard, just as I came across the bodies of the dead cats and shake my head.

"You're going to have to reduce your activity for a while until it heals," the doctor says as he leaves the room. I feel my anxiety rush and I meet Maja's eye. "No gym. No biking or running, no squats, for a few weeks."

Maja rubs my shoulder in sympathy. *Great. Perfect.* Just knowing I'm not able to do anything physical at all to stave off my panic attacks makes my heart race. I don't know how I'm going to manage.

TWENTY ONE

Wednesday, January 15

I MEET VOGEL at the station just after seven thirty. It's quiet once the flurry of activity settles down after shift change and the morning briefing. Assignments have been handed out and the patrol officers head out to their cars, leaving a few of us detectives behind returning phone calls and waiting for forensic results.

"Vogel, we need to talk to Patty Smith again," I say as I hand him a coffee and beckon for him to follow me. I'm moving slowly, thanks to the pain in my left buttock, but I'm trying not to let it show. It's an embarrassing place to get shot.

"I just got in," he whines. "Can't I warm up a bit first?" I smile and keep walking, so he's got no choice but to tag along. As we head to the car I catch him up on what I did last night, and what I now suspect.

"I hate air rifles," Vogel mutters. "There was this guy in my neighbourhood when I was growing up. Hated squirrels and he used to shoot them from his bedroom window. Used an air gun because it was quiet."

"What happened?"

"The idiot shot himself by accident," Vogel smirks. "Bled out before anyone knew what he'd done. Nobody heard the shot."

"Serves him right." I shake my head.

"So you think someone mistook you for a cat?" he jokes.

"Maybe. I am stealthy and nimble."

"And you've got nine lives," he laughs. "Actually I think you might be down to seven now…" He gives me a look, reminding me of the near misses I've had in the past year. Vogel is quiet for a moment. "They might have thought you were one of the volunteers…"

"Like Natalie and Martin Sanger…" I see where he's going. "You mean someone's trying to kill off the feral cat volunteers? That seems pretty far fetched."

Vogel shrugs. "It fits the evidence. Two are dead. Another person shot."

"We need to talk to Patty," I say. "She's the only person who might know what the Sangers were up to. I think they saw something on one of their runs to one of the feral cat colonies, and that they were blackmailing someone. It would explain the two five thousand dollar deposits into their account."

"Do you really think someone would kill two people for only five thousand dollars?" I've known people to be killed for a lot less, but do see Vogel's point.

"Ten thousand. There were two deposits."

"Still. It's not a lot, is it?"

"Maybe whoever they were blackmailing was afraid the demands would keep coming. Decided to put an end to it early."

"What would they have seen?"

"I'm not sure, but I bet Patty knows."

"She's lied to us before. What makes you think she'll tell the truth this time?"

When we arrive at Randy's Ice Fishing Rentals, there aren't any cars in the lot. Randy's truck isn't there either.

"Maybe we're too early?" Vogel suggests. "What time do they open?"

"Martin was always here early, drilling out the holes," I say as I climb out of the car and head for the trailer. "Why would that change? Somebody's still got to do it." I feel uneasy and hope there's nothing wrong. It's probably just a flashback to seeing Martin Sanger frozen in the ice a few days ago. "She's probably inside."

It's clear someone's been here. There are fresh footsteps outside the trailer, but no sign of life. I try the door. "It's unlocked," I call to Vogel as I step in.

Patty is slumped over the desk, her head on the laptop, with a bloody clump of hair hanging in her face. A takeaway cup of coffee is spilled next to her and has dripped over the edge of the table, forming a pool on the floor.

"Vogel! Call 911!" I check and find a faint pulse, then pick her up and drag her outside into the fresh air. I lay her onto the snow and begin to perform chest compressions and mouth-to-mouth resuscitation and keep it up until the ambulance attendants arrive and take over.

Vogel has used the time to look around inside. "You need to see this," he says, beckoning me around the side of the trailer. He points up to the roof where someone has stuffed a rag into the vent pipe. "The exhaust from the propane heater wasn't venting properly. The trailer's full of carbon monoxide." He goes over to tell the paramedics, who immediately turn up Patty's oxygen to a hundred percent.

"It wouldn't take long for her to lose consciousness in there," the paramedic says as they load Patty into the ambulance for the trip to the hospital. "Maybe fifteen minutes at most?"

Randy Delaware arrives in his truck and runs over in a panic when he sees the ambulance. "What happened? What's going on?"

Vogel fills him in while I'm talking to the paramedic.

"Carbon monoxide has no smell," she's telling me. "There'd be no way she'd have any idea she was being poisoned. If you hadn't come by, she'd be dead within the hour. And even though you've got her out early, there's still a risk of heart or brain permanent damage. We'll need to have her examined."

"When did she get here?" Vogel asks Delaware.

"I unlocked the trailer and opened up at seven, just before dawn. I fired up the propane heater, turned on the lights and was already out there drilling out the holes in the ice when Patty arrived at around seven thirty."

"Then where did you go?"

"I meet my buddies for breakfast every day, down at the Riverside Diner. I was there until just now."

"So Patty went in there at seven thirty?" I glance at my watch. "Half an hour ago?"

He shrugs. "Yes, I guess so. I left around then."

"Vogel," I whisper to him. "Patty's left ear was cut, just like the Sangers. Whoever did that would have to have waited, possibly outside, until she was unconscious. Then they came in and cut her ear. There's no sign of a struggle."

"Then they'd have just left, a few minutes before we got here." I nod as Vogel gets it. "We just missed whoever it was." My heart sinks when I look around the trailer. Dozens of footprints, from all the emergency team, Vogel and me, have obliterated any potentials trails we could have followed.

"When are your first rentals, usually?" I ask Delaware.

"Today there's only a few, since it's Wednesday," he says. "They usually arrive by ten-ish."

"Just leave the door open for the next hour or so," Vogel tells him as we leave. "It'll air out and be safe enough, now that we've got the vent cleared."

We walk away so Randy can't hear us. He's standing there looking bewildered, probably because he'll have to spend the day dealing with the computer on his own. The ambulance drives off, followed by two of the patrol cars, leaving Vogel and me.

"Whoever plugged the vent could have done it at any time," Vogel says. "Knowing she'd be in here on her own all day, apart from when she had to step out to deal with customers."

"It's unlikely they were trying to kill Randy," I say. "He's never around. Most days Patty sits in there alone the whole time."

Vogel nods. "First Martin Sanger, and now Patty. Never knew ice fishing was so dangerous."

"Since we can't speak to Patty right now," I suggest. "Why don't we go visit George Campbell and do a little more fishing of a different kind? Since our last visit was cut short so abruptly." Ever since I'd noticed his name on the sign at the freight forwarding yard last night I've felt there has to be something here for us to go on. At least it might be a place to start in finding out what happened to the Sangers. Also, the fact that Elsie Duggan is connected to his mother Lenore Campbell, and that she happened to be conveniently in the hospital the night Natalie Sanger died is just too much of a coincidence.

We drive past Campbell's home address first, thinking we might catch him before he goes into the office but his car's not in the driveway. Vogel knocks on the door and checks the garage, but there's no sign of him, so we head over to his office.

Campbell Global Logistics office is open, but empty as usual. The receptionist looks bored and is watching online videos while pretending to work on her computer.

"Is Mr. Campbell in?" I ask, showing her my ID this time. Vogel just stands beside me, looking tall and intimidating.

She looks alarmed, no doubt remembering our last visit where her boss ended up passed out. "No." She shakes her head. He called me early this morning. Said he was going out of town for a while."

"Any idea where he went?"

She shrugs. "Not really…"

Vogel chuckles. "Does he do this often? Just go off without telling you?"

She looks offended. "I'm perfectly capable of managing in his absence."

Vogel gives her a tight smile.

"Can you please give us some insight into what you do here? What is Global Logistics, exactly?" I interrupt. "I was under the impression Mr. Campbell ran an insurance brokerage."

She smiles. "Yes, he was a broker for a while, years ago. It was the family business, but he doesn't do much of that anymore. Here we manage freight and shipping of goods for businesses."

"So, you're like a middle man? For importers and exporters?"

She shrugs. "More or less. We're a customs brokerage as well, so we also manage tariffs, customs valuations, sales, duties and excise tax payments."

"That sounds complicated." I've learned that flattering people and pretending to be interested in their jobs goes a long way, especially when their jobs are really boring. "You're licensed to do all that?"

"Of course! Mr. Campbell is licensed by the Border Services Agency," she smiles proudly. "Our clients must grant us the authority to act on their behalf. We manage all the intricacies of cross-border shipping and international trade. It's *very* complicated."

"And detailed?"

She rolls her eyes. "You have no idea! We clear shipments, prepare all the documentation, collect duties and taxes, do all the accounting, warehousing, distribution, inspection, storage, insurance…"

"Mind boggling," Vogel interrupts.

Her eyes flick to Vogel. She's unsure if he's mocking her, which he is.

"And this is all international in scope?"

"The majority of our business is air and sea freight out of the country. Mr. Campbell even acts as an intermediary between importers and the various government, like China or Malaysia."

"Could Mr. Campbell have gone abroad, for business?" I ask.

She shakes her head. "I doubt it. He'd have told me. I make all of his travel bookings."

Vogel and I thank her and head back out into the street. I turn back at the last minute and catch the look of disappointment on her face. She'd hoped we were gone for good.

"One more thing," I ask. "What can you tell me about Elsie Duggan? Do you know her?"

The receptionist's lip curls in disdain. "I know *of* her, yes."

"*Of* her? You haven't met?"

She looks surprised. "Certainly not. She's in Las Vegas. Or at least that's where she met Mr. Campbell." Vogel and I exchange a glance and move back in toward her desk. That puts her on her guard and she starts to look panicked. "Why? What has she done?"

"Nothing, to our knowledge," Vogel says. "Her name has come up in our inquiries."

"You say Mr. Campbell met her in Las Vegas? When was that?"

"Last year." She turns to her computer and pulls up a calendar. "He went to a convention on February 8th." She makes a few more keystrokes. "And he travelled there again for business on September 23rd."

"Did you travel there with Mr. Campbell? Did you meet Elsie Duggan?"

"No. Mr. Campbell is very good at tracking his expenses," she says. "There were several dinner receipts with her name on them. I assume she is a business contact or perhaps a vendor." It doesn't sound to me like she believes what she's saying.

"A business contact," I echo. What kind of business, exactly?

"The plot thickens," Vogel says once we're outside. "There's more to the story of Ms. Duggan than we were led to believe."

"So Campbell met her last year, in Vegas. He brings her up here and sets her up as a caregiver to his mother, with some story about hiring her through an ad. Why?"

"And what went wrong?" Vogel says. "Because when we first met Campbell it was clear he hated Elsie Duggan. Whatever he'd planned must have gone sideways."

"I'm not surprised. Elsie is sharp enough to see a better opportunity and act on it, even if it meant screwing Campbell."

"So," Vogel says. "You think Campbell's on the run?" I shrug. "Why? What's he got to get away from?"

"I'm just...curious. When I saw his company name at his freight forwarding yard last night I wondered if there was some connection between him and the Sangers."

Vogel looks puzzled. "You think they saw something at the feral colony by his shipping yard? Something he was up to?"

"It would explain the money going into their account. If they were blackmailing him."

"The five thousand dollar deposits?" Vogel sounds skeptical. "That's not a lot of money to go after if you're blackmailing someone."

"I don't imagine the Sangers had any idea what they were doing. I doubt they'd ever done anything criminal in their lives. Maybe they thought five thousand was a lot of money." Though it doesn't seem like it's worth dying for.

"Okay...so what would they have seen?"

"We need to track him down and find out."

"We'll find him," Vogel says. I know he's right. Campbell won't get far.

TWENTY TWO

OUR FIRST STOP is the hospital. Maybe his mother will know where we should start looking. Lenore is lying in her bed wrapped in a fuchsia cashmere pashmina, surrounded by glossy magazines. She's reading a book on her Kindle and eating chocolate truffles from a box on her bedside table.

"Good Morning Mrs. Campbell," I say when we come in. Her room is heavy with the fragrance of fresh flowers: lilies, roses, freesia and carnations. "How are you today?"

"All things considered?" She laughs then gives me a sharp look as she puts down her Kindle and gives us her full attention. "Are you here about Elsie again?"

"Not today. We're here to ask about your son."

"George," Vogel clarifies.

"I've only got the one. Unfortunately," she says. "What's he done?"

"We just need to ask him some questions."

She raises a skeptical eyebrow. "Uh huh."

The nurse enters the room pushing a medical cart. She picks up a needle and injects something into the IV drip. Lenore Campbell gives her a radiant smile and thanks her.

"Crystallized Penicillin," she tells us. "Two point four million units a day, for fourteen days." Vogel and I exchange a look. Are we allowed to ask what it's for?

"I have Neurosyphilis," she says after an uncomfortable silence. "It's in my brain." She taps the side of her head with a perfectly manicured finger. "My balance is bad, and I'm not allowed to drive anymore. That's why I need Elsie."

"My husband—may he rot in hell—gave it to me, years ago. I never knew I was infected until after he died. He brought it home, from wherever he was fucking around. Of course that meant I have it too now. It was too late to treat by the time I learned about it." She shakes her head.

"Oh sure, I was the *party girl*, but he was the one. All my life I was made to feel less than, like I was trash because I grew up poor and worked in nightclubs. I worked so damn hard to fit into his family. And the bridge club, the fucking symphony, the church groups, fundraising committees for whatever damn charity he thought was important to the family business." Her lip curls in disgust as she looks out the window, remembering.

"The looks I used to get at this hospital when I came to visit before he died. Judging me. Sneering. Looking down their noses at me. Word got around. There's no such thing as patient confidentiality in a small town—don't kid yourself."

She's right of course. I think of Doreen's glee in sharing the story of his syphilis with me. Keeping a secret is a life's work—I should know.

"Everyone loves to see the wealthy take a fall," Vogel says.

"A *fall*?! Honey, I took a swan dive after that." Lenore gives him an appreciative wink. "Fuck 'em all. I decided to live how I want. I have fresh flowers delivered three times a week. I drink champagne and I eat chocolate truffles for breakfast. I'm spending my son's inheritance and I do not give a single fuck." I smile hearing Lorene, an eighty-something year old woman, swear with such lusty defiance. She's a rock star.

She thinks for a moment. "I sometimes think it may be dementia—that's what George tells me anyway. That's what I have to look forward to: syphilitic tertiary dementia, characterized by loss of inhibition, dyskinesia, personality and mood disorders. Oh…and psychosis. It's what happens if you don't get treatment for fifty years. But not quite yet I don't think."

"About your son, Mrs. Campbell," I interrupt her.

"What about him?"

"Does he have a vacation home, or maybe a cottage? Someplace he might go to get away?"

Lorene laughs so hard she chokes. "What's he need to *get away* from, exactly?"

"We just have some questions we need to ask him." I don't see the point in getting her upset. Though it does seem she's actually enjoying herself.

"My son George is weak. He has no integrity," she says. "He loves money, has his eye on getting all of mine, and will do whatever it takes to get more, no matter who gets hurt. He's a chip off the old block," she says, shaking her head. "Just like his father."

The door opens and in walks Elsie, carrying a plate of smoked salmon and cream cheese on sliced bagels, with capers, red onion and dill, wrapped in cling film.

She also has a tote bag and the wire wrapped cork of a champagne bottle is poking out the top.

"Oh goody!" Lenore says. "Breakfast is served." Elsie leans in and Lenore gives her a kiss on the cheek. "Thank you my dear. This is lovely."

Elsie pulls over the table and adjusts it, then raises Lenore's bed so she's able to sit up comfortably. Then she quietly opens the champagne and pours Lorene a full glass, using one of the paper hospital cups. If anyone noticed they'd assume Lorene was drinking ginger ale.

Elsie then pours herself some in a plastic coffee mug, the entire time deliberately ignoring both Vogel and me, as if by sheer force of her will she can make us disappear. I notice a red flush rising up her neck and she keeps giving us sidelong glances. No doubt she's wondering what we're doing here. She looks guilty and I doubt it's because of the champagne.

Lenore tucks into her lox and cream cheese, her eyes sparkling with pleasure. Elsie sits in the chair next her, looking very proprietary. She finally looks at us with feigned disinterest, but doesn't ask a question. I've got to hand it to her, she's definitely a cool one.

"The Detectives are here asking about George," Lenore finally says. Elsie raises an eyebrow. "Apparently he's run off. Disappeared." Lenore looks at her and smiles. "Now what do you think of that?" Elsie shrugs and looks at her fingernails.

It doesn't seem likely either of these two will tell us anything worthwhile, so I get up to leave, with Vogel right behind me. "Enjoy your breakfast Mrs. Campbell." She smiles and waves. "We'll be in touch," I add, looking right at Elsie.

TWENTY THREE

"DO YOU SUPPOSE Kurt Schröder's sobered up yet?" Vogel asks as we leave the hospital. "Why don't we swing over there and have a word with him?"

"It's been twenty four hours. He should have slept it off by now," I agree. Unless he just kept drinking after his visit to the station, once he was dropped off at home by the patrol car.

Vogel drives out of town and up toward Ambrosia Winery. When we first started working together there'd be a few struggles over our roles—who gets to drive or who runs interviews. But we've worked it out for the most part. I prefer it when Vogel drives, since it leaves me time to check email and follow up leads—basically more important and interesting jobs than driving. And, silly though it is, it's important to Vogel that he drives. He feels it impugns his masculinity in some way when I do.

Even though we're learning how to work together, teaming up with another Detective is something I'm still not quite used to. For years when I was a Constable I'd spend all my time alone in a patrol car, since our police force isn't large enough to have two officers in a car at once. But now that I'm a Detective Constable it's common for us to drive together, especially when we're interviewing suspects. I find I miss the solitude; it gave me a lot of time to think. And for better or worse, Vogel never stops talking, most often about his love life, or lack thereof.

There's a new sign hanging at the end of the lane to the winery. It says Closed for the Season. Vogel drives past it up the lane and parks by the farmhouse. There doesn't seem to be anyone around: no activity in the barn, no workers anywhere. The Icewine pressing is over and the grape must and juice will be sitting for the next few days for the sediment to settle before fermentation can begin. Maybe Kurt has given the crew a few days off to rest and taken the time to grieve the death of his wife.

The door opens before we get a chance to knock. Schröder must have seen us driving up the lane. He invites us into a much cleaner kitchen that we were in yesterday. All the empties are gone, the table is clear and the dirty dishes have been washed and put away. I don't smell any alcohol on his breath and his eyes are clear, so I assume he's sobered up.

"When are you going tell me what happened to my wife?" he demands before we can sit down. "Nobody has said a damn thing!"

"I apologize Mr. Schröder," I say in my most tactful voice. "You were…*upset* yesterday morning. It wasn't a good time to speak with you." There's no need to remind him he was blind drunk, not upset.

"You're damn right I was!" he shouts at me. "My wife just died." The fact that he showed up at the station drunk just hours after she died doesn't seem to register with him, or the fact that I let him off a DUI charge. I'm about to shout back in my not-tactful voice when I feel a hand on my shoulder.

"Mr. Schröder," Vogel steps in, seeing I'm going to lose it. I really don't like Kurt Schröder. There's something about his manner, his long hair and unshaved face that reminds me of my uncle and the other dealers and addicts I grew up around in the East Village. I stand down and let Vogel take over. "Are you now able to tell us when you last saw your wife?" Schröder stares at him and blinks.

"After the pressing was done," he says confidently. "We finished up the last grapes, cleaned up the press and we all came in here for a few drinks."

"What time was that?"

"One o'clock," he says firmly as he sits down at the table. I don't believe him. Someone must have given him that information. There's no way he'd remember on his own, not given the shape he was in.

"Can you think of anyone who'd want to hurt your wife? Has she been in any trouble recently? Someone threatening her?"

Kurt Schröder drops his head into his hands. "No!" he says, shaking his head in irritation. "There was nobody..." Then he stops short and stares up at Vogel. "Except..."

I'm standing to one side watching Schröder's body language as Vogel runs the interview. There's something about him that is irritating me and I can't put my finger on it.

"There was something," he whispers with a look of surprise as if it's just coming back to him. "The night that Chinese tourist was killed."

"I saw my wife over by the grape press. It was getting late and I was looking for her because we had to start the tour. The paid guests had arrived and I didn't know where she was. She always did the welcome speech." I can't imagine Renee enjoying that role. The shy woman I'd met would have hated having to give a speech.

"She was talking to someone...and when they saw me, they kind of...hid. It was weird."

"Was it a man or a woman you saw her with?" I ask.

"I couldn't really tell. They were in the shadows." Right. Yet he still managed to recognize his wife. "Then when my wife discovered the body a little while later...I didn't know what to think..." He starts to sob, his face in his hands.

"Mr. Schröder," I interrupt. "Are you implying your wife had something to do with the death of Mei Zhen Lai?"

"Who?"

"The woman who was found in your grape press."

"No way. My wife would never do anything like that," he insists. "But, maybe she saw something?"

"Saw what, exactly?"

"I don't know," he cries. "I don't know." Instinctively I look around for the audience before I realize the show of grief is for Vogel and me.

I look at Vogel and roll my eyes. "Mr. Schröder," I say. "We're going to need you to calm down. What is it you think your wife might have seen?" He just keeps crying and shaking his head.

"Then when I learned how she died...." he buries his face in his hands.

"How did you learn that?"

"Ramon told me," he says through his tears. "I...thought it has to be some kind of a warning. A threat."

"A threat against you? Why?"

He doesn't reply and just stares down at his hands for a long moment. "They are trying to scare us into working with them."

Vogel glances at me, eyebrows raised before continuing with Schröder. "Working with who? To do what?"

"My wife tried to keep it from me." Schröder is staring out the window.

"Keep what from you?" I interrupt before Vogel can ask. I'm getting really impatient with Schröder's drama.

Schröder groans. "I don't want to say anything against my wife," he says. "She was a good person. A wonderful person."

"Say what against your wife?

"She didn't tell me anything. She knew how much pressure I've been under."

I'm getting more irritated by the second. "Mr. Schröder. You need to be more clear. What is it you are trying to say?"

"We've been threatened," he finally whispers. "By a Chinese gang."

I lean back against the counter, my arms crossed. "Really?" I try to keep the sarcasm out of my voice, but Vogel notices and gives me a look.

"What have they threatened you with Mr. Schröder?" Vogel asks, standing between Schröder and me so he can't see my face.

"They want us to work with them. Counterfeiting," he mumbles. "Icewine."

"So you're telling us that someone has been threatening your winery. Trying to force you into working with them to produce fake Icewine?" Schröder nods. "And your wife didn't tell you about it. Instead she tried to handle it on her own?" He nods again. "And that's why she was killed?" Schröder starts to cry again.

We wrap up the interview with Schröder and tell him that another investigative team will be in touch to get a statement from him. Based on what he's just said it's clear that DS Sampson and Sergeant Xiao Chen, along with DS Agu, will need to take over.

I instinctively reject what Kurt Schröder said about his wife. It's just too convenient. I run through the conversation I'd had with Renee in my mind; how she'd spoken of the compromise a marriage demands and how she'd been so supportive of her husband's vision, to the point of sacrificing her beloved peach trees.

On the other hand, I also could see how it might have happened. If she saw it as a way to earn some extra money that would help them keep Ambrosia Winery afloat and provide a financial boost to get them new equipment and expand their facilities, maybe she'd have done it. I don't really know Renee Schröder or how far she'd go to help Kurt achieve his dream.

"Doesn't that seem a little too neat to you?" Vogel says once we're back in the car. "Suddenly the Chinese mob is after them?"

He has a point. "Still, there must be a connection between Renee Schröder's death and the murder of Mei Zhen Lai. Both of them were found dead at Ambrosia, for a start."

Vogel shakes his head. "If you're some Chinese wine

counterfeiter," he begins "And you're trying to find partners here to do business with, I don't think killing your contact at the winery makes a lot of sense."

"No," I agree. "Unless maybe Renee Schröder didn't want to go along with it anymore. Maybe she was going to rat them out—to Mei Zhen Lai."

"And that's why they were both killed." It's certainly a working theory, not that we have any evidence to support it.

"Who else might have had motive to kill Renee Schröder?"

"Safe money's usually on the husband."

"Okay," I smile. "Now we're talking."

"You just don't like the guy," Vogel says.

"No, I don't," I admit. "He doesn't feel right to me," I mutter. I realize I'm being stubborn, but everything in me is rejecting Schröder's story. Vogel keeps talking, probably thinking he's convincing me.

"Gauthier, we already know he was so drunk that night there's no way he could even have managed it," he says. "He couldn't have gone anywhere, let alone kill his wife and string her up in the vineyard. There were witnesses. He was barely able to stand up the next morning. We saw him ourselves." He meets my eye. "Never mind that as far as we know he didn't have a motive."

"He might have been faking it," I say. "Maybe he wasn't as drunk as Figueroa thought. Maybe he got drunk after the deed was done."

I could easily imagine how he did it: Schröder acting drunk, taking the moment to murder his wife when the rest of the crew were partying. "He could have slipped out without being noticed. If any of the crew even noticed he was missing, they'd just think he was checking up on the pressing. He's the boss, they're not about to question him."

I glance at Vogel and see he's considering what I've said. "And his visit to the station the next day was just more window dressing?" he says.

"Exactly. To make sure we'd just think of him as insane with grief, drunk and incapable of anything nefarious. We'd never consider his involvement." Still, as Vogel pointed out, we have no motive and the fact that I don't like Kurt Schröder doesn't count for anything. We just have to wait and see what DS Sampson and Sergeant Xiao Chen have to say after they interview him. Assuming they'll share it with us.

My phone rings and I glance at the display then my heart skips a beat. It's DS Agu. He never fails to put the fear of God into me. I instinctively sit up straight as I answer.

"Gauthier," his voice rumbles down the line. "We've got a match on some prints from Landry's car. It's your *civil libertarian*, Patty Smith." I put the phone on speaker, so Vogel can hear. "Her prints are all over his vehicle. I guess now we know why she refused to give them to us in the first place." I can think of a few other reasons she might have done that, but I'm not going to argue with Agu. I sigh in frustration. If they hadn't put the forensics from the Sanger house onto the back burner we'd have had this information a lot earlier. Patty's prints are probably all over that house.

"You need to bring her in, now."

I clear my throat. This isn't going to go over well. "We would Sir, but she's in hospital. Someone tried to murder her this morning."

TWENTY FOUR

WHEN PATTY REGAINS consciousness the hospital calls to let us know and Vogel and I head over to interview her. It's unlikely she saw anyone stuff the rag into the exhaust vent, but I'm sure she knows why they did it. I also put in a call to Raleigh and have him meet us there. He needs to identify Patty, to see if he recognizes her as the young woman he put into Landry's car that night in December.

The doctors have had Patty on oxygen therapy for the past seven hours to reduce the carbon monoxide levels in her blood and she looks pale and tired when we enter the room. She has a bandage on her left ear and an oxygen mask covers most of her face but she's alert, and she looks frightened.

"Hi Patty," I say from the foot of the bed. "The hospital says you'll be discharged soon. I'll arrange for a car to take you back to Womyn Collective, okay?" I've already called Sophie to let her know what's happened. She and her team will be on hand to take good care of Patty when she arrives.

Vogel steps forward to speak with her and I give way. He seems to have the touch lately, since he was the one who'd convinced her to give up her fingerprints. He speaks to her in a gentle voice.

"How are you feeling Patty?" She shrugs. "Are you up to answering a few questions?" Another shrug. "Someone stuffed a rag into the exhaust vent at the trailer," Vogel says. "Filling it with carbon monoxide, in case you were wondering why you're here." She closes her eyes. "Any idea why someone might want to do that?" Patty just lies there, ignoring us.

I'm impatient and irritated by her lack of response and I push my way in front of Vogel. "Someone tried to kill you Patty. I'd think you'd take a bit more interest."

"Why do you think it was me they were after?" She's mumbling, but I can still hear her through the oxygen mask.

"Stop playing games Patty. Who else would be the target? You're the only one who works in there all day."

She opens her eyes and looks at me. I can see she's considering her options, deciding whether she should tell us the truth.

"Do you have any idea why they'd want you dead?" I repeat the question. She nods. "Do you know something? Did you see something?"

She shakes her head. "Not me." Now I get it. I feel the heady rush of adrenaline I get when I know I'm right.

"The Sangers? Did they see something?" She nods. "At one of the feral cat colonies?" She nods again.

"Do you know what it was?" She shakes her head. "Or who?" Another no.

"Patty," Vogel tries again. "We need you to tell us everything you know. They'll try again if we don't stop them. Next time you might not be so lucky."

"We think Martin and Natalie Sanger were blackmailing someone," I say. "That they were getting paid to keep quiet."

Patty nods. "The money was for the cats," she whispers. That's why the demand was so small. The Sangers weren't experienced criminals. Their only asking for such a measly amount for their silence proved that.

"Whatever," I snap. I'm pushing her hard and I'm not going to let her know my sympathy for the Sangers. "They were extorting money from someone, and it cost them their lives." Patty looks miserable but I'm not letting up. "And after they were both killed, you thought you'd get yourself some of that?" She shakes her head. "So who is it? Who were you extorting money from? And where is the information or whatever they were using to get the money."

"I took it," she mumbles. "When I left the house. But I didn't do anything with it."

"I don't believe you."

"It's true! It's just…after Natalie died…and then what happened to Martin…I panicked."

"I'm not buying it, Patty. I believe you'd run for her life if you were afraid, I believe you'd go into hiding or even leave town. But you don't take blackmail evidence with you unless you're planning on using it. Who were they blackmailing?"

She just looks away. "I don't know who it is. I just have a phone number and the photos Martin and Natalie took."

"Where are these photos?"

"Hidden in the trailer."

At least they're safe there. The trailer has been secured as part of a crime scene, and I'm going to make sure there's a constable on watch until we get a chance to look it over tomorrow.

"Why would anyone want to kill you Patty?" I already know the answer.

Patty starts to cry. Tears roll down her cheeks and get caught up in the oxygen mask. "I heard his voice in the kitchen that morning. The morning you found Natalie. And I saw a guy out on the ice with Martin that morning."

"Who was it?"

"I don't know."

"Was it the Chinese men?"

"There weren't any Chinese men. I lied."

"You *lied*? Why? To confuse the investigation?" She nods, looking miserable. "Patty, you almost got yourself killed."

"I'd seen that woman in town, the one who died. She was having a coffee with Renee Schröder. I had no idea who she was, I just thought…I don't know…" So that's what gave Patty the idea to lie about hearing someone speaking in Chinese the morning Natalie Sanger was attacked.

I look over at Vogel to see if he's caught that. So Renee Schröder and Mei Zhen Lai did meet. Why was the agent speaking with Renee? Trying to catch her and her partners? Getting her to turn them in? Or was it something else entirely?

Does that mean Kurt Schröder is telling the truth? One thing it does tell me is that Renee had lied to me when she'd said she didn't recognize Mei Zhen Lai.

There's a knock on the door and I get up to answer it. It's Raleigh. He beckons me out into the hall.

"I've been watching through the glass," he says. "That girl you're talking to? I'm positive that's the one who went into Landry's car that night."

"Okay," I say as I go to pull up a photo of Landry off my phone. "I want you to come back in there with me."

Raleigh looks down at his shoes, hoping to avoid the situation and the shame it will bring on him. But he doesn't have a choice.

I know from the way he looked over at me during the briefing earlier that he hasn't told DS Agu yet. It will be better for him if he can at least say the girl he put into Landry's car that night didn't die in the cellar. And if it transpires that Patty is the one who escaped, the one who killed Landry and got away, then that's also a good ending to his story. It'll certainly mitigate whatever disciplinary action they are likely to take against him.

I reenter the hospital room, with Raleigh trailing behind me. Vogel sizes up the situation immediately and knows where this is going.

"Patty, this is Detective Raleigh. Can you please tell me if you recognize him?"

She looks confused and her eyes dart back and forth between Vogel and I before she turns to look at Raleigh. A long moment of silence passes.

"Why?" she finally asks. "Why do you want to know if I recognize him?"

"Please just answer the question."

"Yes. I recognize him," she mumbles. "But I don't know his name."

"Can you please tell me where you know him from?"

Patty exhales loudly. "A while ago, when I first came to town, I was in trouble. I'd lost all my money and had nowhere to go. I came up to him outside a coffee shop I asked him for a ride to a shelter."

I thank Raleigh and he leaves the room. I hope he's gone to confess to Agu, but I suspect he's back behind the glass, seeing where the rest of the interview goes and exactly how bad he looks.

"Then what happened?"

"He didn't feel like doing it. I guess he needed to get himself a doughnut and a coffee," she mutters. "Some guy he knew offered to help out, so he put me into his car and walked away."

"And did this guy give you a ride to the shelter?"

She shakes her head. "I put my backpack into his trunk and got in the car. He started driving me out of town," she says, her brow furrowed. "And I asked him if this was the right way. I mean, why was he taking me out into the country? He said yes, it was the right road, and that he'd lived in town for his whole life and knew all the shortcuts."

Patty picks at her fingernails for a minute, remembering that night. "I got a creepy vibe off him and I started to freak out. When he came to a stop at some country intersection I jumped out of the car and ran into the bushes at the side of the road. I was afraid he was going to come after me, but then another car came up behind him and blew their horn because he was just stopped there. So then he took off."

"I lost all my stuff. My clothes, boots, everything I owned."

"You were lucky you got out like you did," Vogel says.

"It wasn't *luck*," Patty says. "I trusted my instincts." She grimaces. "But I shouldn't have gotten in that car in the first place. I only did it because that cop said it would be okay."

I slide a photo of James Landry across the table to her. "Is this the man from the car?"

"Yeah, that's him."

We now have an explanation for how Patty's prints got inside Landry's car. She isn't the one we're looking for—the one that got away. Agu will be disappointed. It looks like Landry found someone else that night. Unless Patty is lying to us. She could have been in Landry's car, like she and Raleigh said. But who's to say she didn't end up at that farmhouse, in the cellar. She still could be the one who killed Cellar Man.

My phone and Vogel's both ring at the same time. I'm afraid to look in case it's Agu, demanding an update on Patty Smith and Landry.

"DeGroot?"

"You'd better come into the station," he says. "FSU found a match to some of the fingerprints at Cellar Man's place. They belong to Landry's wife."

TWENTY FIVE

"BUT SHE SAID she'd never been there, didn't she?"

Agu nods. He's leaning against the table in front of the white board, and he looks exhausted. This Landry case is a twenty-four hour a day investigation and his feet are being held to the fire every day for it and the counterfeit wine case. I'm sure the pressure to get it solved is intense. And now, with this sudden discovery, it's taken a very strange turn sideways.

"She did say that, yes," Agu says. "She claimed she didn't even know her husband owned the house." He spreads his hands. "I guess she lied."

"FSU got around to testing the prints on the exterior of the doorframe to the locked cellar room. It wasn't deemed a high priority area, as compared to the murder weapon or the interior of the room. Or the focus on finding the identities of Landry's victims."

"So," Agu says. "Gauthier, you're with me and Evans. DeGroot, you're with Vogel." We head out in two cars. That tells me Agu is planning on bringing Mary Hauptman in—either for *voluntary questioning* at the station, or under arrest. I hope she has a lawyer.

Mary Hauptman answers the door herself this time, looking pale and tired. Her wrists are heavily bandaged from her suicide attempt. When she catches my glance she pulls down the sleeves of her cardigan, trying to hide them.

She stands aside and lets Agu, Evans and me pass. The others remain outside in the second car. Mary's eye flick toward the two police cruisers. She doesn't seem surprised.

The house is dark and quiet—no television on, no lights, and no-one else home.

"Where are your daughter and grandchildren Ms. Hauptman? Are they home?"

She shakes her head. "They've been staying at my son-in-law's parents' place." She doesn't need to say any more. I'm sure they are keeping the grandchildren away from her, from the darkness she's carrying. And maybe that's not a bad thing. I sit next to the wicker baskets of children's toys in the living room and hope the stain of shame won't permeate everything and ruin their lives, but I don't hold out much hope.

"Ms. Hauptman," Agu begins. "You told us you've never been to the farmhouse." A small sigh escapes her lips and her shoulders relax as she exhales in relief. She knows why we're here. She knows what we've found. She's been waiting for this moment. "But we've now found your fingerprint on the door. How do you explain that?"

"I was there," she whispers after a moment. "I killed him."

Evans quickly pulls out his notebook and checks the time on his watch. He also starts recording the interview on his phone, but she'll be brought into the station for a formal videotaped interview later. Agu silently watches Mary Hauptman, waiting for her to continue.

"I suspected he was up to something for a long time. I thought he had another woman. But, I just...didn't want to know." She wrings her hands and pulls down her cardigan sleeves again. "I just let him carry on. I didn't know what else to do. Confront him? Threaten to leave him? We'd been married almost thirty years."

"It wasn't all the time," she says, her voice a hoarse whisper. "He'd go for months without going out at night. He'd stay home with me and we'd watch television together, or we'd go out to a movie. And I'd think it was over—whatever affair he was having, that it was done. That he'd now come back to me, come back to his senses and he'd left her, whoever she was."

"Who did you think he was seeing?" Agu asks.

"I just thought it was someone from his work. I didn't know. Maybe a woman he met at the office, or who worked as an adjuster for one of the insurance companies."

She clears her throat "I followed him out there last year. It took me a long time to get to that point, to be able to do that. I thought that the house belonged to the woman he was seeing, the one he was cheating on me with. But I never went back after that one time.

"Then, about a month ago he didn't come home one night… and I got so angry. It was our wedding anniversary…and he didn't come home!

"So I drove out there. I saw his car in the driveway. Then while I was waiting on the road I saw a young woman—much younger than I ever imagined he'd be involved with—run out of the house, get into his car and drive away. I remember thinking *Where's she off to? Why is he with her? On **our** wedding anniversary?*

"All the things I'd been putting up with ran through my mind and I left my car on the road and marched right into that house. I was going to have it out with him, right then and there.

"But when I got inside, there was nobody home. There was no furniture in the house, no lights on anywhere. It was so…strange. I didn't know what to think. "Then I saw a light on in the basement, so I went down the stairs. I saw a key lying on the floor in front of a heavy door.

"I picked it up and unlocked the door. And I saw…that room. What was in there." She stares into the middle distance, remembering that night. "He was lying there on the floor by the bed, moaning. He knew who I was. He said my name. And he looked up at me, asking for help.

"I was horrified. I just…couldn't grasp what I was seeing, what he'd been doing there, who he really was. I saw the wooden chair leg lying there. I picked it up and...I hit him with it. Again and again. I don't even remember how many times I hit him. He stopped moving."

"Is that when you lost your scarf?"

She just stares at Agu. "What scarf?" Her hand goes to her throat. "Maybe. I don't remember."

I believe her story; it's clear she's guilty but the evidence still has to add up.

"There weren't any of your fingerprints on the weapon Mrs. Landry," Agu asks for clarification. "How is that possible?"

"I was wearing my gloves. It was cold that night."

"So how did you manage to leave a print behind on the door-frame?" asks Vogel.

"I did?" She thinks for a moment. "I dropped the key when I was locking the door behind me. I had to take my glove off to pick it up. I remembered to wipe the key," she whispers. "I guess forgot I'd touched the door frame."

"What did you do then? After you locked the door?"

"I went home," she says. "But I reported him missing the next morning. I made sure to throw out all the clothes I'd been wearing, in case there was any blood on them, for when the police came to investigate. But that never happened. Nobody ever asked." She seems surprised by that.

"Ms. Hauptman," Agu says. "You need to come with us now. Please get your coat."

She complies without hesitation; she goes into the closet and pulls out a worn parka then she slips her feet out of her house slippers and into a pair of winter boots.

"I would have come forward you know," she says as we escort her out to the waiting car. "If you ever charged anyone for killing him. I wasn't going to let an innocent person take the blame." Again I believe her.

TWENTY SIX

Thursday, January 16

AS I OPEN the back door to the station I notice the temperature is warmer than when we'd come in, just a few hours earlier. There's a strong wind blowing in from the south and I pray it'll break this cold spell.

"Hey Vogel," I tease him. "The weather's warming up just in time for your trip to the tropics." He shakes his head in disgust.

"Figures. And by the time I'm home it'll be freezing cold again."

"This has been one hell of a day," I mutter to Vogel as I search for my car keys in my handbag. "Starting with one attempted murder and ending with a confession to another one. I just want to go home and have a hot bath."

Vogel glances at his watch. "It's only just after five. Feels like it's midnight." He struggles into his coat as he pushed open the door. "Is the Landry case officially wrapped up?"

"Yes," I say as I follow him out the door. "She's confessed. In custody."

"What's going to happen to her?"

"Your guess is as good as mine. The Crown Attorney will have to decide what to charge her with. Second degree murder?"

Vogel nods in agreement. "I doubt they're going to give her

a medal, but maybe they'll reduce it to manslaughter, based on the circumstances."

Now that Mary Hauptman's been charged maybe the media circus outside the station will stop. I'm sure they'll still harass her daughter and neighbours, at least for a while until the story has run its course, but once we've issued the official statement there's not much more for the police to say on the matter. The ball will be handed off to the Crown prosecuting attorneys, once we've passed over all the evidence we've compiled, along with Mary Hauptman's confession of course.

It's funny how the media has changed their coverage of Mrs. Landry, who they've been painting as Cellar Man's widow and possible accomplice. Now she's almost a hero—the wronged wife who took action and exacted revenge on her evil husband when she realized what he'd been doing. She took the law into her own hands, went from zero to hero. I'm not sure how much of an impact the court of public opinion holds, but I hope it helps reduce her sentence.

Vogel drives off and I sit in my car for moment longer, waiting for the engine to warm up. I check my phone and reply to a text from Maja. She's pulling a late shift at the clinic tonight, and won't be home until after eight. So there's no rush to get home; nobody's waiting for me.

I think back over the day, reviewing where we've managed to end up. The Cellar Man case is over, except for the hours of paper-work. That leaves more time and energy for the Unit to devote to the murders of both the Sangers and Renee Schröder and Mei Zhen Lai. That's good; many hands make light work and Vogel and I can only get so much accomplished on our own.

In our briefing this afternoon Agu still insisted I stay on the missing persons inquiry into who the young woman who escaped Landry could possibly be. It's a waste of my time and energy but he wants to wrap things up. I'll do the minimum, just to make sure I stay on his good side, but it seems like a pointless exercise, just the sort of task he'd assign to the newest member of the Unit.

I suddenly remember what started my day—the visit to the trailer. I'd wanted to ask Patty about Campbell Global Logistics, to see if that feral colony was the one the Sangers might have seen something. And with all that happened today, it had slipped out of my mind. We'd gone to George Campbell's office and found he'd gone away; the visit to his mother didn't shed any light on where he might be.

It occurs to me that I need to check his house again. Maybe he's back home. Just because he told his receptionist he wasn't coming into the office for a few days doesn't mean he's gone to Jamaica. He might just as easily be sitting on the couch, drinking wine and binge-watching Netflix. His house is just a few blocks away on the other side of the Clarence Street Bridge. At least it's on my way home.

I do a slow drive by his bungalow and don't see any lights on inside, so I turn around and park in front. There's a car in the drive-way—a brand new Audi R8 coupe. When I walk past I touch the hood; it's still warm. It looks like George Campbell just got home.

I peer through the window and see a flashlight moving around inside the house. I pull back and watch as the light moves around, first from the back of the house where I assume the kitchen is, then into the living and dining rooms. What the hell is George Campbell doing, going around his own house in the dark with a flashlight? Hasn't he paid the electric bill? Has his power been cut off?

When the flashlight goes down the hall I decide I've had enough and I ring the doorbell. There's no answer, so I knock. When he doesn't answer on the second knock I go around through the gate to the back door. There are no security or exterior lights on, but the snow is bright enough to reflect the moonlight. I knock on the back door, again with no luck.

I'm not legally allowed to enter the premises without a warrant unless a life-threatening emergency exists inside or there is imminent risk of harm to a member of the public. Or unless I'm invited. None of those fit the bill, but who's to say different? I turn the doorknob and find it unlocked, so I slip inside.

I pause on the threshold, listening for the sound of anyone inside. If the car in the driveway is anything to go by, George Campbell is here. I flip the switch on the wall and the overhead light in the kitchen comes on. So, the power's not cut off. I feel the adrenaline rush up my spine as I draw my weapon and creep into the room. Something is not right.

The room is empty and there's just a single dirty coffee mug in the sink. I walk through into the dining room and find George Campbell dead on the floor. He's got a shotgun wound to the chest, but there's no sign of a gun anywhere, and neither of his ears have been cut. I reach down to feel for a pulse even though I already know there won't be one. His body is cold; he's been dead for hours. So whose car is in the driveway?

I freeze and listen intently. The furnace is on and I hear the warm air being pushed up through the vents. The refrigerator motor kicks in and the clock on the kitchen wall ticks. Then there's a faint noise coming from the closet next to the front door. I walk over and pull open the closet door. Hiding behind the coats I find Elsie Duggan. She looks terrified.

I motion with my gun. "Please step out of there, Elsie." She complies, her eyes locked on my weapon. She's carrying a stuffed gym bag that she leaves on the floor.

"What are you doing here?"

"Lenore wanted me to get something for her." She indicates the gym bag.

"Really?" I can't even pretend to believe her. "What could that possibly be?"

She doesn't respond. "Elsie, it's easy enough for me to check. Lenore may care for you very much, but I don't think she'll cover for you if you killed her son."

"I didn't kill him! I just got here." I know she's probably telling the truth, but I don't want to make this easy for her. The car's hood is still warm, meaning she'd just driven it. George has been dead for hours and there's no shotgun anywhere in sight. "Anyway, Lorene didn't even like him."

"No. She didn't. But still, he was her son." Elsie just rolls her eyes. "So, what are you doing here?" She sighs and sits in a chair then looks up at me, waiting. I can tell she's decided to cooperate.

"What's in there?" I point my gun toward the gym bag. "Open it."

Elsie sighs and bends down to unzip and pull the bag open. I nose it open with my toe. Inside is a silver dinner service, including a teapot and a few silver picture frames. Things easy for her to sell.

"How do you know George Campbell? I understand you met in Las Vegas?" Her eyes widen in surprise and I can see she's thinking hard about how much of the truth to tell. Then she shrugs, probably having calculated there's no risk in telling all of it.

"He hired me to assist his mother," Elsie says with a sly smile. "And to get close to her."

"Why?"

"Money," she laughs. "He wants her money." Elsie glances at the body on the floor. "Wanted."

"And what were you supposed to do?"

She shrugs. "He seemed to think I could convince her to make him Power of Attorney."

"Now? Doesn't she already have a Will?"

"She did. But she had her lawyer revoke it a few years ago."

I nod. That makes sense. "Lorene probably revoked her Will when she first learned she had syphilis. She did say she was going to spend his inheritance…"

"Yeah, I think so."

"So Lorene currently has no Will and no Power of Attorney, so when her syphilis does cause the inevitable dementia, if she even lives that long, it'll be too late to make one anyway."

"…Because she'll be no longer competent." Elsie finishes my thought. "That's how George explained it to me anyway."

"Poor George," I say insincerely. "I guess he was in a real pickle. If he didn't stop Lorene's spending her money it would all be gone. And there's nothing he could do about it." Elsie shrugs and studies her nails. "But, since he's her son and only heir, the money will go to him anyway. Eventually."

"Whatever's left," Elsie smirks.

George Campbell was a creep, but this scheme with Elsie isn't what killed him. Whoever shot him wasn't after Lorene's estate or her money.

Elsie is sitting at the table, as cool as if she's got ice water flowing in her veins.

"George hired you to *assist his mother*?" She nods. "Assist her to do what, exactly? To fall down the stairs?"

"I didn't do that." She insists. "It was all him." She's probably telling the truth about that. I bet she made the most of that information too.

"And then you told Lenore about it." Elsie shrugs.

Elsie's a complete opportunist who's been working both sides—that's why George Campbell was so angry with her when we'd first interviewed him. He hired her to do a job for him and she screwed him.

"Why'd you tell her?"

"I like Lenore. And what George was doing was wrong."

"But he was paying you." Another nod. "Probably a lot more than the twenty dollars an hour he told us?"

She scoffs. "Definitely."

"And that's why you were stealing his silver?"

"He owed me." She looks down at his body. "And I'm not in any Will."

"So you thought you'd just help yourself?"

She nods. "Pretty much."

"How'd you know it'd be safe to come and steal this stuff? That Campbell wouldn't be home?"

Elsie laughs. "You came to Lorene looking for him. Said he'd gone away." She shrugs. "Seemed like an appropriate time."

That could be true. I can't get a read on her. Elsie definitely knows more than she's saying, but what she's saying isn't necessarily even true.

It's even possible she killed him herself, on an earlier visit. Then she decided to come back later at a more convenient time to rob the house, once she'd disposed of the weapon. We'll need to search Lenore Campbell's house for a shotgun, just in case.

Still, I don't really see any need to arrest and charge her with theft. She'll be better off looking after Lenore than sitting in jail. It's not as if George Campbell's going to press charges anyway.

"Elsie, you need to leave, now." She looks at me in surprise. "I'm calling this in and it's better for you if you aren't anywhere around when the police arrive."

"Where should I go? Home?"

"Go see Lorene. Sit with her tonight."

She picks up the gym bag and starts to head toward the door.

"Wait a minute," I say. She stops, her shoulders tense. "You might want to leave that here." She turns to me with a smile and I know something's not right.

"What else is in that bag Elsie?" Her smile fades. "Open it all the way." Stuffed at the bottom is a pink winter jacket and snow pants.

I raise my eyebrow. "Campbell's? Doesn't seem like his style."

"He made me give it back," Elsie scoffs. "He thought he'd return it, since it was only worn once. Cheapskate." She gives me a sly look, waiting for me to figure it out.

"Campbell had you dress up in this? When? Last Saturday night?" She shrugs. "He wanted you to join the group of volunteer pickers at Ambrosia. To pretend to be Mei Zhen Lai? Why?"

Elsie looks bored. "He paid me. I didn't ask why."

"And after she was found dead, you never thought about telling us?"

"It wasn't my business."

"I'm still trying to figure out exactly what your business is."

"Give me a break." She rolls her eyes. "It wasn't personal. I didn't even know her."

"Weren't you afraid of repercussions? What if George Campbell or whoever he's working with decide to come after you, tying off loose ends to make sure you don't talk?"

"I'm not afraid of George Campbell."

I look down at the body. "No, I guess not." I can't believe how cold she is, going through Campbell's place in the dark, stepping over his dead body to steal his silver. Elsie's fearless and she certainly isn't afraid of me either.

Elsie looks toward the door, eager to leave. I don't think she killed George Campbell and I have lots of reasons to detain her, though only attempted theft might ever stick. She could just lie and say Lorene sent her anyway. It's not worth the paperwork.

"Go home Elsie." I know where to find her. She doesn't need to be told twice. I hear the back door close and in a minute the headlights of the Audi are backing up out of the driveway and turning down the street.

I shove the bag under the sideboard with my foot. If I know Elsie, she'll be back for it later, or at least she'll try.

I call it into the station then send a quick text to Maja.

Looks like I'll be a bit late tonight.

While I'm waiting for back up I review the situation. George Campbell is dead from a shotgun blast to his chest. There's no gun at the scene, so whoever did it took the weapon with them, as well as the expended shell casing. Which means it'll be impossible for ballistics to match the weapon that fired the fatal shot. A shotgun's a noisy weapon though. I wonder if any of the neighbours might have heard anything then realize that on a cold January night, with the doors and windows closed tight and most likely their televisions on, it's unlikely.

So where is Campbell's car? The Audi in the driveway is clearly Lorene's, since Elsie just drove off in it. Did whoever shoot Campbell steal his car? I suppose it'll be found dumped somewhere, wiped clean, which means the killer arrived here on foot. Carrying a shotgun? That makes no sense. Or there were two of them—one drove off in the vehicle they arrived in and the other took Campbell's car. But why bother? It's just another way to leave trace evidence behind and get yourself caught. That tells me that whoever did it wasn't too smart. Unless they planned on selling it, which they could only do if they had connections to chop shops and dealers in stolen vehicles. But that certainly isn't your average citizen's kind of connection.

The death of George Campbell could easily have been put down to his having interrupted a robbery, if I hadn't come around when I did. The car missing and the silver—thanks to Elsie, and we'd never even know about the pink coat. But that's not what happened here. I just don't know who did it, or why.

What's really troubling me is the pink outfit. Why did George Campbell want Elsie to impersonate Mei Zhen Lai? Obviously to make the rest of the guests think she'd been at the event the night her body was found. Sure, Elsie isn't Asian, but she has dark hair. The bright pink coat is enough to make an impression on most people, and it worked. DS Raleigh said that most of the guests remembered her being there.

The only reason I can think of for Campbell wanting to make it seem like Mei Zhen Lai was there is to confuse us about the time she died. I'm sure he had no understanding of forensic pathology and how they can determine time of death. Maybe he was hoping her body wouldn't be discovered so soon, and maybe not even at Ambrosia. Mei Zhen Lai was already dead—days before she was found, and Campbell knew it. It's probable he killed her, or someone he was working with did. But why? And why was her body dumped at Ambrosia? Anyone finding it would immediately connect it to the Icewine investigation.

Unless whoever dumped it there already knew about the investigation. Someone like Renee Schröder. Could she have done it? To protect her farm and silence Mei Zhen Lai? If what her husband said was true, maybe it was Renee who killed the Chinese investigator and hid her body in the grape press. I flash on the new foundation for the barn extension Kurt Schröder was about to pour, once the harvest was over. Was Renee's plan to bury the body in that cement?

I look down at Campbell's body, lying on the dining room floor and run through all the pieces in my mind, to see how they fit. Whoever shot Campbell must have been in on whatever this scheme is. Blackmail. The Sangers. Seeing something at GCL shipping yard. Campbell hiring Elsie to impersonate Mei Zhen Lai, to confuse us about time of death. Then that means Campbell must have been involved with Renee Schröder, if she killed the Chinese investigator. But she was already dead, so she couldn't have killed Campbell.

Was it Elsie after all? Is that why George Campbell's ear wasn't cut? All of the victims had their ears cut, even Patty. Why didn't George Campbell? Did the killer bring a shotgun but forget his knife? Or is his death not connected, unlikely as that seems.

What would Elsie's motive be? Killing George Campbell would clear the way for Elsie to move in and take over Lorene Campbell's life. But she's already managed to do that. There's no need for her to get blood on her hands.

I feel a rush of irritation at Elsie, at her evasions and her lies. Not to mention how her impersonation of Mei Zhen Lai wasted a lot of our time. Just like Patty Smith. First she tells us she was only at the Sangers for a couple of days, then we find out it's been weeks. Then she admits Martin and Natalie were blackmailing someone, but denies knowing any more about it. Yet for some reason she makes off with the evidence and hides it, supposedly to protect them? It's more like she wanted to carry on with the extortion herself. And she still won't tell us the truth, even though someone's just tried to kill her. First thing in the morning I'm going to get that evidence out of the trailer myself, then the truth will come out.

TWENTY SEVEN

I GOT HOME really late since I had to hang around while FSU processed the crime scene at George Campbell's. Then I spent what was left of the night at home with Maja, watching television and drinking wine. At least I pretended to watch television, but my mind was mostly reviewing the puzzle, going over and over who connects to whom, and how the cases might even connect to one another.

I've decided to go in late this morning. After all, I've earned it after working late last night. Maja's gone to the clinic and I'm just having my second coffee when my phone rings. It's Sophie, from Womyn Collective.

"Hi Lucy," she says. "I thought you said Patty was being discharged today."

"She is…" My pulse starts to race as I glance at the clock on the wall. "Hours ago. Isn't she there?"

"Nope. I've been waiting for a while now. No sign of her."

"Okay, thanks for letting me know Sophie." I hang up and call dispatch.

"Did someone send a car to pick up Patty Smith at the hospital earlier today?" I wait a minute then dispatch comes back on the line.

"Yes, we did. But she was already gone." And no one thought to let me know? My blood starts to boil and I'm about to tear a strip off her but I bite my tongue. There's no point in taking it out on the dispatcher.

I hang up the phone. So Patty must have discharged herself earlier, before the constable arrived to take her to Womyn. Why? Where did she go?

When I'd seen her in the hospital she wasn't very cooperative, and I know she was definitely frightened. So why would a young woman who was afraid for her safety, who someone had already tried to kill, not want to be driven to a place where she'd be looked after and protected? What did she have to do that was so important that she'd take that risk?

Where would she have gone? There's only one place I can think of: Randy's Ice Fishing Rentals. She's gone to get the evidence.

When I get out of the car I sniff the breeze like a dog scenting the air. As predicted there's a warm wind blowing in from the southern US, and I can feel the temperature is rising quickly. It's the January thaw, more or less on schedule. Every winter, we get a sudden and very brief warming spell that gets all of our hopes up that winter is already over. It never is.

Last week we were frozen in the middle of the polar vortex and now the forecast is for a sudden temperature shift, with high winds forcing the temperature up to thirteen degrees Celsius—a twenty-degree rise in two days. In a good year the thaw will last for about a week before it drops again once February arrives. We lose our parkas and balaclavas, put away our snow boots and puffy coats and venture out in spring jackets, if only for a few days.

The false spring melts snow and causes local rivers and streams to overflow their banks and basements to flood. The warm southern air causes fog thick enough to cancel flights and cause serious car accidents on our roads. After the first thrill of warmth, the resulting chaos is enough to make us wish for winter again—which is a good thing since it's definitely coming back.

I knock on the trailer door and step inside. Patty's there, as I expected. She's not happy to see me.

"I just heard from Sophie. She tells me you didn't show up there when you were discharged. Why didn't you go to Womyn, Patty?"

"I had some business to take care of."

"What kind of business?"

She shrugs and I try to shock her into a reaction. "George Campbell is dead." She visibly pales.

"Who?" she asks trying to sound cool, but the break in he voice gives her away.

Patty's not much of an actress. She knows who George Campbell was. "Did you kill him?"

Patty looks horrified. "No!"

"Are you sure? I think he might have been the one who tried to kill you, right here in this very trailer."

"Why would he do that?" She won't meet my eye.

The door opens and Randy Delaware comes in, carrying a five-foot long steel bar with a wide wedged end.

"Hi Randy," I say. "What's that? It looks…menacing."

"It's a spud. We use it to chip ice holes," he says. "It's fast and easy, low tech. We can make fishing holes the old school way. And I use it to test the ice."

He turns to Patty. "We've got to move, now. Grab your ice picks."

She stands and grabs for a set of ice claws that are lying on the table. She loops the string around her neck and tucks the dangling picks into her pockets to keep them from getting in the way.

"What's happening?"

"The lake ice isn't safe. We've got to pull in the shanties."

"Are you sure? It looks safe to me."

Delaware smiles. "You're an expert on ice?" I shake my head. That's something I definitely am not. "It's breaking up fast. The currents flowing underneath the surface are melting the ice from below."

I know the marine units keep their eye on the ice all winter. Any change in the wind direction or increase in temperature can make the ice unstable and dangerous. Signs get posted cautioning the public to stay off the ice and sometimes temporary fences are erected to keep people away from riverbanks. I just never knew it happened this quickly.

"I was just testing it," Delaware continues, holding up his spud. "Conditions can change really fast when we get the January thaw. It's Stage 4 now, in a few hours it'll go to 5 or even 6."

"What's that even mean?"

Delaware turns to Patty for an answer. I guess it's a test, to see if she'd been listening to his training.

"Stage four is weakening ice. Vehicles break through," Patty explains, rolling her eyes. "Stage five is rotten ice. People go through."

"What is means is that we're closed until it goes below zero for a few days," Delaware laughs. "I don't need to lose my fishing shanties through the lake! Let's go Patty!"

"That's it for the year?" Pulling in the shanties seems like a permanent decision.

"I'll put them back when the cold returns. If it returns," Delaware says.

"Dude," Patty laughs. "This is January in Canada. The cold will return."

Patty's right. Last year's January thaw ended when a brutal cold front came in from the West bringing freezing rain with hundred kilometer per hour winds that took down power lines and felled trees.

She's about to step out of the trailer to follow Delaware onto the ice when I call her back. "Patty, I need to talk to you."

"I have to help Randy," she snaps. "Leave me alone."

She storms out, heading onto the ice on Gravelly Bay.

I stand in the doorway of the trailer and watch as Delaware attaches a chain to the shanty nearest to shore and winches it in, sliding it over the ice until it's on shore. The shanties all have runners fitted to their undersides, made from two by twelve pieces of lumber with old cross country skis screwed to their bottoms, to make it easy to slide them across the ice.

As I'm watching them work I feel freezing water dripping onto my head. Several huge icicles lined up along the roof of the trailer starting to melt in the rising temperatures. I step to one side so the drip falls onto the augers and ice cutting tools stacked neatly up against the side of the trailer. I assume they'll be locked into the trailer once the shanties are secured.

In less than an hour Delaware and Patty have managed to tow all of the shanties off the ice and secure them on the beach. Gravelly Bay looks empty, the ice just a sheet of white with a few holes that haven't frozen over scattered across its surface.

They're red faced and sweating from exertion when they return to the trailer, but they're both smiling. Delaware waves to me and keeps walking to his truck, leaving Patty to keep an eye on the things for the rest of the day. She doesn't look pleased to find me still waiting to talk to her and she pushes past me, heading inside.

I lean on the doorframe, blocking her way out in case she decides to run for it.

"I thought about having a look through the trailer when you were out there working, for the photographs you said you'd hidden in here. But something tells me you already removed them. Am I right?" I try to meet her eye. "That's the *business* you had to take care of, right?"

Patty does her best to ignore me. She sits at the table and fires up the computer, checking emails and the contact form for the Randy's Ice Rentals website.

"Gravelly Bay is less than a kilometer from the hospital. So is George Campbell's house. Not too far for you to walk once you'd discharged yourself."

"I think you came here and got the evidence the Sangers used to extort money from Campbell, then you went over to his house. Did you decide to confront him? To try and get some money for yourself like Sangers?" There's still the question of the shotgun—where she'd found one and what she'd done with it, but I know I'll figure out soon enough.

Patty's back tenses, but she doesn't say anything.

"My first question is, did Campbell kill the Sangers?" I have a hard time imagining fat, sweaty George Campbell overpowering Martin Sanger and holding his head down in the ice hole until he was dead.

"My other question is, did you kill Campbell?" Silence.

"Patty, I'm only trying to help you here. These people, whoever they are, are dangerous. Five people are dead and it's pretty clear you're next."

Patty doesn't move. She continues to stare at the computer screen, pretending I'm not even there.

"*Fuck it*, I'm out of here," I say as I storm out. I can waste my time at the station. At least there's coffee there.

TWENTY EIGHT

NEEDLES OF SLEET pelt my face as I walk to the car, but I'm so angry I can barely feel them. Patty is an idiot. I know she's lying. I know she's hiding something. And, I know whoever tried to kill her—if it wasn't George Campbell that is, will try to do it again. What does she know? Why won't she tell me? Is she protecting someone? Who?

The sky is heavily overcast, indicating a storm is coming. What kind of storm we get will depend on the temperature when it hits. If it gets warmer it could be rain. If it drops suddenly it might become freezing rain. Or if it gets steadily colder we'll get snow and our January thaw might be over as suddenly as it began.

I should go into the station, but I'm too angry to sit around and do paperwork, let alone continue with the tedious missing persons investigation Agu assigned me to. Even though Mrs. Landry—or Mary Hauptman, has confessed to the murder, we still have at least one loose end: Who is the one that got away? We know she isn't the one who killed James Landry but she certainly struck him with the chair leg and locked him into the cellar before she ran off.

The only description Mary Hauptman was able to give us is that she looked to be young and had dark hair. She was quite far away when the woman ran out of the house and got into Landry's car, so I suppose we can count ourselves lucky we even got that much.

I've isolated my search to missing women under thirty-five who aren't redheads or blondes, and who disappeared in the country in the last six months. It was disturbing to learn there are almost fifty names, just as a start, and my heart isn't in it. Honestly, I feel like she should just be allowed to disappear. She managed to escape Landry and she isn't the one killed him, so why do we need to find out who she is anyway? They aren't enough hours in a day to get essential work done, so why are we wasting time looking for someone who isn't guilty of a crime and doesn't want to be found?

I need a distraction, someplace to go, but the only place that comes to mind is just as likely to make me even angrier. I decide to go for it anyway. I'm going to visit Doreen. I put the car into low gear and start to climb the icy road up the escarpment to Pelham Woods Retirement Home.

This time I arrive without coffee or donuts and Doreen is not impressed. I find her in her room, with the television on the weather channel and the sound off.

"And it's pissing down freezing rain," she mutters. "I can't even step out for a smoke."

"Sorry," I throw up my hands. "I can't control the weather."

"Never asked you to," she snaps. "You shouldn't have driven up here in it. It's dangerous."

I don't reply, mostly because she's right. By the time I'd driven too far to turn back I regretted my impulse to come see her. Driving back to town at this point will be even worse, unless the salters and sanders have been out. I may as well sit tight at Pelham Woods for a while until the roads are safe.

"So why'd you come?" Doreen asks. She knows me well enough by now to know there's a reason.

"I just need to talk something through."

She smiles and slides open the door to her small balcony, then pulls up a chair in front of it and lights a cigarette. "Go ahead. I'm ready." Doreen's a sharp observer of people and situations. She thinks like I do, which makes her a great sounding board. And she knows how to keep a secret better than anyone, apart from me.

I laugh. Doreen's willing to defy the Pelham Woods management to make sure she gets her nicotine fix. I pity anyone who dares to reprimand her again.

"George Campbell is dead. I found him last night." She raises her eyebrow, curious to know more. "Shotgun wound to the chest."

"Was his ear cut?"

"No, it wasn't. Not sure what that means."

"Maybe it was a different killer? Different motive?"

"Both Martin and Natalie Sanger had their ears cut. So did Renee Schröder, and Mei Zhen Lai. And Patty Smith—her ear was cut, too…

"…but thanks to you she didn't die."

I shrug. "I thought it had to do with the feral cat thing. But then Renee Schröder was killed and as far as I know she had nothing to do with them…"

"Sure she did," Doreen interrupts. "She was volunteering with that cat rescue group at the time I worked with her."

"The feral cat rescue? The one run by Natalie Sanger?"

"The very one. She used to bring cats back to her parents' farm after they were neutered and let them live in the barn to catch mice." Doreen is thinking as she smokes, trying to retrieve some fragment of memory. "I think she even took in a whole feral cat colony one time. Relocated them all at once to the family farm." She shakes her head at the memory. "But she had to give it up after she married Kurt."

"Why?"

Doreen shrugs. "He's allergic? I don't know." Why does this feel important I wonder? But I can't make any connection.

"Renee was so soft hearted. And stubborn! You have no idea," Doreen continues with a smile. "Would not let up. Kept trying to get me to take in some stray cats they were trying to find homes for."

"And you didn't take one?"

Doreen's cat comes out of the bedroom and rubs up against her legs. She reaches down and absently pats his head.

"No. I didn't want one at the time. Then this old guy started coming around my place and we got along fine, so…" She spreads her hands. "The rest is history."

"What else can you tell me about Renee Schröder? You said she was a nurse?"

Doreen nods. "She started maybe ten years ago, just when I was ready to retire. She was down to earth, no airs and graces. Came from farming so she knew about hard work. Her family ran a peach farm for years. Left it to her when they died, like their parents did before them. That's the way it's always been around here." .

"You knew her well?"

"Well enough," Doreen shrugs. "We worked on the surgical floor together for a while. I liked her. She was quiet. Shy. It was a surprise when she and Kurt got together. I guess it was a case of opposites attracting."

"What about Kurt? You knew him too?"

"Kurt was always a bad boy," Doreen says with a chuckle. "Oh, you know. Not *criminal*. Just sowing his wild oats. He couldn't wait to get out of here, go see the world. He played guitar in bands, touring around. I heard he even worked on cruise ships for a while."

"Then what happened?"

"He came home," she shrugs. "I guess that whole rock and roll lifestyle got old." I know all about *bad boys,* since I come from the East Village, where most of the trouble and crime come from in our town.

Doreen lights another cigarette and there's a loud pounding on the wall from the suite next door. I guess her neighbour isn't pleased about the cigarette smoke.

"*Fuck off!*" Doreen shouts as she pounds the wall to make sure they get the message.

"And when Kurt came back home…" I prompt her.

"There was nothing waiting for him. He'd sold out his shares in the family winery, and had nothing to come home to. So he got a job in the hospital, in the maintenance department. Quite the comedown for a young man who left town thinking he was going to be this big rock star. But that's where he met Renee, so that worked out well for him."

"He didn't go back to wine making?" I'm trying to make the connection to Ambrosia Winery.

Doreen shrugs. "Well…Kurt tried to go back to work for his brother for a while. Didn't work out. But then he married Renee and they started to turn her family farm into a winery."

"How competitive do you suppose Kurt is with his brother? Renee mentioned something…"

Doreen nods. "Very, I'd guess. Kurt's that kind of guy."

I nod, thinking it through out loud. "His brother has been winning awards at these international wine competitions. Meanwhile Kurt and Renee are struggling just to keep Ambrosia Winery going, are doing whatever they can to promote the business, but they aren't doing so well; they're late paying their workers and I bet they're late on other bills too. I wonder how far he'd be willing to go to get the money he needed to keep the winery afloat."

"I think he'd go as far as he had to, to make some quick cash," Doreen says. "Kurt isn't a patient man. He's into shortcuts. I'd say that's why he married Renee. It was an easy way to get some land."

"Land he's turning over as fast as he can from fruit to grapes," I say. "Even though his wife wasn't happy about it."

"We have a witness who says she saw Renee meeting with the Chinese investigator," I say. "But when I interviewed Renee she said she didn't even recognize her. What does that say?"

"So she lied to the police?" Doreen laughs. "Who doesn't? Maybe she was afraid?"

"Of being found out? You mean she was involved in the wine fraud?"

"No way. I just don't believe that.'

"Then what?"

"Maybe she was afraid of Kurt." Doreen looks at me. "Maybe she found out—from this Chinese investigator—that Kurt was involved in the counterfeiting."

"And that's why she was trying to take over the bookkeeping," I say, getting excited. "So she could find evidence? One of the crew told me he'd heard Kurt and Renee arguing about taxes and the government. Maybe that's what he heard—Renee accusing Kurt of being involved."

"Maybe she wasn't as afraid as she should have been," Doreen says. "Maybe Kurt killed the investigator? He found out she suspected him?"

I nod, considering the possibility. "And he conveniently has a building site at the winery where he could hide the body. Renee accidentally found the body and recognized her right way. She must have known right away it had been Kurt." How did she feel? Did she confront him? Is that how she ended up dead, strung up in the netting?

Doreen's sharp eyes study me. "You think he killed Renee too?"

I have no problem imagining he'd done it. "I'd bet on it. If Kurt could kill Mei Zhen Lai, then he could kill his wife. Maybe she was going to tell someone."

I think back to Kurt Schröder's rambling interview. "He did his best to make it look like his wife may have been involved in something—behind his back, of course. Claimed he knew nothing about it. Acted like he was scared of this *Chinese gang*..."

Doreen laughs. "Between the two of them, there's no question who's the likeliest suspect. Renee'd never hurt a fly, much less be involved in some kind of international wine fraud."

"Yeah," I agree. "I didn't really know her but I can't see it."

"Or maybe," Doreen continues. "Kurt just saw a convenient way to get rid of his wife. I'm sure he inherits the farm now. No need to argue with his wife about what to plant. Which I guess gives him another motive."

My mind is racing, considering how Kurt would benefit from Renee's death. "And so he kills her, then cuts her ear to make it look like it's connected to the other deaths?" Doreen shrugs.

"But why'd he do it?" I'm thinking out loud. "All it did was link all the crimes when we may never have gotten there... If he hadn't cut Mei Zhen Lai's ear, no one would have connected it to the Sangers." I'm thinking out loud. "It was a bad move. A stupid move..."

"He's not a smart guy," Doreen interrupts. "He'd do something dumb like that. Try and make it look like a serial killer had done it or whatever."

My blood runs cold. "Except there's no way he could have known about the Sangers' or Patty's ears being cut..."

"Unless he did it." Doreen finishes my sentence.

"Or someone told him about it. It wasn't reported in the media, but maybe someone at the other crime scenes saw it. You said he worked at the hospital. Maybe he's still got buddies there?"

"*Works* at the hospital," Doreen corrects me. "He's still working there as far as I know. So was Renee. They needed the cash since the winery wasn't making any money yet."

"Kurt Schröder works at the hospital," I echo. "Patty Smith said she was scared off on the night Natalie Sanger was killed, by a hospital maintenance worker."

Doreen laughs. "He wouldn't have been working at night. Maintenance staff only work day shifts."

My mind is racing. Of course Kurt had been at the hospital that night. It would have been a simple thing for him to hang around, pretending to mop the floor or whatever, then to slip in and smother Natalie when the constable left her room unattended. Who'd even notice a maintenance worker in the hallway mopping while he waited for his moment to strike? But why would he kill Natalie?

"I feel like there's a connection I'm missing. Like it's right in front of me and I can't see it." Doreen takes a deep drag off her cigarette. I've never seen anyone enjoy smoking like she does. "What can you tell me about George Campbell?"

"I don't really know him. We didn't travel in the same circles, if you know what I mean." She shrugs. "I've heard he wasn't very good at business, at least not compared to his father and grandfather."

"His mother said he was weak and had no integrity."

"A mother knows her son." Doreen looks out the window at the falling rain. I know what she's thinking about, but I'm not going to open old wounds.

We sit in silence and I finally put the pieces together. Schröder told us that story about the Chinese gangs trying to force him and Renee into some fraud scheme, and like all the best lies, it was half-true. There was a fraud scheme, but it wasn't one they were being forced into. Kurt Schröder was a willing participant.

But Kurt wasn't doing it alone. He wasn't capable of it. He needed someone else, like a customs broker who was in a position to secure the necessary documentation, to falsify the required import and export permits and clearances. Kurt had a partner: George Campbell. A partner he had to get rid of once things started to get complicated.

George Campbell brought in bulk wine and had it shipped to Ambrosia. It was mixed there, bottled in Canadian glass, with VQA labels, then exported to China as Icewine. Campbell took care of all the paperwork, the freight forwarding and even the warehousing. He probably even managed the cargo insurance for it all. Everything flowed through George Campbell, who was now dead.

And whatever Natalie and Martin Sanger had seen at Campbell's shipping yard, whatever they were blackmailing him with, connects all of it together. Schröder must be the one they'd seen, the one they had photos of. It's all connected and it has to do with

Icewine. Kurt Schröder is involved up to his neck in it. He killed Mei Zhen Lai when she got too close, and then he killed Renee too.

And the only link connecting it all back to Kurt Schröder is Patty. She has information that implicates Kurt in all of it. She's in serious trouble. I grab my coat and head for the door.

"Drive safely," Doreen calls after me. "And you're welcome!" There's another pounding on her wall. "*Fuck off!*" she shouts again as she pounds back.

TWENTY NINE

THE LIGHT IS fading as I arrive in the parking lot. The wind has been picking up all day, rising in intensity with strong gusts up to ninety kilometers an hour. It's driving sleet as the drizzly rain is starting to freeze with the drop in temperature.

The road is already slick and I have to make a hard turn to the right to avoid a collision with Delaware, who's leaving in a big hurry, spraying gravel in his rush to get away. Where's he off to in this weather? He'd better slow down or he'll end up in a ditch.

I leave the car and run toward the trailer, slipping and almost ending up on my back as soon as I step onto the pavement. The gravel parking lot at least offered some traction, but the paving along the waterfront is already slick from the freezing rain and I find myself sliding out of control, slipping toward the edge of the frozen lake. I manage to catch myself by grabbing hold of a shrub and stand there, my heart pounding in panic. I hate ice. I hate the feeling that I have no control, that my feet aren't planted firmly on the ground. I feel my pulse racing and I struggle to calm down and get myself under control.

The second I exhale in relief and feel I'm not falling, that I'll be okay, I fall flat onto my back, knocking the wind out of myself. Luckily I don't hit my head, but it's a struggle to get up on my feet again and I have to crawl as far as the edge of the pavement before I'm able to find something to hang onto and pull myself upright.

I drag myself up the steps of the trailer and knock. I know Delaware's gone, but Patty had better still be in there. I need to talk to her and this is the likeliest spot I can think of finding her, before it's too late.

Nobody answers and I knock again, feeling my temper flare. Damn Patty. I know she's in there, probably ignoring me and hoping I'll just give up and leave. She doesn't even know the danger she's in. I push open the door and find her, eyes wide in terror, with a knife held to her throat. The knife is in the hand of Kurt Schröder.

"Put the knife down, Kurt," I say, as I quickly scan the trailer. He just smiles and shakes his head. I quickly draw my weapon and aim it squarely at him.

"Do you think you can shoot me before I kill her?" he says. "Want to bet?" My mind is racing as I consider my options, and his. The knife is pressed into Patty's carotid artery. He's holding Patty in front of him and I'm not able to get a clean shot.

"Delaware will be back at any minute," I say, hoping it's true. "He's just gone to Canadian Tire to buy some rope and chain. He just told me, out in the parking lot."

Kurt smirks.

"No, he won't." For a bad moment I'm afraid Delaware is in league with Kurt. "I spiked two of his tires and he's only got one spare. By the time Delaware gets to wherever he's going they'll be flat. And when gets back here, it'll be too late for both of you."

"Now, I need you to put down your gun, turn around and walk out. We'll be right behind you." I hesitate for a moment then Patty cries out as he presses the blade against her throat. I place the gun on the table and raise my hands, then slowly turn and go back down the steps.

The wind off Gravelly Bay whips my hair into my eyes and I feel the sting of ice pellets on my cheeks. It's now dark, apart from the few security lights in the parking lot. The heavy cloud cover from the freezing rainstorm has obscured the moon and stars. I can hear them coming a few paces behind me. Patty is struggling and whimpering in fear as Kurt shoves her along. Out of the corner of my eye I see him pick up Delaware's ice chipping spud in his free hand.

"Keep walking," Schröder says. "Out onto the ice." A wave of terror washes over me. I don't want to step out onto the ice, especially knowing it's now unsafe. My anxiety and dread start to mount and threaten to overwhelm me. I'm afraid I'll collapse into a full-blown panic attack. "Move it," he hisses, his voice full of menace.

Even though the wind is roaring I immediately hear a crack as I step out onto the ice and I freeze.

"Go on," he yells and I force myself to take another step. I slide my feet along, as if skating on my boots. It feels more stable than trying to lift my foot off the ice.

A few minutes pass that feel like an hour as I make my way further and further from shore, with Schröder and Patty behind me. The faint lights from the parking lot cast a weak glow in the distance and all I can see is the sleet in front of my face.

"This'll do," Schröder says and I stop. We're out by where the ice shanties had stood earlier this morning. Nothing is left but the faint outlines of the holes, now slowly freezing over.

"Here." He hands me the ice spud. "Start chipping." I can't believe what he's telling me to do at first and I freeze, in horrified disbelief. "Make the hole bigger," he shouts. I stare at him, squinting into the freezing rain. He's several feet away, still holding the knife on Patty.

I've never used an ice spud and I clumsily start to chip away at the hole. My left shoulder is aching from the cold and my injury and I'm struggling to do as he's ordered. I work as slowly as I can, trying to buy myself some time to think of some way out of this, some way to escape Schröder before he kills both of us, because I know that's exactly what he's planning to do. He's going kill Patty and me, and make it look like an accident.

"Why are you doing this Kurt?" I dare a quick glance up at him and see he's smirking. "You think killing me..."

"And her," he gives Patty a shake and she yelps in fear.

"You're not going to get away with it. People know I'm here. My partner knows about the blackmail, and about how you killed the Sangers and the Chinese investigator. And your wife." The smirk falls away as his face turns to stone.

He doesn't say anything for a moment. The only sound is the spud as it hits the ice.

"The ice is getting soft." His voice is quiet. "Accidents happen when we have a quick thaw like this. I had nothing to do with Patty falling through the ice," he gives her another shake. "Or with you going in to save her." He smiles. "Nobody knows I'm here. Randy never saw me. I didn't drive over."

He's right, about everything. Nobody knows I'm here. And the ice is soft, thanks to the rain and warm temperatures all day. When I chip it with the ice spud large chunks fall away into the hole even though I'm trying to prevent it. Once a piece near my feet breaks off and I have to jump back before I fall into the water myself. I hear Schröder laugh and I think of swinging the ice spud wide to hit him in the head. But I know there's little chance I'd even manage to connect, let alone do it without him killing Patty first.

"That'll do," he says. "Now take off your gloves and throw them in." I know what he wants, to make sure I'll have no protection, so my hands will become numb from the cold in case I decide to fight him. I do as he asks then, full of dread, I turn to face him.

"What are you going to do now?"

"I'm going to throw her in." He grins and in that second Patty is flung deep into the black water, but the wind is so loud I can barely hear the splash. She doesn't even scream.

The second Patty's in the water I launch myself at Schröder, knocking him off his feet. He slips on the ice and goes down on his back as the knife falls from his hand. I kick the knife into the hole then I'm on top of him, punching and biting and scratching as if my life depends on it, which it does.

I hear Patty splashing in the water as she comes up for air, gasping in shock at the freezing cold water.

"Patty," I shout as I'm fighting Schröder. "Use your ice picks! Climb out!" Then Schröder's fist connects with my jaw and I fall back, almost blacking out. I'm on my back as he scrambles to his feet. He struggles as he slips and falls once, then again, on the slick surface.

Patty stabs the claws into the ice then lifts her upper body up over the edge. She's pulled herself half out when Schröder comes for her again, kicking her back into the hole. She's fallen back into the water and I get to my feet and tackle Schröder again. We're wrestling at the edge of the hole as Patty manages to drag herself up out of the water and roll until she's far away from the edge of the hole, on solid ice. She stands and is frozen in place, unsure what to do—to try and help me or to escape.

"Run!" I scream at her. She hesitates for a split second then takes off across the ice.

Schröder is torn. Should he follow Patty or finish me off? He gets to his feet and is about to follow her then thinks better of it. He sees the ice spud lying a few feet away and he grabs it then points it at me.

"Get up," he says. I clamber to my feet, keeping my eyes on him as he thrusts the spud at me, again and again. He's grinning as I step back, trying to avoid the pointed metal rod. I don't dare go for him again, not with him holding that. He's lost the knife, but the spud can just as easily kill me.

Should I try and make a run for it, go around him and head for the shore? I can't run on this ice; I can barely walk, but then neither can he. We'd have the same disadvantage. I decide that's my best option and I push off ready to sprint when I hear a sickening crack as the ice gives way under me and I fall through into the icy black water.

My worst nightmare has come true and I'm underwater, unable to breathe in the icy blackness. The dark cold lake is beneath me, around me, trying to pull me down. I know I'll be swept away under the ice. I'm going to die.

I surface, eyes streaming and gasping for air. I start to hyperventilate. My heart is racing and I can't get my breathing under control. I know what this is—it's the cold shock response and I struggle to get my breathing under control, to deliberately slow it down from this panicked choking. I reach for something to grab hold of so I don't slip under the surface.

Schröder is there, standing close to the hole. He's holding the ice spud and he stabs at my hands when I try to grab for the edge. He spikes at me, jabbing with the ice spud and just missing my hand when there's a shout. It's Patty, calling from the trailer, her voice almost lost in the wind.

"I called 911!" Patty screams again. "The police are on their way."

Schröder's head turns when he hears her voice and I reach up out of the water. I grab his ankle and pull, hard. He slips and falls onto his back and then I'm dragging him, trying to pull myself out of the water but instead he's sliding toward me into the hole. He's strong, stronger than me, but I'm holding on with everything I've got. My left shoulder is an agony of pain but I'm not letting go of him.

Schröder is roaring in rage as he's kicking at me with his free leg, trying to break free and he connects with my forearm. I hear a crack and I let go as he scrambles back to his feet. He pulls himself upright, but he makes the mistake of standing up so he can run to the trailer to get Patty and the ice gives way under him. But only his leg goes through and he takes a last look at me flailing around in the hole before he takes off after Patty. If he manages to kill her and escape before the police arrive then he'll be safe. I'm no threat to him. He knows I'll be dead soon. He takes off running toward the trailer.

I try to stay calm. I take deep breaths and keep my head above water. Panic is the enemy. Panic is what will kill me faster than hypothermia. I know I've got less than fifteen minutes, more likely ten at most, if I'm lucky. My muscles will get weak and I'll lose coordination and strength, before all the blood flows from my extremities into my core in order to preserve heat. My muscles and nerves won't work well and I'll lose meaningful movement until I can no longer grip anything or even tread water. Then I'll slip under the surface and drown just like Heather did, all those years ago. I'll join her, after all this time.

I kick my feet and reach both my arms out onto the ice, digging into it with my nails, trying desperately to get a grip. My shoulder is weak and throbbing and it feels like my arm is fractured from where he kicked me, but I manage to get my shoulders, then my chest up onto the ice. Then I reach forward again, spreading my weight while kicking my legs as if I'm swimming onto the ice. I'm out of the water as far as my hips when I feel the ice start to crack under me, giving way. If I fall back in now I won't have the strength to drag myself out again. I freeze for a heartbeat in terror then I roll as quickly as I can, away from the black hole.

Once I'm far enough away I get to my hands and knees and crawl toward shore. I'm terrified to stand upright. But I'm not moving fast enough and I know I need to run if I have any hope of saving Patty. I get to my feet and start to run through the sleety darkness toward the lights of shore. My clothes are soaked and starting to freeze right on me. My coat is so heavy I pull it off and drop it on the ice and keep moving toward shore.

When I get closer to the trailer I see Schröder has hold of Patty. She's fighting him off, biting and scratching as she tries to defend herself. Then he gets her by the throat and starts choking her. Patty's eyes are closed in the struggle so she doesn't even see me coming up behind Schröder. I pick up the spud from where he's dropped it but my hands are so numb I can barely get a grip on it as I swing and strike him. I'm aiming for his head but I'm so weak I can't raise the spud high enough and the blow just glances off his shoulder. Schröder spins around and knocks it out of my hand then he comes for me.

He shoves me up against the side of the trailer, and starts hitting the back of my head on the wall as I'm flailing and scrambling around blindly, trying to grab for something, anything to use against him. I reach up and connect with one of the large dripping icicles. I break it off in my hand and lash out at him, hitting at his face and stabbing it toward his eyes. Schröder reels back screaming, with blood on his face. Then he slips on the ice and falls back hard, hitting his head on the sharp edge of the auger lying next to the trailer.

I come at him again, ready to hit him once more but see his eyes are wide open and blood is staining the snow around his head. I put down the icicle. Schröder won't be coming after anyone now.

I stumble around to the front of the trailer and find Patty, lying on her side in the snow. She's barely breathing. I sit her upright as the police sirens and flashing lights from the emergency vehicles fill the parking lot.

"Patty," I shake her. "It's okay. You're safe."

THIRTY

Friday, January 17

THE AMBULANCE ATTENDANTS have wrapped Patty and me in heated blankets to help prevent hypothermia, but I'm so hot and flushed from my fight with Schröder I doubt there's much risk of that, despite my having been in the water so long. My arm is aching and I hold it against my chest. I know I'll be heading to the hospital for a cast tonight.

"Why didn't you just tell me the truth, Patty?" I say once we're alone. "Just tell me what you'd heard that morning when we found Natalie? Or that you'd seen Renee downtown talking with the Chinese investigator." If she had we'd never had ended up here tonight.

"I didn't see the point," Patty whispers. "They were both dead, I thought. Then after I found out that Natalie wasn't dead, that she might recover, I didn't want to tell you the truth about what I'd heard. I didn't want to get Natalie into trouble. I thought you'd think she was responsible for what happened to Martin."

"She's not exactly innocent," I mutter, but Patty doesn't hear me.

"And then you decided to blackmail Campbell yourself, after Natalie died?" She shrugs. "I was desperate. I needed the money."

"How did you get in touch with him after Natalie died?"

"I just called the phone number on that slip of paper I took from the Sangers. It was simple."

Simple. Everyone in this mess is looking for an easy road, a simple way to make money, to get by. Patty. Natalie Sanger. Elsie. Campbell. Kurt Schröder, looking for some quick cash so he could beat his brother at wine making. Make enough to start winning awards himself, once he made enough cash to build the winery. He didn't have the patience it takes to achieve mastery, so he went for the short cut.

It never works. Poor Renee Schröder, a woman who wasn't looking for a fast score. She just worked hard every day, doing an honest day's work, and she still ended up dead.

"Patty, you need to give me that evidence. The photographs Natalie took." She nods and goes inside without hesitation. Nothing like almost getting murdered—again—to make someone co-operate. She's gone for a couple of minutes while the paramedics check my vitals one last time to make sure I'm okay and put my arm into a sling. When she returns she hands me a grocery bag wrapped around an envelope of photographs, like those developed at a pharmacy or department store.

I unwrap and flip through them, looking at grainy images of the Campbell Global Logistics shipping yard, taken through the chain link fence. It's night and there's snow on the ground. There's a time stamp printed on the bottom of the photograph: December 27. So, two weeks before Martin Sanger was killed. There are images of Kurt Schröder and George Campbell loading pallets of wine into a shipping container. Whatever they're doing could be innocent enough, without context for what's going on. It doesn't seem like anything to be worth blackmailing someone over.

I guess the Natalie Sanger made a point of checking back the next night they were at the feral cat colony. Maybe they'd even hidden so they could take the photographs. Then I get to another set of photos, clearly taken on a different night. The time stamp now reads January 3, two weeks ago.

They are of Schröder and Campbell carrying the limp body of a woman wearing a pink winter coat and pants and placing her into a shipping container, then locking the door. Either Mei Zhen Lai was already dead by that point, or she froze to death in the container that night. So this is what Natalie Sanger was using to extort money from Campbell.

Now I understand why Mei Zhen Lai's body ended up in the grape press at Ambrosia Winery. Schröder and Campbell were going to bury her in the new concrete floor of the barn. Kurt probably thought it would be safe to leave her body in the old grape press until the harvest was over, but when Renee found the body, and of course immediately recognized her, he had to kill Renee too, before she told anyone.

Poor Renee, first learning that your husband was suspected of being involved in an international wine fraud, then finding the body and knowing it had to have been him who'd killed her. How she'd managed to keep it together, to pretend everything was okay when we met her just showed how strong she'd been. But she should have just told us the whole story when we interviewed her. What was she hoping for? That somehow Kurt would be able to explain it away, tell her how it was all a big misunderstanding?

"They took them on her phone," Patty says. "That's why they look so grainy."

"Natalie told me that the first night she saw them they thought something strange was going on. She couldn't figure out why anyone would be in the shipping yard after hours. It looked suspicious, so they made a point of coming back again. To keep an eye on them."

"And they thought it might make them some money?"

"Natalie did. I don't think Martin even knew about it." Even more reason to feel pity for Martin Sanger. He was tortured and murdered to give up information he didn't even have.

DS Agu and Vogel arrive at the same time as FSU. Vogel hands me a coffee.

"Thought you might need warming up." I nod my thanks and take a sip, then share it with Patty.

"Gauthier," Agu begins, shaking his head. We've been here before and I brace myself for a dressing down or a reprimand for my foolish or impulsive actions, and especially for leaving the suspect dead, again. "I'm glad you're okay," he says as he gives my shoulder a hard squeeze.

Patty is taken away by the paramedic and Agu leans in to speak to me.

"Could she be our girl, from Landry's farm?" He nods toward Patty.

I'm careful not to say anything. Agu shoots Vogel and me a sharp look. "It's okay Gauthier, Raleigh told me the whole story. I respect your wanting him to tell me himself, but you and Vogel should have come forward right away."

"Sorry, Sir."

"Is she the one that got away?"

"I don't know, Sir. She told us that she'd run away, that she got out of Landry's car, leaving all of her stuff behind."

"We only have her word for that. Landry might have got her into that cellar. Maybe she's afraid to get into trouble, if thinks she killed him."

I watch as Patty's blood pressure is checked again. She's saying nothing, as usual, doing her best to ignore the paramedic's cheerful small talk. What do I know about her? Who is she really? She's lied to us repeatedly. She covered up the truth about Natalie Sanger's blackmail then she even tried to do the same thing herself. Patty Smith, if that's even her real name, is no angel.

"It's possible, Sir. But how will we ever learn the truth?"

He sighs and leaves me alone, then goes over to watch the Coroner examine Kurt Schröder's body. There's no question about time or cause of death in his case. Schröder died instantly when the back of his neck connected with the edge of the auger, severing his spinal cord. It's better than he deserved, in my opinion.

Vogel perches next to me and gives me a hug. "That coffee didn't do you any good. This'll help warm you up," he laughs. "I know you don't like people in your personal space, but this time you need to make an exception." He looks at me and lowers his voice. "Gauthier, you've got to be more careful. It would have been too easy for you to die out there in that lake." I nod and tears well up in my eyes. I wipe them away before anyone can see. I hand him the package of photographs and he looks through them.

"So," he changes to his professional voice, probably to spare me more embarrassment more than anything. Vogel is a sensitive guy, for all his faults. "Were the Sangers blackmailing Schröder?"

"I'm pretty sure she went after Campbell. It was his freight yard, and I'd say he looks like he has more cash, which may not even have been true, but whatever. According to Patty it was Natalie Sanger's scheme. I think Martin just got caught up in it, poor guy. "

"A look through his bank records will turn something up. It should be pretty interesting for the RCMP and the Fraud Unit. If Campbell and Schröder were involved in the Icewine fraud, there'll be a lot of cash unaccounted for." The RCMP will step in and go through his business, books, and house with fine-toothed comb. I know the case won't be ours any longer, at least none of it that touches on the Icewine fraud.

"Poor Natalie Sanger. I don't think she had one clue about the kind of people she was dealing with." I shake my head. "Looks like Campbell sent his partner—Kurt Schröder, after them to make sure the blackmail stopped and the evidence disappeared."

"Yeah," Vogel agrees. "Campbell didn't look like he had it in him. But Schröder…" He shivers dramatically. "Still I don't get it," Vogel says. "Why did he cut their ears?"

"I think he did it the first time when he was torturing Martin Sanger. Maybe to get him to say where the photographs were hidden."

"And the rest of them?"

"Maybe it seemed like fun to him, and a way to confuse us." I flash on the image of Renee Schröder, with blood dripping down her blond hair. "Or he got a kick out of it, trying to make it look like the killings have something to do with the ferals."

"What, like some crazy cat lady was going around killing people? A feral cat serial killer?" he laughs. "That's lame."

"Kurt Schröder wasn't that bright. Campbell was the brains behind the operation, I'm pretty sure. I don't think he got his hands dirty..." I stop talking as an idea pops into my head.

"What?" Vogel prompts me. "What are you thinking?"

"Patty is the only one who had her right ear cut," I'm thinking aloud. "Now why would that be? And whoever it was did a sloppy job. Like they weren't used to it, or they were afraid. Even the method of killing was different—no blow to the head, no brute force. Someone wanted to kill Patty without getting their hands dirty."

"You think Campbell did it?"

I nod. "Yes. It doesn't look like Kurt Schröder's style. Maybe he forced Campbell into doing it."

"So he'd have blood on his hands too."

"It's a good way to keep him loyal. Bind them together in this."

"How did Schröder even know about the TNR thing, with cutting the ear? I don't see him as a guy who'd like to know or care about feral cats."

"His wife used to be one of the volunteers. She kept bringing cats out to the farm, to catch mice."

"And seeing their notched ears gave him ideas." He thinks for a moment. "So why didn't he cut Campbell's ear?"

I shrug. "Maybe he forgot his knife? He remembered to bring his shotgun along. Maybe Schröder was losing it by then—he'd killed the Sangers, and Mei Zhen Lai. Then he had to kill his own wife..."

"Why'd he do that? String up his own wife like that? And then cut her ear? That's cold."

"Patty told me she'd seen Renee Schröder downtown, talking with a Chinese woman. Maybe Mei Zhen Lai approached her and then she confronted Kurt about it."

"So he decided to kill her? To stop her from talking to anyone?"

"I don't think that she'd have been a willing participant in the fraud, or in the cover up of Mei Zhen Lai's death. I bet she'd have said something after she found her body in the grape press."

"So that's it then," Vogel says. "All wrapped up in time for me to get away on time for my vacation."

I laugh. "Unless the paperwork takes us two weeks, I'm sure you'll be fine."

"There's only one thing," I say, glancing over at Patty. "Agu is still after the one who got away from Landry."

"I don't think she'll ever be found," Vogel says. "If she hasn't come forward yet, she never will."

"There's no risk for her to come forward any longer. Especially now that the news is out that Landry's wife is responsible for his death."

"Whoever she is, she's got her own reasons for keeping quiet about what happened to her in that cellar."

I look up and see that Maja has arrived, but this time not in her role as Coroner. She rushes over and gives me a hug, then shoves me back so she can look at my face.

"Relax," I laugh. "I'm fine. I've already been examined by medical professionals!" She's doing a good job of hiding her emotions. Nobody would have the slightest hint of our personal relationship.

"You seem fine," Maja says with a wry expression. "But I'm going to hear it from them directly if that's okay with you." She heads over to the ambulance and starts talking with the attendants.

I know we'll be released in a few minutes. I'm feeling no pain, thanks to whatever the ambulance attendants gave me for my arm.

"Vogel, can I borrow your phone for a second?"

"Where's yours?"

"At the bottom of Gravelly Bay."

He shakes his head. "Gauthier, that's the second phone you've lost this year. Hope the department will cover the cost of this replacement."

He hands his over and I put in a call to Sophie at Womyn Collective. I'm going to have Patty sent over in a patrol car. Sophie will need to know she's on her way and that she'll need some extra care when she arrives. Then I ask one of the constables to take Patty over as soon as the ambulance attendant says it's okay.

We've found out who the killers were, and can now put this Icewine fraud case, and I hope the Landry case, to rest. I know Agu wants me to persevere with the missing persons and try to find out who our missing woman is, but I have no intention of doing so. I'll just let it slide until something else comes along to give the Homicide Unit another focus.

I can't wait to get home and have a good night's sleep. Put my anxiety back into its cage and get back on track with my life. For the first time since this all started I feel like the world is taking on its proper shape.

Patty is released and allowed to go home so I walk her over to the police car. When we're out of earshot of anyone I put my hand on her arm. She turns to me.

"Who are you Patty? Why are you really here?" She stares at me, her eyes wide in alarm. "What are you even doing here in town? You've got no money. No place to stay. You don't know anyone here. And you're willing to risk your life blackmailing Campbell and Schröder just to get some cash."

She says nothing for a moment, which isn't unusual for Patty. Then she sighs. "I'm here to find my family. I came to town looking for my father."

I hadn't expected that. "I thought you came for the Icewine harvest."

"That was just a way to make some money while I'm here. I know wine; my stepfather is a winemaker in the Okanagan Valley."

"Your *father*?!" Well that seems like something positive I can get behind. "Okay, then. We'll help however we can," I say, glancing toward the Vogel and Agu who are making their way toward us. "What's your father's name?"

"McAlpine. Scott McAlpine."

My mind goes dark and I stumble against her, spilling the rest of my coffee. It's a name I'd hoped to never hear again.

THIRTY ONE

Saturday, January 18

THIS TIME WHEN I go into Lenore Campbell's hospital room there's no scent of fresh flowers and no music playing. Lenore's hair hasn't been styled and she's not wearing lipstick; it's the first time I've seen her without it.

"I'm sorry for your loss," I say. The woman has lost her only son, and even though he was a terrible human being who may have tried to kill her he's the only relative she had.

"Loss," she echoes. "Not much of one I'm afraid." Which makes it even worse. At least Lorene Campbell is a realist. She doesn't bat an eye when I explain the wine fraud to her, and George Campbell's role in it all.

"I'm not surprised," she says when I've told her the whole story. "He's just like his father and that whole rich, shady family." She sighs and lays her head back on the pillow. "People think because of what I used to do for a living that I'm sketchy. Not me. It's the rich bastards who run this town and it always has been. They're the ones you've got to keep an eye on." I agree with her a hundred percent. It's certainly been my experience.

She stares out the window for a moment, watching the clouds scudding across the sky.

"I know there was no way George found someone like Elsie through an ad in the local paper, like he said. I wasn't born yesterday," she shakes her head. "That boy never inherited his brains from me, that's for sure. I wondered what he was up to, like I always have. Didn't take long to figure out, after it happened."

"You mean when you fell down the stairs?

"Yes. When I *fell*." She gives me an arch look. "He tampered with the carpet somehow, so I'd trip. Fixed it all back up after so there was no trace. I assume he did it so he could bring Elsie into the house."

"To do what?" Elsie has admitted as much to me, but I'm not going to share that with Lenore. What would be the point?

"Maybe get her to change my Will? Charm me to do George's bidding?"

"Did Elsie tell you what really happened?"

"She did."

"And you believe her?"

"A mother knows her son." It's the second time I've heard that in as many days. Lenore looks out the window again, blinking to keep back her tears.

"Where is Elsie?" Shouldn't she be here at Lenore's bedside, pouring her champagne and feeding her bagels and lox?

"Gone. With my money and my car." I can't say I'm completely surprised. But I did think Elsie sincerely liked Lenore. "She forged my signature on the car ownership, used my bank card to clean out the cash in my chequing account and drove off into the sunset. The bank called me this morning."

"Do you want to press charges?"

"No. Let her have it! I'm not using it anyway." Lenore chuckles at Elsie's audacity. "It's only money. And one thing I've learned is money's not worth much in this life."

She stops laughing and for a moment looks every minute of her age. "I'm sorry she's gone though. I was hoping to go on a cruise, to see Bali and Tahiti. I was going to take Elsie with me." She has tears in her eyes. "But she had other ideas."

Lenore stares out the window for a moment. "Maybe she'll come back." Then she quickly shakes her head. "No, I'm just being soft. I know I'll never see her again."

"I knew that girl had something. She's just like me. Or like I could have been if I hadn't settled. Chosen marriage. *Respectability.*" She spits out the last word as if it tastes bitter.

"You know I've already put her into my Will," Lenore says. "Elsie doesn't even know.

She'll get everything I have: the money, the house. Everything." I wonder if Elsie would have stuck around if she'd known that, and whether that would have been a good thing. Much better if she's stayed for Lenore, not Lenore's money.

As I turn to leave as Lenore's phone lights up. I hear her gasp and I glance at the display: **Elsie.** Lenore grins and me and winks and as the door closes behind me I hear her laugh.

"You're coming home?! When?"

We searched Ambrosia Winery and the Schröder's house over the next few days and found George Campbell's car, hidden in an outbuilding at the winery. Kurt had probably been planning on selling it somehow. He never was too smart. He also had a large collection of shotguns and air rifles, in case I needed any more proof he's the one who'd shot me and the cats. I imagine he was at the feral colony, either trying to kill them all or at least ensure they'd be moved to another location, to prevent any future accidental witnesses to whatever he and Campbell were up to. Whether he shot me by mistake or deliberately I'll never know. Shooting a police officer would only shine a spotlight on the area, which you'd think was the last thing he wanted. But again, Kurt Schröder was never smart.

Renee's phone was buried in Kurt's sock drawer. I assume he'd hidden it after he killed her, probably intending to go through it and find any evidence of who else she might have been talking to, besides Mei Zhen Lai. But all we found was evidence they'd met a few times for coffee. The call Ramon Figueroa saw her making the night she was killed turned out to be to the pizza delivery company; they'd made a mistake with the order. But I'm guessing Kurt saw her making the call and jumped to conclusions. He thought she was calling the RCMP to rat him out, and that's why he killed her. I suspect Renee might never even have exposed Kurt and turned him in, but he couldn't take the chance.

Kurt's brother is taking over running Ambrosia Winery, at least for the short term, now that both Renee and Kurt are dead. Since they had no children the land will probably end up going to him in the end, once everything shakes down. Apparently he's thinking of turning over the land back to stone fruit, since so many of the region's peach and cherry farms have gone over to grapes. I hope the irony of that keeps Kurt spinning in his grave.

Mei Zhen Lai's must have approached Renee about the counterfeit operation. She'd probably discovered Kurt and Campbell were partnering in the production and shipping of the product and she was trying to get evidence through Renee. That's why Renee had been trying to take over the bookkeeping and administration at Ambrosia, so she'd have access to the files.

Now they're all dead— Mei Zhen Lai, Renee Schröder, George Campbell and Kurt Schröder. And the Sangers of course, and all for what? To protect their illegal Icewine operation? We don't even know what they made from it yet, but whatever the amount was, if you divide it by the six people who are dead, the value of each human life would be pitifully small.

When I drive up the lane at Womyn Collective Farm Patty is already on the porch, smoking a cigarette. I'm sure it's not her first of the day and she's probably trying to calm her nerves. I'm taking her to meet Doreen, Scott McAlpine's mother and her paternal grandmother.

"Hi," she says as she slides into the front seat. "What are these?"

"Two coffees and cinnamon buns, from Green Bean Cafe. Doreen's favourite."

Patty looks at me suspiciously. "How do you know?"

"Doreen and I go way back," I say, evading the question. It's a fact, but it's certainly not the entire truth. It's as much as I'm willing to share right now.

When I'd broken the news to Doreen she was stunned, then as happy as I've ever seen her. Her wrinkled and careworn face lit up with happiness. In the course of the year I've known her, she's gone from being completely alone to having two granddaughters. But I made it clear she had to keep our connection a secret.

"Don't tell her anything about me, okay?" I'd made her promise. "I'm not ready for having a half-sister. I'm barely ready for you, Grandma."

"Honey, nobody's ready for the likes of me," Doreen had laughed. But she understands better than anyone ever could why we can't tell the truth about our relationship. It will lead to too many questions that I'll never be ready to answer.

"Thank you for your help," Patty says. "In finding her."

"You're welcome. It wasn't difficult," I say. "There weren't many Scott McAlpines in the area in that time period." I don't mention that he had a criminal record longer than most, for assault, drugs, trafficking and theft. I'm not sure she needs to know now, or ever. I often wish I'd never found out myself.

"How is it that your parents met?" I know that Patty is from British Columbia, and as far as I know Scott McAlpine never got out that way.

"Before I was born my mother was working here, at one of the clubs in Niagara Falls."

"Clubs?"

"She was a stripper. And an addict." Patty raises her chin defiantly, daring me to judge her. I'm certainly not going to. I've come from similar and have no false pride about my background.

"She met my father here, got pregnant, but moved out to Vancouver and had me. She got clean. Raised me."

"Why Vancouver?" I'm half afraid she's going to tell me that's the farthest she could go to get away from McAlpine. I've learned so many bad things about him that nothing would surprise me, but it still hurts every time I do.

I keep glancing at Patty as I drive, trying to look for the family resemblance. She's coloured her hair dark, but I can see from her pale skin and freckles she's got the same Scots heritage as Doreen. I bet she's a natural redhead, like me. Patty told me that her mother hadn't named Scott McAlpine on her birth certificate; I assume she wanted to sever any connection to him and maybe even to make sure he couldn't try to claim his daughter, though that idea is laughable given what I know of him.

"Family," Patty says. "My grandmother is still out there. My other grandmother, I guess." She stares out the window as we drive along the top of the escarpment. Far below, through gaps in the trees we get glimpses of the distant lake, the water deep blue in the winter sunlight. "My mother married a wine maker out in the Okanagan Valley," Patty continues. "I grew up in the winery and learned all about Icewine there. That's how I got the job with at Ambrosia."

"Where is your mother now?" I'm pretty sure I know the answer.

"Dead. Hepatitis C, from when she was a user. Before she died, she told me about her past, about my father, where he lived. So I came out to find him."

I've managed to calm down since Patty told me her father's name, though the shock was intense. I thought about the timeline and tried to confirm her story as best I could before I'd even mentioned it to Doreen. Scott McAlpine had moved out of the East Village leaving my mother pregnant, but was still in town for years before he disappeared. Patty is five years younger than me. I know he'd worked as a bouncer in strip clubs, alongside his unofficial job as a drug dealer. It's certainly plausible that he'd become involved with a stripper and gotten her pregnant. There's always a DNA test if there was any question, but for me it's indisputable. What woman would tell her daughter she was the offspring of someone like Scott McAlpine unless it was true? It's hardly something to be proud of.

So this morning I called Patty and told her we'd managed to track down her grandmother, the mother of Scott McAlpine. I said Scott had left the area years ago, but didn't share what I know about what happened to him, and where he is now. If Doreen wants to someday, that's her business, but she'll have to keep me out of it.

When we arrive at Pelham Woods I walk Patty up to the door of Doreen's suite and knock twice. She's expecting us.

"Come in," I hear her hoarse voice through the door. I open it and let Patty in. She's nervous and the tray of coffee and cinnamon buns is shaking in her hand.

"Nice to meet you," Doreen says as she slides open her window. I can hear the emotion, breaking in her voice. As I close the door I also see a photo album on the coffee table.

"Want a cigarette?" I hear as I close the door behind me.

THIRTY TWO

SO SOMEBODY FOUND you after all. That's a shame. I hoped you'd rot in that cellar, your corpse putrefying then turning to dust. Unfound forever, like the women whose lives you stole. It looks like I don't even get to get the satisfaction for having killed you, which is another shame really. It's the least I was owed after what you did to me, and to the rest of us. How many were there? The newspapers say seven. Seven of us, eight if you count me. Do I even count? Since I'm the one who got away?

I don't seem to, at least when you listen to the news. There's barely any mention of me. Just the dead ones, or at least the ones they've managed to identify. And the wife who killed you. I'm not sure how I feel about that. Cheated, I suppose. Feels like I deserve a medal for what I managed, for how I escaped and for what I did to you.

The frozen fields and rivers fly past as I stare through the glass, everything a blur of white and black and grey. Is the landscape moving or am I? I watch the expanse of white outside, framed by the window. Similar to the view I had for all the time I was trapped in that cellar, but this time I can take all three hundred and sixty degrees of sight, everything behind me and everything I'm facing. I see it all now. Everything is out there for me, more than an empty field that stretches miles into the far distance. I'm no longer marking time. There's a future reaching into the horizon and I'm not waiting.

ACKNOWLEDGEMENTS

Thank you to my dear friend Martha Mason, who welcomed me into her beautiful family cottage on Lake Erie, which provided the inspiration for the Niagara Noir series. The characters and situations in this novel are my own invention and any mistakes in the book are my own.

I'm grateful to Dr. Sammy Barakat for his pharmaceutical and medical advice, and for his support over the years.

Thanks also to the Damonza team for fabulous cover design and formatting and to Lucy Dauman—whose early editorial comments and support made such a difference in the finished novel and helped me turn The One That Got Away into a novel I'm very proud to share.

Most of all, I'm grateful to my mother for inspiring me with a love of reading and of books, and to my children for their love and support.

ABOUT THE AUTHOR

Liza Drozdov is the author of Blood Relative and Dark Water, both in the Niagara Noir series. She worked as a bookseller and book publicist, as a garden designer and a college professor, and as a producer of lifestyle television, before settling down to writing full-time. She lives in Oakville, Ontario.

www.lizadrozdov.com

www.twitter.com/lizadrozdov
instagram.com/lizadrozdov
facebook.com/lizadrozdov